DEVIL'S GUARD

AFGHANISTAN

ERIC MEYER

First published in the United Kingdom in 2012 by Swordworks Books.

ISBN 978-1-911092-51-3

Typeset by Swordworks Books
Printed and bound in the UK & US
A catalogue record of this book is available from the British Library

Cover design by Swordworks Books
www.swordworks.co.uk

DEVIL'S GUARD
AFGHANISTAN

ERIC MEYER

CHAPTER ONE

I am considering two promises. One is the promise of God, the other of Bush. The promise of God is that my land is vast...the promise of Bush is that there is no place on Earth where I can hide that he won't find me. We shall see which promise is fulfilled.

Mullah Omar

The man looked at the assembled group, watching carefully as they returned his gaze. He was tall, at least six-three, and lean, yet he was different from them for other reasons. Not because of the patch he sometimes used to cover his one useless eye. Not for his black robes and black and gray patterned turban, which were little different from the clothes of his companions. Not for his beard streaked with gray, which was no longer than the other beards in this room. It was for the power that emanated from him, from his gaze, and the way he held himself; the awesome mental strength that seemed to flow from him to inspire and command those he led. Until the Americans came, he was Head of the Supreme Council of Afghanistan. Now, he had even more power, the power to change political shape of the entire world.

"I am ill."

Three words, yet they sent a ripple of fear into the assembly. He held up his hand.

"No, I am not about to die, but I will have to travel to a location where I can receive treatment. It is essential that I regain the strength to continue the fight to drive out the infidels. I need a band of fedayeen, men I can trust to be my personal bodyguard. I will ask for volunteers when this meeting is over."

He knew there would be no shortage of volunteers for his proposed band of fanatics, the fedayeen, who would guard him with their lives. It would give them, and their families, everlasting prestige if they lived and an assurance of immortality if they did not.

"Next, our intelligence about the American intentions has dried up. We have lost so many men over the past few months that we are fighting blind."

Commander Abdul Qadir held up his hand. He was in his early forties, bearded and sinewy, like the men he led. His sunbaked face was lined and cruel.

"We have a man who expects to be appointed to the traitor Barzai's personal staff very soon. As soon as he is in place, our information will flow once more."

Omar nodded. "That is good, Commander Qadir. As soon as you have anything, let me know straight away. In the meantime, I want you to make certain that the areas we control between Jalalabad and the Khyber Pass are kept clear of the infidels. It is important you do not fail. If any NATO patrols are sent into the area, you know what to do."

"You are going to Pakistan again?"

Omar stared at him. "Perhaps, perhaps not. I will keep you informed. Let me know about the informant in the palace, and enlarge your operations in that area. That is all."

He got up, stiffly. All of them remarked how tired he looked. Some were terrified; they could not lose this man, the man who was hunted by every resource the foreign infidels could employ. He was Afghanistan, and they had vowed to protect him to the last breath in their bodies. They laughed aloud when they heard the question translated into Pashto, the question that was uppermost in American minds. For the infidels would never learn the answer to the problem that vexed them more than any other.

"Where is Mullah Omar?"

* * *

"How are things going, Max?" she asked me.

I smiled at Avizeh, the pretty young woman who ran our shoestring operation in Kandahar. She wore a clean, white dress that accentuated the olive tint of her skin. Her hair hung loose under the obligatory headscarf, and unusually for the local women, she wore gold hoops in her ears.

"Going? They're fine, everything's good."

She kept the skeptical look on her face. I sighed. "Ok, it's not so good, but I'm hoping things will pick up."

"Hah!" she grimaced. "If I lose this job, I don't know what I will do."

"You won't lose it, we're fine."

"Fine! Do you think I haven't seen the overdue bills, Max? We're in trouble, aren't we?"

I nodded. "Yes, we're not so good. Rachel hasn't been paid in weeks, and we're struggling to find the money for the aviation gas."

"I hope we keep the airline afloat. If I have to look for another job, it will be difficult."

"For you? Surely not!" Avizeh was fluent in English, Pashtu, Dari and Thai. She was also very efficient; anyone would be glad to hire her, and not just for her looks.

"You know what they call me in town? A dog washer."

"What are you talking about? What's a dog washer?"

"You know that Muslims regard keeping dogs in the house as unclean?"

I nodded.

"They say that those Afghans like me, who work for a Westerner, are put to work washing dogs, menial and unclean work. It is a great insult."

"I'm sure it is. I'm sorry, Avizeh. I promise you I'll do my best to keep things going."

Rachel, my co-pilot, came into the hangar. A former Air Force pilot, she'd been dumped after an accident left her grounded with only one eye and a permanent limp. To compensate for any shortcomings, the feisty brunette, short and barely five feet tall, possessed a dark beauty both on the inside and the outside that could light up a room. I wondered daily which particular god had been smiling on me the day I managed to recruit her for Helene Air.

"We're all ready to go, Max. I'm not sure about the refueling. We'll need two stops, I'd guess."

I grimaced. "Let's hope the budget can squeeze it. It's a long haul to Vietnam. Did you find out about the cargo? I'd be more comfortable if I knew what we were carrying in the hold."

"Not a chance, I'm sorry. The crates are secure, but I'd guess we already know what's inside."

Yes, we had a good idea. Drugs, in the form of raw opium. It was both the scourge and the salvation of

Afghanistan, a deadly dichotomy of wealth for the people who ran the rackets, and a slow agonizing death for the consumers. After 911, a politician stated that Afghanistan exported more than five hundred tons of opium each year. The invasion would be justified if meant stopping that 'evil' trade. They'd reported that eleven years later, exports were running at over eight thousand tons a year. We refused to carry drugs but were adult enough to know that some cargoes would be bales of opium sealed inside wooden crates, and we couldn't check every one.

"Let's hope the Vietnamese customs officials have been paid off," I added grimly.

She smiled. "You know it'll be fine. It's what keeps this part of the world spinning."

"You mean drugs or pay-offs?"

"Both. Around here, it's one and the same."

She stopped speaking as a pair of fighters flew off the airfield in a roll of kerosene-fueled thunder, NATO Tornado ground attack aircraft. We hardly took any notice these days, just waited until the noise abated and then carried on speaking. Kandahar served NATO and the ISAF forces as a military airfield, as well as a civilian airport for Southern Afghanistan.

"Do you fancy a drink before we leave? It could be a long time before we get the chance."

I could see her considering it, the Air Force fighter jock that she'd been struggling with the co-pilot for a backwater airline that she'd become. The Air Force lost.

"I'd love one," she smiled.

"Can we take your car? My SUV is out of action again. I'm waiting for a new gearbox."

"Yeah, sure. Let's go."

We walked outside, or rather, I walked and Rachel limped, but it was very slight. She didn't need two good legs because there was no doubt in his mind that her beauty would attract admirers wherever she went, limp or no limp.

We drove slowly through the streets of downtown Kandahar. I still found it strange, where almost everyone seemed to carry a weapon. Foreigner-filled SUVs jostled for position with ancient timber carts pulled by donkeys and sometimes Afghans. We found our way to our usual haunt, the Millennium bar. Some people argued it was named after the Millennium Falcon, Han Solo's ship from Star Wars. I was certain it was a throwback to the year two thousand, and the name was no more exciting than that; like the rest of Afghanistan, a stale reminder of a stale past. We ordered drinks and a meal. It wouldn't do to fly on an empty stomach.

"What the hell are we doing?" Rachel asked out of the blue.

"Doing? We're eating and drinking."

"No, I meant in Afghanistan. Look at the place! It's a toilet, after all these years."

"It's better than it was under the Taliban. Women couldn't go outside without a burqa or a male chaperone. Men were forced to pray or they were punished. They had to grow beards and cut their hair according to the religious rules. There was no music. It was banned. No TV, no photographs, of people, anyway. No gambling, for sure, and you know how these people love to bet on bird and dog fights. The poor bastards couldn't even fly a kite."

"So that's what NATO and ISAF is fighting for. The right to watch TV and bet on a cock fight."

I looked at her. "What's up? You've been here for several months, so you know what it's like."

She shrugged. "I don't know. I'm just feeling down about it all. You know that stadium we went to, last time we flew into Kabul?"

"Sure, we watched a soccer match. It ended in a riot, as I recall, and we had to make a run for it."

"Right. The Taliban used it for public executions, where they'd behead criminals, including women, and cut off the hands of alleged thieves. The whole place is soaked in blood."

I couldn't think of an answer for that, and just then the food arrived. The waiter put two plates down in front of us. As far as I could make out, it was an orange oil slick of potatoes and meat that turned out to be mostly gristle. Maybe Rachel was right.

We finished our unappetizing meal in silence and drove

back to Kandahar International. The aircraft sat waiting outside the hangar, a de Havilland Twin Otter. She was a 19-passenger short take-off and landing utility aircraft developed by de Havilland, produced by Viking Air. The aircraft's fixed tricycle undercarriage, STOL abilities and high rate of climb had made it a successful cargo and passenger carrying aircraft. She was tough and reliable, and able to take the knocks and bangs in a country like this one where smooth tarmac was just a dream in most places. We finished the walkaround inspection and climbed into the cockpit for the pre-flight checks.

"I miss Jahandrah. He was a good man," Rachel murmured as we were checking the flap operation."

He'd been our maintenance engineer, a local Afghan, one of those men born with oil running through their veins. He could fix everything, from a kid's cycle to the turboprop engine of a cargo aircraft. Since he'd been gone, we'd relied on maintaining the aircraft ourselves or calling in someone when we were out of our depth. There was usually someone from the ground crews willing to earn a few extra bucks.

"What happened to him, did you even find out?" she continued.

I nodded. "Avizeh told me the whole story. He was a Tajik, and as you know they're mostly Pashtuns around here. It was a vendetta, something that happened during the Soviet occupation. One of the Tajiks accused a local

Pashtun leader of cowardice, and you know what they're like where their macho pride is concerned. Never forget an insult. He was gunned down going home from work."

"Poor bastard," she said. "I suppose the cops never found out who did it?"

I shook my head. "They're mostly Pashtuns around here. They wouldn't life a finger for a Tajik."

"Fucking assholes," she exclaimed. I'd noticed her swearing more of late. It was a natural reaction to the dismal chaos that surrounded us, a defense mechanism almost like a talisman against the evils of the Afghan conflict.

We had to wait for clearance, a flight of NATO helicopters came clattering in to land, disgorging scores of weary troops almost the moment they hit the concrete, American Airborne Infantry.

"They look so young," Rachel muttered.

"You're not so old yourself," I reminded her with a grin.

"Yeah, but I'm not spending my time in some FOB, waiting for an enemy contact to start shooting at me."

A forward operating base, or FOB, was often nothing more than a flyblown pile of rocks and sandbags with rudimentary protection for its defenders. The troops hated them.

The headphones came to life. "Helene Air, hold for take-off. We have to clear an obstruction on the runway. There will be a short delay."

I looked across at the tower, something about the guy's voice didn't sound right. He was nervous, so what wasn't he telling me? I looked across the expanse of the airfield and saw that halfway along the runway there was a vehicle lumbering in our direction. A BTR-80, an eight wheeled amphibious armored personnel carrier designed in the Soviet Union. They sent thousands of them to Afghanistan in the 1980s, and there were a few around in use by the Afghan National Army, the ANA. During the mujahedeen resistance to the Soviets, the rebels stole hundred of them and put them to use against their former owners. But there was something badly wrong with this one. It was in the middle of a friendly, well-defended airfield. Yet it was battened down, as if it was going into action. In any case, the Afghan Army had no part of the defenses inside the airfield.

"Rachel, emergency power! Get her off the ground."

She hadn't been a fighter pilot for nothing. She slammed the throttles forward, released the brakes and the aircraft began picking up speed.

"What's up?" she asked, concentrating on keeping the aircraft as level as possible as we bumped over the rough taxiway heading for the tarmac, and the onrushing BTR. It seemed huge and deadly, like a prehistoric monster thirsting for blood. Our blood.

"That APC, there's something wrong. It's ANA, yet she's buttoned up ready for action."

"Insurgents?

"It could be, so I'd prefer to be out of here while the military deal with them."

We had picked up speed and then we were on the smoother surface of the main runway. The BTR was still hurtling towards us. A hatch opened, and a turbaned head appeared. We watched as someone passed out an RPG missile launcher to him. He pointed it in our direction, and there was no doubt now about their intentions.

"Oh Christ!" Rachel exclaimed. "He's going to launch that thing at us."

"I can see that." She was handling the aircraft well, keeping it on a straight, accelerating path for a take-off; if the BTR hadn't been about to open fire on us. It was on a path that was slightly converging with us, and I calculated the angles in my head.

"Turn five degrees to port, now!"

"But we'll be heading straight for him," she objected.

"It'll make us a smaller target, head on. Don't give him the whole of the fuselage to shoot at."

"Got it."

She touched the rudder bar, and the aircraft moved so that it was head on to the armored vehicle. There was nothing we could do. We had to wait and pray that he missed.

He missed. The sudden spurt of flame and smoke as he fired, the certainty that we could see the missile speeding the short distance towards us; everything conspired to force Rachel to swerve the aircraft away. Yet it would only have opened up the length of our fuselage as an easy target, and with iron resolve she kept the aircraft on course. The missile zoomed over the top of the cockpit, missing us by only a few feet.

"Veer away now," I shouted. "Get her airborne before he takes another shot."

I was happy to leave her piloting the aircraft. Her reflexes were honed to a fine level of acuity that I couldn't hope to match from my experience flying lumbering cargo transports. I watched the enemy and called the shots, and she handled the Twin Otter as if it was a thoroughbred Ferrari racing car. We vectored away from the APC, all the time picking up speed to that crucial factor, V1, when we could rotate off the runway and fly out of trouble. But he'd altered course too.

"He's coming towards us, Max."

"I see him. Stay on course."

"He'll hit us!"

"I don't think so."

But there was another danger. From inside the vehicle, someone had passed the missileer another rocket, which he prepared to fire. I looked down at the ground speed indicator. Almost. I checked the shooter and could see he was having trouble preparing his missile as their vehicle jolted over the rough ground at the side of the tarmac.

A convoy of four Humvees with roof mounted fifty caliber machine guns were rushing towards the enemy to intercept, but they would be too late for us. I glanced at the indicator again and calculated the approach of the BTR. Maybe Rachel was right.

"Rotate! Level off just above the tarmac."

If we clawed for height, we'd be a sitting target. She pulled back gently, and the aircraft lifted to fly just above ground effect, slowly gaining altitude as the wings felt the lift from our forward speed. A dark shape appeared in the windshield. The BTR, he'd gone clear underneath us. We both watched the shooter as he in turn looked up at us. The missile was almost ready to fire, and I could swear I could see his finger tighten on the trigger.

"Ten degrees port, now!"

She made the adjustment to the rudder, the wing slid around and she chalked up her first kill. The starboard wheel on the aircraft's fixed undercarriage swung around and smashed against the head that stared up at us. He didn't see it coming. One moment we could almost count the blackened, rotting teeth fixed in a frozen snarl, and then the wheel caught him, dashing his head against the iron rim of the hatch. His RPG was thrown off the body of the vehicle to tumble uselessly to the ground. Rachel pulled back a little on the stick, and we started to gain height now that the danger from the missile had gone.

"Christ, look at them go!"

I followed Rachel's gaze to watch the Humvees bracket the BTR with a hail of heavy, steel jacketed rounds from their fifty calibers. The thin armor of the Soviet vehicle was no match for the modern weaponry; the BTR slewed around, went up on four wheels and then overturned. The guns kept firing, and a sheet of flame and smoke leapt up from the beleaguered APC.

"Yeah, they aced the sucker!" Rachel cheered. Ever the fighter jock, she couldn't help but gloat over the defeated enemy. "I reckon that was a suicide mission. Those Afghans must be getting desperate."

"A suicide mission, for sure. They couldn't hope to escape from a heavily defended airfield. But not Afghan, they don't believe in dying in the fight against the foreign infidels, not if they can avoid it. But the foreign fighters, volunteers, they'd offer to carry out that kind of a mission."

"Foreign fighters? Who'd be stupid enough to fight for this crazy country?"

"Islamists have been flocking here for years. Chechens, Bosnian Muslims, even some Americans and Brits."

"They should have asked me," she said with some bitterness. "I could have told them the place is not worth fighting for."

"Amen to that."

She'd been here for less than six months. She'd spent most of that time working day and night to keep the airline running, flying more hours than safety or sanity would allow; the rest of the time prowling around the aircraft in an old set of my overalls, checking and rechecking that it was not coming apart at the seams. The repairs we had to make would not have cleared a CAA inspection, even if the guy had a white stick and a trained Labrador to guide him.

The headphones crackled again. "Helene Air, you took off without permission. You must observe proper procedure when using Kandahar International Airport. Your actions could have jeopardized safety, and I will be forced to make a note in the operational log."

We exchanged glances, and both of us collapsed into laughter. Before Rachel could make an acid retort that would upset them, I switched to transmit.

"Our apologies, Kandahar International. It was a misunderstanding. It won't happen again."

There was a hesitation, and then a few seconds later they continued. "Very well. NATO liaison says they were aware of your emergency, so perhaps it will not be entered in the log. Climb to five thousand feet and turn one hundred and eighty degrees to overfly Kabul. Have a good flight."

"Thank you, Kabul International. Helene Air, out."

"You were pretty good back there, Max. Where did you say you served?"

"Thai military, nothing special."

"Hah! You must tell me about it sometime. You'd make

one mean fighter pilot."

No, I wouldn't, not now. At the time, I'd wanted my military career to be something special, and had volunteered for Special Forces. I'd enjoyed the unconventional soldiering that came with special operations, until a joint mission that took us across Cambodia to their border with Vietnam. I'd never know if we'd crossed the border in error, but the Vietnamese Army trooper that had pointed a gun in my face was no error, and I'd shot him, twice. I still woke with nightmares thinking about him. Was he really going to shoot, or was it just a threat? Did he have a family, a wife and kids? Were they now impoverished because of his death? I'd started drinking heavily until I was invalided out. I'd eased off the booze, but the memories had stayed. And when that missileer was aiming at us, I could almost see the face of the man I'd killed superimposed on his face. No, I hadn't been cool. The truth was I'd been anything but cool. All I'd seen was more kids about to lose a father.

"Maybe," I acknowledged with a tight smile. I left Rachel to carry on flying the Twin Otter and closed my eyes to think. But all I saw was a father, a husband, and the wife and kids he left behind. It was no problem for Rachel. She lived for flying. Flying was the only activity that kept her sane through the miseries of Afghanistan, despite the mind-numbing hard work and perpetual danger.

As we climbed towards our cruising altitude, I looked down at a long line of vehicles kicking up dust along the road. Officially, it was known as a Highway, but the reality was different. A one-lane dirt road that was too dusty in the summer and frequently a quagmire in winter. It looked like a NATO fuel convoy. At least they hadn't ambushed that one in the mountains.

"What's our refueling schedule?" she asked, her memory jogged by the lumbering line of tankers. "I assume you've planned where we're going to stop for gas?"

"Oh yeah, the refueling stops. I estimate we'll be fine to reach Islamabad, so you'll need to take her up high to clear the Hindu Kush. After Pakistan, we'll land at Dhaka in Bangladesh and tank up again, that should do us for out final destination."

"You looking forward to seeing the sights of the Saigon cesspit?"

I smiled. She was, like most Americans, and not enamored of the communist regime that had taken over Vietnam in 1975, not that I found much to like about the new rulers of the People's Democratic Republic of Vietnam. Despite their corruption and ramshackle lifestyles, the southerners were in general easy going. Not so the northerners, who were from a different race and different culture. Why was it that totalitarian governments always named themselves democratic? Weird.

"I doubt we'll have much time for that. We only have time to fly in, unload, and fly out again."

"Have you ever been to Saigon?"

I looked across at her. I'd been there several times before. After all, my family had something of a history in that city.

"I have, yes."

"Like it?"

"Compared to Afghanistan, it's not so bad. But it's not like the old days, or so they tell me. I gather it was once known as the Paris of the east."

"I'd like to see it sometime," she mused.

"From the flight deck of a B52 bomber?"

She grinned. "Now you're talking, buster."

A short while later, she asked me a question about Afghanistan. "I mean, what the hell's their problem? Don't they want the kinds of things we're trying to do for them? Schools, roads, industry, and sanitation?"

I nodded. "Sure they do, some of them. But those things are not their priorities. You have to remember that they've successfully repelled a number of invaders, including the British and the Russians, so the people and the warlords think they're invincible. They hate and distrust foreigners. They're only friendly to their own people, those that are born to the life. And even then, their life is all about fighting. Afghan men learn to fight as soon as they learn to breathe. It's an automatic reflex with many of them. They fight with dogs, cockerels. You name it, and they fight it. They play polo with the head of a goat. I've even seen them pit tiny birds against each other, so small they'd fit in your hand. They've fought for centuries, so long that I doubt many of them can even remember what they're fighting for. Certainly not a new road or village school."

"So you don't think there's any hope?"

"There's always hope. I guess they want to be left alone, to work it out for themselves. No drugs, no foreign armies, no foreign Islamists stirring up trouble, just Afghanistan for the Afghans."

"At least they'd only kill each other," she grunted.

"That'd be progress, wouldn't it?"

She laughed. I liked it when she laughed. I liked it a lot.

* * *

The phone was ringing, and for a short time he was tempted not to answer it. He'd only arrived at his folk's place the night before, and he was on furlough. Second Lieutenant, Class of 2012, United States Military Academy at West Point. He'd made it, after all the hard work, the good grades at school, then college, a real struggle for his parents. He'd worked his ass off too, pumping gas in the local garage, and then off to West Point for the endless series of grueling entrance tests. The biggest moment was when the letter popped into the box. He was admitted. Now all he had to do was work his butt off some more, and he'd been a real, live military officer. He intended to enter the survey branch. He wanted to study archaeology after his military service, and maybe he could take a second career as a college professor. Everyone loved a soldier, well, most people did. The Vietnam days were long gone, and now it was a profession that people admired, as they should. He'd missed the cut for the engineers, and instead had been assigned to infantry. They told him that he'd be posted to Fort Benning. 'There's plenty to survey down there, Second Lieutenant. It's a big place. Keep your head down and your nose clean. If a vacancy comes up in the survey branch, you'll be the first to know'. That was fine with him. He'd go wherever he was sent. At least he wasn't sweating his ass off in some foreign hellhole. They were bringing the boys back from those places, since the war was over in Iraq, and Kosovo that was a tiny police action. And they wouldn't send him to Afghanistan, not a fledgling second lieutenant. They wanted real soldiers over there, not nerds like him. He sometimes wished he was a bit tougher, but maybe it saved him from some of the, let's face it, more uncomfortable assignments. When they wanted a warrior, they were inclined to overlook him. He remembered that mom and dad had got up early to go to church, as it was Sunday, so he picked up the phone.

"Hello?"

"Second Lieutenant Rains?"

How did they get his number? Oh yeah, he always had to leave a contact number.

"Yes, I'm Rains."

"Corporal Reardon from HQ, Sir. I have your new assignment."

He smiled. They'd all told him about the army screw-ups.

"That's good of you, Corporal, but I already have my assignment. I'm due to report to Benning in forty-eight hours."

"Yes, Sir. I mean, no, Sir. That's been changed."

"Oh, really? Where are they sending me?"

Christ! That was quick. This could be it, the survey unit he'd wanted.

"Afghanistan, Sir. You need to return to headquarters ASAP. You're ordered to fly out tomorrow."

"No, there must be some mistake. I'm not down for combat, Corporal, it's..."

"You're an infantry officer, Sir?"

"Well, yes, I guess so."

"There's no mistake, Sir. You're taking over a platoon of infantry, Lieutenant. They're moving up to Camp Phoenix in Kabul as soon as you join them. Your written orders will be ready for you when you report here. Thank you, Sir. Have a good trip."

He decided to take an ice cold shower. He needed to clear his head. Fuck! It was crazy. Rains checked his appearance in the full-length mirror. Did he look like a combat soldier, really? He was pale and thin to the point of being gaunt, fair and blonde, a legacy of his Scandinavian ancestors. His hair was short, not quite a buzz cut, combed straight back. No, he looked like an associate professor of archaeology. At that moment, he wished to Christ it were just a dream. He couldn't even shoot straight, and he'd sure never fired a shot in anger. Damn what was he to do? He thought for a few moments. He was a second lieutenant in the United States Army. He'd follow his orders. But what would he actually DO? He hadn't got the faintest idea.

CHAPTER TWO

Operations in Iraq and Afghanistan and the war on terrorism have reduced the pace of military transformation and have revealed our lack of preparation for defensive and stability operations. This Administration has overextended our military.

The President of the United States of America

The Situation Room at the White House looked strange in its unaccustomed emptiness. Mathew Mann, the Chairman of the Joint Chiefs, glanced around at the cold, gray, bare walls and the naked electronic screens; at the solid, institutional furniture, executive quality, that would seat the horde of senior administration apparatchiks who made the decisions about who would live. And who would die. He caught his reflection in the mirrored glass wall opposite where he sat. He was looking at a trim six-footer with black hair, cut so short it was little more than a shadow on top of his head. His eyes were dark, and he liked to think of them as veiled. Especially when he played poker, or politics, which were essentially the same game. Bluff and counter bluff for high stakes. He loved his country, his job, and the Army. Some said he mixed up his priorities at times, but he was not a man who spent a great deal of time soul-searching. He knew that behind his back, he was nicknamed 'Action Mann'. It wasn't a name that caused him any difficulty. He knew he was getting old when he felt irritated that the air conditioning hadn't been adjusted to account for the empty room, for the small group that was gathered for this meeting. He smiled at his frailty.

The room was designed to cope with the raised adrenaline, perspiration, even the fear of a large number of political and military hangers-on. Even with his tunic buttoned up, he felt the cold, almost as cold as the chilly Washington. He grinned to himself; he was getting too old for this particular kind of armchair warfare. There were only two others present, the President, as elegant, fit and trim as ever; a handsome, dark Othello, who weaved the spells that changed their lives, and not always for the better. Although he knew that Barrani was a good man. The Secretary of State sat near to him. Short, trim and power dressed as usual, her fragrance even managing to overpower the aircon in this place. But this morning her usually immaculate blonde hair and perfect makeup were slightly askew, which was no surprise given the early hour. The President had a full diary, so when he wanted to discuss one of his pet concerns it had to be fitted in outside of normal working hours, like this morning, at ten minutes after six. He realized they were both staring at him, and he made an effort to stop the woolgathering. What was the question? Damn, he should have paid attention. These people were not used to asking twice.

"Could you repeat the question, Mr. President? I'm not quite clear on what you're looking for here."

President Barrani stared at him, a lawyer's stare. "General, I said that I'm less than satisfied with our progress in Afghanistan. It seems to me that every time we attack the enemy, especially the leaders, the important targets, they fade into the mountains and just wait for us to leave. Then they start shooting again, taking back territory we've spilled blood to win. What are you doing about it? And what's more to the point, where is Mullah Omar? Now that bin Laden is gone he's the man the Taliban look to for leadership."

He wanted to give an honest answer, but he'd liked to do a whole lot of things, except that his hands were constrained. Tied by the politicians in Kabul, the United Nations, and here in DC.

"We're doing everything we can, Sir. But we do have to

consider the political implications of our every action. If we get it wrong, it makes life difficult for the soldiers on the front line."

"That's crap, General, and you know it!" Mrs. Chalmers leaned forward and glared at him, another lawyer's stare. "The President asked what you're doing. All you've told him is what you're not doing. I'll ask the same question. What are you doing about it?"

The General sighed. Ok, if they wanted it, they'd get it. "Nothing." He looked at both of them. "The rules we operate under prevent us from taking the kind of direct action that's needed."

Barrani smiled. "At least that sounds like an honest answer, General. Now tell us, what would you do if your hands weren't tied by the politicians?"

General Mann nodded. So it was to be that kind of meeting; they wanted honest answers. Answers they could beat him over the head with later. It explained the lack of any staffers and the numerous assistants that were always thick on the ground at this kind of a head to head.

"You want the absolute truth?"

They both nodded emphatically. "Go ahead, General, tell it like it is," the President ordered him.

"Yes, Sir. It's really simple. The only way to contain the enemy in Afghanistan is to cut off the head. Kill the leaders. It's a tactic we used in Vietnam, when we were allowed to, the so-called Black-ops."

"General, I seem to recall we lost in Vietnam," Mrs. Chalmers reminded him. He grimaced. Sure, it was the public perception, that the US had lost that war. But it was only half right, and also half wrong.

"We lost the Vietnam war politically, Ma'am. Only politically! In military terms, we won every single battle. And the Black-ops operations were a success, every one of them. It was the single most effective weapon in our armory."

Oliver Barrani wore a thoughtful expression. "So in effect, you're saying that we need to adopt this Black-ops method of working in Afghanistan? Send in undercover teams, Special Forces, I assume, to assassinate the leadership of the Taliban?"

The General sighed with relief, at last, a politician who understood the military reality.

"Exactly, Mr. President."

Harriet Chalmers cut across them. "Is there no other way to gain the initiative, General? Surely an undercover assassination program isn't likely to earn us a good press."

Mann replied to her challenge. "You're right, if it gets reported, but undercover means that it never finds its way into the press. As far as I know, there's only one way to ensure a good press."

"And what's that, General?" Oliver Barrani asked, sensing an opportunity for political gain.

"It's obvious, Mr. President. We need to win the war.

Everyone loves a winner. As for assassination, that's just another name for fighting battles. In war, you kill people, period. The Islamists started it by killing plenty of our folks in the World Trade Center. I'm saying we should finish it. Killing the leaders is the fastest, most economical way of achieving that end."

Harriet Chalmers made to object, but Barrani waved her down.

"What are the figures?"

Mann smiled inside. That word 'economical' had caught his ear, as intended. He spent some time comparing the costs of a limited number of Strike Teams as opposed to Main Force Battle Groups and aircraft, including drones. Even as he spoke, the figures sounded impressive to him, and he'd written many of them himself. Eventually, the President held up his hand.

"Enough. You're saying we get the biggest bang for our bucks? That's good enough for me. Draw up a plan, General. We'll go down that route."

"But Mr. President, the United Nations will never…"

The President stopped Mrs. Chalmers' objection dead by finishing her sentence.

"Will never know anything about it," he grinned. He turned to Mann. "Is that clear? This is to be kept undercover. You can do that?"

The General shook his head. "Not one hundred percent, Sir, no. Something always leaks out, but enough to make it deniable. I'll make sure we use contractors to go in and carry out the strikes. No American troops need be involved."

"You mean mercenaries?" The Secretary's sneer was enough to show her feelings for that kind of soldiering.

"I mean contractors," he replied firmly. "We've been using them for a long time, and nobody has shown any objections so far. Especially when it means less of our troops being flown back in body bags."

Barrani nodded. "Contractors are fine by me, General. How about transport, getting these people in?"

"We'll use small, commercial air transport outfits. There are one or two flying around the country carrying a range of cargo and passengers. They'll do most things if the price is right."

"Good, keep me informed, General."

The President stood up and the others followed. Harriet Chalmers looked grim, but Mann shrugged to himself. She'd just have to deal with it, and make it right with her opposite numbers in the United Nations. She was welcome to that side of things. He knew what he'd do with that bunch of whining chair polishers. It wasn't anything pleasant. He started towards the door, to return to the Pentagon so he could pursue the real business of the American military. As he exited the room, a question surfaced in his mind, one that nagged at him on a daily basis, and one that needed to be answered if they were ever going to win this war. 'Where is Mullah Omar?'

* * *

Our flight from Kandahar International Airport, Afghanistan to Ho Chi Minh City, Vietnam, was uneventful, as it should have been. We had the two stops to refuel, but for once, there were no foul-ups; no problems with paperwork, no officials claiming that the 'consideration' we had to pay them to avoid any screw-ups wasn't enough. The de Havilland Twin Otter flew well too, which was as good as we could expect given the constant shortage of money for spare parts and maintenance. The tough little high wing cargo aircraft was robust and reliable, the pride of our tiny fleet. The cockpit was Spartan but comfortable, and a huge improvement on the old C47 Dakotas that we'd flown in the early days.

We even had comfortable leather seats, a heater that worked and a degree of soundproofing. And best of all, the war had been over for a long time, so they didn't shoot at you these days when you flew over Vietnam; the way they'd shot at my grandfather when he flew numerous missions across the country. I could see Rachel smiling as I stared down at the steaming hell that was the jungles of Vietnam. What was it really like for my ancestor, fighting for the French during the Indochina War? I turned to look at her.

"You're wondering why I look at that awful sea of green, so I may as well tell you. My grandfather was a soldier in the French Foreign Legion, and he fought in those jungles."

"Really? What was his name?"

"Jurgen Hoffman."

"Right. I thought you said your grandfather owned the airline. Your grandmother took over after he was killed, didn't she?"

"That's right," I replied. "But before he ran the airline, he was a soldier."

"How could he have been French, with a name like Jurgen Hoffman?"

"Most Legionnaires weren't French. They came from almost every country in the world. Still do, I believe. He was a German. In fact, before he joined the Legion, he was an officer in the Waffen-SS."

She looked at me sharply. "He was a colorful guy, your grandfather! Care to tell me more about him?"

It was something I preferred to keep to myself, but it was a long flight, and I saw no reason for her not to know. She got little enough from my almost bankrupt airline. If she didn't receive her pension from the US Air Force, she'd certainly starve. Wages were not our number one priority, so they often had to be postponed to pay the fuel bills; as well as the bills for aircraft spares, equipment and the never ending bribes that sapped the strength from all of South East Asia.

"He came to Indochina in the French Foreign Legion, fighting as a sergeant in 'A' company, Second Battalion, 13th Half Brigade. At the time he was on the run, evading the hunt for Nazi SS officers that took place after the end of the Second World War. I should add that my grandfather was no war criminal. He was a Sturmbannführer in Waffen-SS Das Reich, a Panzer Infantry division. But it was enough to put him on the wanted list of the Allies after the German collapse."

Rachel grimaced. "That must have been pretty tough for him."

I nodded. "It was. My grandmother told me a number of the tales he'd passed on to her. Stories of how hard it was back then, fleeing before the victorious Russian hordes, fighting a series of desperate rearguard actions that saw more and more of his comrades slaughtered for no reason, other than Adolf Hitler's stubborn lunacy. Like a lot of other SS troopers, he found a bolthole in the French Foreign Legion, which until 1947 didn't ask too many questions about links to the Waffen-SS. He fought through the jungles we're flying over right now, against the Viet Minh. They were the communists back then, before they became the Vietcong. After the French debacle at Dien Bien Phu, when the Legion pulled out, he went south to Saigon, with the French wife he'd met in North Vietnam. Her name was Helene, and she was my grandmother. He used his discharge pay from the Legion to buy a couple of worn out cargo aircraft, and they started this airline. They were looking for a peaceful life, for a time to prosper and start a family, and a chance to help to build the two newly created countries - South and North Vietnam. But Ho Chi Minh had other ideas, and there would not be any peace."

"And then we Americans came along."

"Yes, then the Americans came," I agreed. "They exploited my grandfather ruthlessly, and he had to struggle to keep afloat while they fought their proxy war against the Russian surrogate, North Vietnam. In 1973 my grandparents moved their operations to Thailand. They could see the inevitable communist invasion of the south was about to happen. My grandfather continued flying in and out of Vietnam. In fact, my grandmother often flew as his co-pilot."

"She was a commercial pilot, too?" Rachel asked, surprised.

I chuckled. "She was a pilot, that's for sure, and a damn good one. I believe she only ever got her private pilot's ticket, but that's more than many of these local pilots had. The rules around here are different than in the States."

"Obviously. So what happened to him?"

"He was killed during the mad scramble to escape the North Vietnamese communists when his aircraft, carrying refugees, was shot down by a North Vietnamese Mig 17. My grandmother was flying co-pilot for him that day, and she told me she held him in her arms as he lay dying in the wrecked cabin of the aircraft. Amongst the passengers on board was their daughter, Sophie, my future mother. When my grandmother Helene died, Sophie wasn't interested in the business, so I inherited the airline."

"How about your father, what happened to him?"

"I never met him. My mother never told me his name, but I understood he was the son of one of my grandfather's comrades who fought with him in Vietnam."

"That's strange, why did she keep it quiet?"

I shrugged. "I've no idea. All I know is that she was a single parent when I was born."

"He went off with someone else, eh?" she said sympathetically. "That's real tough."

"No, my mother told me he was killed when his aircraft was shot down by the Russians. He was flying a cargo into Afghanistan in the early days."

"Jesus Christ, the fucking communists again!"

"Yeah, it was during their invasion. He was just in the wrong place at the wrong time. It wasn't even one of our own aircraft. I guess he was just doing someone else a favor."

I realized what a dismal story it was, so many deaths in this small part of the world, South East Asia. Yet we were still here and still fighting. I sometimes wondered what it was all for, what were we doing here. I never found the answers. Maybe it was something in the blood. Or was it a challenge, like asking a mountaineer why he risked his life to climb Everest? 'Just because it was there,' they'd reply. Were we all mad? I could still remember my mother trying to hide her bitterness when she told me about my father. It was the last time I'd seen her, two years ago, in Paris, where she now lived.

Rachel was silent for a time, and then she said, "You've had some rotten luck in your family, Max. And now the airline's almost out of money. Is it really that serious, are we in trouble?"

We'd located to Afghanistan, to Kandahar, when work became scarce. It was a dangerous and hard business in Afghanistan, but if you lived, it should be possible to earn enough cash to pay back the bankers and finance companies and move on to a sane environment. But you also needed some luck, and lately that commodity had been in short supply. I smiled at her, trying to make light of it all.

"I'm lucky enough to have a fantastic co-pilot, Rachel, and God only know why you work for me."

"It sure ain't the money, buddy," Rachel smiled back. "The way things are going I reckon I might even have to pay you to let me fly. I guess you ought to know, it's the exact opposite of the way business is normally done."

"Things will get better, Rachel. It won't always be like this."

She stared at me. Then she broke out in a gale of

laughter. "In your dreams, buster. The only way we'll see any money out of this outfit will be if you win the lottery."

"I don't do the lottery," I protested.

She nodded. "Why had I guessed that? Maybe it's time you did."

"So why do you stay with me?" I asked her, knowing the answer already.

"Because you let me fly, Max. No one else will." She looked at me closely and grinned. "The pilot is pretty handsome too."

"Get out of here, Rachel."

"No, I mean it," she said earnestly. "You're a nice looking guy."

I looked back at the jungle to hide my embarrassment. I wanted to mumble, 'The co-pilot isn't so bad either'. But I kept silent.

We droned on for another hour, and I dozed, thinking about what it would have been like, fighting down in those steaming jungles, the heat, and the humidity. Snakes. Vietcong. Rachel touched my arm. "The starboard engine's running a little rough, and we're overdue for a service, Max. It's not going to get any better. Can we get it looked at in Saigon?"

I shook my head. "I doubt it. We're already overdue with our maintenance bills. And don't mention the name Saigon while we're there, you know how it upsets the locals."

She looked grim. "I couldn't give a shit about the locals."

I glanced across at her, curious about the dislike in her voice.

"Was your father in Vietnam? He was a pilot, wasn't he?"

"Yes, he was. I never saw him either. I'm told he was a red-hot pilot, but he died of cancer soon after I was born. What a waste!"

I wondered did she mean a waste that he'd died, or that it was from something as mundane as an illness? Then there was the other thing. She'd told me before that she found me attractive, but I had a business to run. I stared into her eyes, trying to make her understand why it couldn't be. Except they were such beautiful eyes, and it wasn't the first time I'd noticed, even though I knew that one of them was false. Which one?

"So we both know life can be crap, but we also know we have to move on."

She nodded and looked out through the cockpit window. She was using extreme care to fly the aircraft, squinting ahead into the cloud and mists that hung over the Vietnamese jungle, like an old, wet army blanket. She had a slight squint because of the eye she'd lost in the accident that ended her Air Force career, the same accident that had damaged her leg. She had changed back into civilian clothes and turned her back on her military career, leaving with a slight limp, a small pension and a hefty compensation check.

"We really should get it checked out before it goes altogether."

"I know, but it'll have to wait. You know how things are."

She didn't reply, for the downpour came suddenly, as it often did in this country. Sheets of rain fell in furious torrents so that we were flying into an angry wall of swirling water. The wipers struggled to cope, and I rechecked our heading and distance to run. Our destination, Tan Son Nhat International Airport, lay only fifty miles in front of us, but in the worsening storm I had doubts we'd be able to make a safe landing. I began working out alternatives even though it would cause problems to our schedule, and may cost us the next cargo that was waiting for us in Ho Chi Minh City. There was nothing suitable, so I contacted Tan Son Nhat.

"This is Helene Air Twin Otter en route for Tan Son Nhat. We're fifty miles out and caught in a rainstorm. Can you suggest an alternative?"

There was a brief silence. Then, "Rainstorm? What rainstorm?"

The voice was shrill, scathing. As if I was mad. Then again, maybe anyone who flew into this godforsaken country was mad.

"We are fifty miles west of Ho Chi Minh City, flying through a heavy rainstorm."

"Rainstorm? There no rainstorm here, Mister. You blind?"

English is the universal language of air traffic control the world over, but the English that they spoke at Tan Son Nhat ATC was unlike any I'd heard before. Even so, it was obvious the storm hadn't reached our destination, so we could stay on course. I touched the transmit key.

"Understood, Tan Son Nhat. We are approaching the airfield, ETA approximately ten minutes. Will call when we're on final approach."

"Sure, you do that, Mister. Rainstorm!" he snorted as he signed off.

We continued on through the heavy rain and sure enough, five miles out of the airport it eased, and we finished the journey in brilliant sunshine. We touched down and taxied to the freight terminal, where there were loaders from a local mineral exploitation company waiting outside the company hangar to unload our cargo of drilling equipment and tools. As the last of the wooden crates were hauled though the aircraft doors, they started to drag our return load, mineral samples, into the cargo bay. Rachel and I relaxed, munching our way through sandwiches and drinking cans of soda while we sat watching the process of loading from a couple of wooden boxes outside the hangar.

"It must have been something in its day," she murmured. It was obvious she was reminiscing about her Air Force days. "I can imagine the F4s taking off, Hueys shuttling troops to the battlefields, and Cobra gunships setting out to give them fire support."

"It would sure have been busier," I replied. "But I doubt a few passenger jets and the occasional Boeing 747 annoy the locals like the constant military traffic used to."

"We were fighting for their freedom. They should have been more grateful," she snapped, a tinge of bitterness in her voice.

I looked at her, surprised at her vehemence, but before I could respond a Vietnamese official stalked up to us; he'd been out of sight, coming from round back of the hangar. A small squad of soldiers, a sergeant and four troopers followed him. All of them were armed with AK-47s, the iconic Soviet assault rifle. With their banana shaped magazine, they were the most recognizable weapons in the world, and their solid rate of fire and 7.62mm bullets made them both lethal and effective.

"Don't move. Let's see what they want," I whispered to Rachel.

She nodded.

"Why you no show passport when arrive?" he snarled.

His face was pockmarked with childhood acne, and his teeth, like most Vietnamese, were either crooked, black or non-existent. Afghanistan was little different, another poverty stricken flyspeck of a country, and another American foreign war. Some of the older Vietnamese had been fortunate enough to benefit from American medicine during the war, but not this one. He was bow legged, legacy of a poor diet, and a paunch betrayed the amount of time he spent behind a desk. I held out my hand.

"Hi, my name's Max Hoffman. Pleased to meet you."

He looked at my hand, surprised at the unusual courtesy. His expression deepened into a sneer as he ignored it. "Why you no show passport?"

I sighed. He was one of those. "You know we have an arrangement. When we land and don't have to leave the airport, you don't need to see our passports."

"You show passport."

"Very well. Rachel, would you pass down my briefcase from the cockpit."

"Sure."

She limped to the ladder, climbed up into the fuselage, and went forward to locate the case where I kept all of our papers. I didn't want to let this awkward official out of my sight; something about him spelled 'trouble'. The cargo handlers watched him carefully as they continued to unload, but I could see something more in their expressions. Fear, yes, but fear of what? She brought down the case, and I showed him our two passports, hers American and mine French. He scrutinized the documents, and then checked our licenses.

"You airline was in Vietnam?"

"That's correct. Saigon."

I could have bitten off my tongue as I said it, but that's what it said on my passport. He looked up sharply.

"Ho Chi Minh City."

"Of course," I replied smoothly. "The city had a different name when the airline was here, that's all. It says Saigon on the original licenses."

He glared at me, then handed the passport and licenses back. He picked up Rachel's passport and stared at it.

"American."

It was a statement, and one word that dripped with contempt. For him, maybe, the war wasn't over. Perhaps he'd lost relatives to the American bombing. It wasn't unusual. Or maybe he was just an arrogant, ill-mannered pig, like many of these petty bureaucrats in communist dictatorships.

"Yeah, that's right, buster, I'm American. Any problems with that?" Rachel's voice was hard as flint, and he glared at her. Then he relaxed and smiled.

"No problems now. Americans we have problems, we kill."

I could see Rachel start to limp towards him, so I took her in my arms, putting my lips close to her ear.

"Not now, Rachel. We're not out of here yet. Just cool down and forget him."

She tried to shake me off. "Motherfucking sonofabitch, these people couldn't hold a candle to Americans. I hope they all rot in their pissant slave state."

"What? What she say?"

I smiled at him. "Nothing, my fiancée is not feeling well, that's all. Women!"

I raised my eyebrows and grinned. He gave me a suspicious frown. It was a moment when things could have gone either way, but at last he nodded. Like most Asian men, he was a raving macho misogynist, and women were of course weak. Then he lost interest in Rachel and swung back to the soldiers.

"Sergeant, order your men to search the aircraft, the cargo, everything!"

"Why do you want to search the aircraft?"

He swung back and stared at me. "You mind own business."

I felt Rachel pulling at me and realized I was still holding on to her. I released her, and she gave me an angry glare. "Why did you do that, Max? I could have dealt with him."

"I'm sure you could, Rachel, but his soldiers could have caused you a few problems."

She grunted but made no reply, and we watched them pull wooden crates off the load waiting to be taken on board then jimmy open the lids. Two soldiers boarded the aircraft and started to hunt through the cabin and cockpit, but I knew there was nothing for them to find.

"What the hell are they looking for? They don't do this normally, do they? Christ, I thought Afghanistan was bad, but at least they leave you alone there."

I shook my head. "It's the first time they've done this. I've no idea. I guess we'll find out soon enough."

She looked doubtful. "Maybe. And what's this fiancée business all about?"

I gave her a weak grin. "Rachel, I was trying to defuse the situation. These people have a certain respect for couples, so it made a difference that he thought you were my fiancée. That gave me the right to explain things on your behalf. I just want to load up and get out of here."

"I copy that, it's a god-awful place."

"It's actually a wonderful place, so my grandmother told me. It's just these people who made it into a living hell."

She nodded. I was about to speak again when there was a sudden commotion. One of the soldiers had ripped the lid from a huge wooden crate to inspect the contents when a man jumped out of the box. The soldier froze in surprise, and the man took the opportunity to sprint away. The sergeant looked around and barked orders; his troopers ratcheted rounds into their rifles and lifted them to take aim. The man was running towards us. I started to shout at the troopers to hold their fire, but two shots cracked out in quick succession. A bullet whistled between us, and I dragged Rachel to the ground as the man rushed past us. More shots cracked out, and there was a cry of agony. I looked around and saw the runner was down. The Vietnamese soldiers ran across to him and looked down. I could see he was badly wounded, squirming in agony. To my horror, the sergeant took out his pistol, a Soviet Makarov automatic. He pointed it at the wounded man's head and pulled the trigger. The explosion sounded loud. The airfield was in that second in the middle of a lull, nothing landed or took off. There was only the loud report from the pistol, the meaty 'smack' as the bullet hit him in the back of the head, and then he was still. We climbed to our feet, and I heard Rachel muttering some obscene insult to the sergeant, but she wisely kept well away from him, and he didn't hear it. He barked an order, and two of his men dragged the body away. The customs officer stared at us and pointed at the pool of blood on the ground where the man had fallen.

"American." He smiled. I shook my head. The victim wasn't American, of course, but his meaning was clear. He grinned at us.

"Now you in Afghanistan. Like Vietnam. More Americans. All dead." His smile became a belly laugh, and he almost choked. I found myself willing him to keel over, gasping for breath, but he recovered. I could hear Rachel murmuring, "Motherfucker." We both turned to look as a truck drove around the corner and approached our aircraft. A man climbed out, and he was unmistakably American, and unmistakably Ivy League. He walked over to me and held out his hand. "Hi, I'm Ed Walker. This is my cargo you're taking to Peshawar."

I took his hand. "Max Jurgen. I'm the pilot and owner of Helene Air."

He stared at me, and I stared back at him. He was tall. I was six feet, and he loomed over me, maybe three inches taller. Good looking too, ramrod erect, confident, as he would have been taught since prep school. Blonde hair and blue eyes, I could imagine the girls falling over themselves to catch his eye. I was dark haired and Mediterranean, Rachel told me I was a good-looking six-footer that women would find attractive, but I almost felt like a peasant against his patrician features. Almost. Unlike him, I wasn't a slime ball.

He could have been an American corporate executive. The kind that worked on Wall Street, and the kind that almost singlehandedly destroyed the American economy. Masters of the Universe, I believe they were called; pale, WASP face, button down Ralph Lauren, tweed jacket with leather elbow patches and polished leather Oxford brogues. This guy would have taken me for a bellhop if he'd seen me on the street. CIA, he had to be. They were still very much in evidence all over South East Asia, especially Afghanistan, but even here in Vietnam.

"What's the cargo we'll be carrying, Mr. Walker?"

"Cargo? Oh, this and that, nothing special. One moment, there's something I need to finalize."

He strode over to the sergeant and spoke quietly to him in Vietnamese. I spoke some of the language, enough to get by, and enough to know that Ed Walker was fluent, and as one would expect of a CIA officer working in this neck of the woods. I watched the American hand the sergeant an envelope. There was an exchange of smiles, a warm handshake, and then the soldiers left. Walker came back to Rachel and me.

"Those guys won't be back. They were looking for defectors."

Rachel stared at him. "If I lived in this lousy place, I'd sure defect as fast as my legs would carry me."

He nodded. "I hear you, and I couldn't agree more. It's no pleasure park. Tell me, how soon can we leave? I have a connection to make, and I don't want to be late."

"Where are you headed?" I asked him.

He pulled a face. "After Peshawar? Afghanistan."

"Right. You wouldn't want to be late arriving in that Asian paradise," I said deadpanned.

He chuckled. "Yeah, I know what you mean. Duty calls, so that's where I have to go."

"What line of business are you in, Mr. Walker?"

He glanced at me briefly. "Nothing special, this and that."

I gave him a smile.

He went away to check the cargo, barking orders at the cargo handlers who had returned as soon as the soldiers disappeared. I showed him to the row of jump seats in the cabin, just behind the cockpit bulkhead, and made sure he knew to buckle in before take-off. Then I forgot about him. When I sat down in the left hand seat, Rachel started the engines, and I called the tower for clearance. I got the same wise guy as before.

"You clear to take-off, Helene Air. No rain, you safe."

Before his microphone clicked off, I could hear him laughing. I was tempted to suggest a course in etiquette and manners for the bastard, but I left it at that. Maybe one day he'd be flying through a tropical rainstorm and be so scared he'd shit his pants. I hoped so. Rachel took control of the aircraft, and we took off, starting the long haul back to Peshawar, in Pakistan. Close to the border with Afghanistan, it had become a vital hub for drugs and arms trading. Even the Taliban had an office there, or so it was rumored. When I went aft to check the cargo, Ed Walker was in the middle of a call on what had to be a satellite phone. He was crouched near a window to get a signal, but when he saw me coming, he said a couple of words and hung up. I nodded a greeting.

"Handy gadgets, the satphones. Everything ok back here?"

"Sure, I'm good. How long before we reach Peshawar?"

"We're on course, Mr. Walker, but it'll be a few hours yet."

"Good, good. They're waiting for me on the tarmac. As soon as I land, they'll transfer the cargo, and I can get on my way to Kabul."

"Nice place."

He smiled. "Yeah."

"Tell me, Mr. Walker, what kind of cargo would you carry from Vietnam to Peshawar? It's got me beat."

He eyed me for a few moments. I thought I saw a little curl to his lips, a small sneer. He saw me as little more than a chauffeur, a guy to drive his aircraft and carry his bags.

"You saw me pay off that customs guy back in Tan Son Nhat?" he replied at last.

I nodded. "I saw."

"Right. It's that kind of a cargo."

I went back to the cockpit. If he wanted to be Mr. Mysterious, that was up to him. He was beginning to irritate me, anyway. Maybe he thought he was James Bond. That was fine by me, as long as he paid up promptly and kept out of my hair. We landed twice to refuel, and then we took off on the final leg to Peshawar. I contacted Air Traffic Control, and Rachel settled into final approach. I let her take the de Havilland in; she just loved to fly, flying anything and everything. I was convinced she'd pay me to let her work for the airline if I insisted. In fact she almost did. We landed on the long runway and taxied to the commercial hangars. The cockpit door opened, and Walker came through into the cockpit.

"You're looking for a Cessna Caravan. It should be parked behind the main cargo hangars. If you'd taxi over there, we can make the transfer."

"That shouldn't be a problem. Rachel, can you take it?"

She nodded. "Sure, I'm on it. I can't see a Cessna yet." She stared out of the windshield. "Wait, yeah, it's over there. Ok, I'll get as near as I can."

I was surprised that Walker was using such a small aircraft, but it was his choice. We came up to it. There were half a dozen armed men lounging on the ground nearby. When we stopped, and I opened the cargo door, they were waiting and climbed up to start unloading the crates, carrying them across to the Cessna. It was the larger version, the Grand Caravan, and I noted the thick, balloon tires and toughened suspension legs. So that's why they were using her, it was the perfect aircraft for Special Forces or mercenary operations. She would land on rough ground and only needed a crew of one, the pilot. The Caravan would take a cargo of soldiers and equipment virtually anywhere, including the rough strips in the interior of Afghanistan. I wondered what Walker was up to, what kind of horrors he was planning to visit on the folk of that beleaguered country. It was always the civilians who suffered, especially when these Ivy League 'Masters of War' set out to make their mark on the battlefield. They would consider any innocent village in Afghanistan to be their personal battlefield, and they'd stop at nothing to forge their reputation before returning to Langley for a high-level management position. These people had virtually invented the phrase 'collateral damage' all on their own.

Walker glanced at me. "What do you think of her? I'm told the Cessna's a good aircraft, but we only just acquired it, so I guess we'll have to see."

I nodded. "I've seen them around. They're ideal for rough field landings with those big tires fitted. You've got auxiliary tanks?"

He shrugged. "Search me. I've got a driver to take care of those things."

Yes, he would have. I was surprised he didn't use the word 'chauffeur'. I gave him a polite nod and started back to take care of the Twin Otter. They finished the unloading, and Rachel taxied over to our hangar we used in Peshawar, which was our secondary base of operations. I was glad we wouldn't be ferrying Walker into Afghanistan for some murky operation. Helene Air may be struggling to keep afloat, but we refused to carry drug shipments, weapons or mercenaries, at least, knowingly. I was well aware that some of the cargos we carried would probably be considered illicit, but I couldn't police our customers if they hid their true intentions. It kept our hands clean, and nobody died as a result of the way we earned our living, or failed to earn a living, anyway. Two men came across the tarmac and intercepted me as I was walking back to our aircraft. They both wore suits, shirts and ties, and shoes that were at least half clean. I knew at once it couldn't be anything good, not when someone dressed in a suit, collar and tie approached you in Peshawar.

"Mr. Hoffman? Max Hoffman?"

"Yes, I'm Hoffman."

"We are from the bank's head office in Kabul. We heard you were landing here and came out to meet you. This is for you."

They handed me a document. I opened it and read the writing, in Pashto and English. I couldn't understand the legalese at first.

"What is it, what does this mean?"

One of them gave me a polite smile. "It is a notice of bankruptcy, Mr. Hoffman. Your business is in liquidation. The bank will sell the assets and notify you if there is any surplus money due to you. I'm sorry, but from what I've seen, I doubt you even have enough to cover your debts."

I felt as if he'd punched me in the stomach. "But, I have contracts. How can I go on flying?"

His smile left him, and his expression now was hard. "Oh, you won't be doing any more flying. You're finished. The business no longer belongs to you. Please, do not go near the aircraft, any of them. They are no longer your property. You may remove your personal effects from your offices, but it must be done right away. The liquidators will be here at any moment. Good day, Mr. Hoffman."

I walked back to our hangar. Each step felt like lead. I was walking through a thick soup, so that my legs moved only with difficulty, every step slow and forced. Rachel saw me approach and came up to me.

"What's up, Max? Are you ill?"

"The airline, we're finished. It's gone."

"What? What the hell do you mean? How can we be finished?"

"The bank, they've seized it to pay off the debts. It's bankrupt, and we're not even allowed near the aircraft. We have to get our possessions and that's it, the end."

"Jesus Christ, I don't believe it. The bastards, how could they do that?"

I didn't answer her at first. I felt the same way, yet of course they could do it. The banks owned our souls these days, and they could do anything they wanted. I looked around at the hangar, the Twin Otter, our pride and joy, then back at Rachel.

"I think we should sort out our possessions. The liquidators are due any moment."

"What do we do then, Max?"

"I don't know. Look for a job, I guess."

I noticed Ed Walker looking across at me. He'd seen the two suits hand me the document. He must have seen my expression, so he knew exactly what was going on. Damn him, of all people, I wished he hadn't just witnessed my downfall. He nodded politely enough, then walked to the Cessna Caravan and climbed aboard. The engine was already ticking over, and it slowly taxied out to the main runway to wait for clearance to take-off. I had a battered

Jeep Wrangler parked near to our hangar. It seemed crazy to keep a facility in Peshawar when we had a hangar in Kandahar, but the bureaucracies of both Afghanistan and Pakistan meant that it actually cost less than the need for separate paperwork when we flew between the two countries. I offered Rachel a lift into town, and she accepted. When we were driving towards Peshawar town center, I asked her where she wanted to be taken. She looked into my eyes.

"I want to find a bar, Max. Then I want to get drunk. You gonna join me?"

"Sure. I've nothing else to do. Let's go."

But two hours later, and after almost an entire bottle of Bourbon, it still didn't feel any better.

* * *

Dwight Rains slapped the dust from his uniform. If anyone ever asked him about his first impression of Afghanistan, what it was like, that one word was what he'd use by way of a reply. Dust. It got everywhere, covered everything, and it was like a living, breathing organism. He stepped into the brigade office and saluted the officer who sat behind the desk. Major Evan Fairchild glanced up, and Rains noticed the chest full of medal ribbons. He wondered what this man had done to deserve them. No doubt he'd find out soon enough.

"Second Lieutenant Rains, Sir, I'm reporting in for assignment as per instructions."

Fairchild flipped a casual acknowledgement. "What's your strength, Rains?"

"Thirty-two men, including the platoon sergeant, Sir."

"Where are the rest of them?"

"That's all I came out with, Sir. The platoon is under strength at present."

"I see. I was told they were sending forty men in four squads. You'll have to make do, but if you take any casualties, it could cause you problems. Let's hope it won't come to that. Your men are settling into their quarters?"

"They are, Sir, yes."

"That's a pity. As soon as they're ready, I want a convoy escort. We're sending some heavy equipment out to Kandahar, and you'll be taking care of them. You're up to scratch on the Strykers?"

Rains nodded. The IAV Stryker was an eight-wheeled armored fighting vehicle, produced by General Dynamics Land Systems, and in use by the United States Army. The vehicle was named for two American servicemen, both named Stryker, who posthumously received the Medal of Honor during both World War Two and the Vietnam War. They were becoming essential in the strange kind of war fought in Afghanistan. The hull was constructed from high-hardness steel that offered good protection against heavy incoming fire, especially from the front. In addition to this, Strykers were also equipped with bolt-on ceramic armor that offered further protection from IEDs, Improvised Explosive Devices, and incoming artillery and rockets. Best of all was the remote operation of the turret guns from inside the vehicle. For soldiers who wanted to survive the constant threat from insurgents, the Stryker was without peer in the day-to-day threats ISAF soldiers faced.

"That's good news, Rains. You wouldn't survive for very long here in the old M113s. They're worse than useless against the kind of hardware the Taliban use against us."

"I thought they'd got rid of them, the M113s. They're Vietnam era museum pieces," Rains exclaimed, then almost bit off his tongue. This veteran combat soldier didn't need telling about his own equipment, but he just nodded.

"They're not ideal, you're right, but against small arms fire they're ok. We just use them for local transport, and they're good against snipers. Out in the countryside, they're deathtraps, though, so we never use them outside the city. What do you think of your new home, Phoenix Base?"

He was smiling as he asked the question. It was a shithole, but it wasn't for the new second lieutenant to criticize. Camp Phoenix was an installation located in the capital, Kabul, about six miles from the Kabul International Airport. It was a mess of concrete fortifications, barbed wire and inside, the various buildings that housed the US soldiers. Maybe not the most miserable place on this earth, Rains reflected, but it would certainly be up there with the leaders. And the people! As he'd driven through the teeming streets, he'd been surprised at the angry glances the locals darted at him, at his American military vehicle. He hadn't expected much, but not the outward shows of hatred for all things American.

"It's interesting."

"It is that. Make sure your men attend to their security," Major Fairchild continued. "Last year three suicide bombers were killed by the base defenders during an attack on the camp. Two self-detonated, causing little damage, and we killed the third one, but it could happen at any time."

"I'll tell the men to keep alert, Sir."

"Right. As soon as they're settled, report to the armor park, and I'll make sure your Strykers are ready for you. You'll need to take three, and that's eleven men per vehicle, which is about par for the course. The convoy you're escorting is Afghan National Army regulars, and they're driving ten trucks with equipment that's needed yesterday in Kandahar. Any questions?"

"What time do we leave, Sir?"

"I assume this is your first operational assignment?"

"Yes, Sir," he replied, feeling like he was standing in front of his headmaster.

"As fast as you can get it together, Lieutenant. It's two hundred miles. If you leave right way, you'll be there before dark. Don't leave it any later, the Taliban eat up convoys that travel at night."

"I'll get the men moving, Sir."

"That's what I would do if I were you, Rains. And watch out for the civilians, that means don't go running any jingle trucks off the road."

"Jingle trucks, Sir?"

"The Major nodded. "You'll see plenty of them around. They're painted up like it's Halloween, weird colors, like sixties pop-art. Some of 'em have bells festooned over the bodywork, and they jingle like crazy. Jingle trucks, they call 'em."

"Yes, Sir."

"Good luck."

They exchanged salutes. Rains left the building, back out into the camp, and back out into a whirlwind of dust, noise, troops racing back and forth; and the heavy tension in the air that was almost thick enough to bear a load.

CHAPTER THREE

We have gone forth from our shores repeatedly over the last hundred years and we've done this as recently as the last year in Afghanistan and put wonderful young men and women at risk, many of whom have lost their lives, and we have asked for nothing except enough ground to bury them in.

Colin Powell

"These figures do you no credit, General," President Hamid Barzai snapped. "You were given this post on the understanding you would deal with these rebels. Yet every day brings some new outrage. People are afraid to walk outside their homes, even close to the Presidential Palace. Why have you failed?"

Lt. Gen. Mohammed Kadim was short, in his late forties and built like a wrestler, bald, with hard muscles and an erect stance. A career soldier, he was of the same tribe as his President, who made him the Army Chief of Staff, the man charged with beating the Taliban scourge in the country of Afghanistan. He met his President's eyes and then looked away. He could see that Barzai was boiling with rage. It was not the time to argue facts and figures with his fellow Pashtun. The President wanted results. Results that Kadim didn't have.

"Sir, we are making good progress against the rebels, yet they are so numerous. I need more resources. Resources that I am constantly denied." He glanced at Abdul Rahim Wardak, the thin, elegantly dressed soldier turned politician. He wanted President Barzai to be in no doubt about where to place the blame. Barzai gazed at the Minister of Defense. "Well?"

"General Kadim had twenty-eight percent more troops on his strength than he had this time last year, but it seems to make little difference. Sometimes I wonder where all of these extra troops are. They seem to be ghosts."

It was a lethal shot at the General. There was a long tradition of claiming pay for non-existent soldiers in the Afghan Army. Kadim reacted angrily.

"Every single soldier on my strength can be accounted for, Sir. They are not ghosts, and the blood they shed in this war is very real."

Barzai grunted. "We shall see. Perhaps it is time I ordered an inspection of your troops to find out what they are doing to stop these attacks getting any worse. But there is some hope, I am happy to inform you."

His advisors looked up with interest. Maybe he had a plan that would take the pressure from their departments. Mullah Rahim Massoud, the fourth man in the meeting, sighed.

"Not the Americans again? I would like to think we could solve some of our problems without their clumsy interference."

"Without their clumsy interference, none of us would be here, and the Taliban would be sitting in this room!" Barzai fired back at him. "Yes, the Americans are extending a helping hand to us again. They are, of course, unwilling to deploy more troops to our country. Their tactic will be to use private security forces to attack the Taliban in their lairs, in their homes and strongholds. Chop of the head of the snake, and the body will die. That's their plan."

"Mercenaries!" Mullah Massoud spat out; not realizing it was an uncanny echo of the American Secretary of State's view of the use of private security forces.

"Perhaps so," Barzai continued. "But whatever you wish to call them, they could strike a blow against our enemies that will bring them to the negotiating table."

"If they are successful," General Kadim added with a morose tone. Inside, he was thinking why the Americans again? But he knew the answer. His own people couldn't be trusted. As many as a quarter of them were Taliban sympathizers, and some of those were sleeper agents, waiting for an order from Mullah Omar to strike a blow against the infidels. This included him, because of his alliance with the Americans.

"Whether they are or not," Barzai said briskly, "they cannot make matters any worse than they are. And every Taliban leader they kill helps our cause."

"What do you want of us?" the Minister of Defense interjected, making certain that his ministry wasn't excluded from any changes of policy. Or increases in funding.

"Nothing, Minister. I just want you to be aware of the operation, so that if you come across it, you will do nothing to hinder it, and perhaps even offer our help if it is needed."

"It would be better if we are not involved in this business," Mullah Massoud offered. "Our people will not take kindly to hearing of the involvement of mercenaries in our struggle."

Barzai turned his piercing gaze on the Mullah, and then he glared at the others. "I agree. This is why I want to be certain that word of this will not go outside of this room. This matter is between the four of us, and if you wish to continue in your present posts, make certain it remains that way."

They all nodded their agreement, and they all wondered how they could use the information to their advantage. Or to the disadvantage of their opponents, which meant everyone in this room, apart from themselves.

"One more matter, General Kadim. Make certain you remember your prime assignment."

Kadim, puzzled, turned back to Barzai. "Sir?"

"You have a simple question to resolve, General. I trust you make it your number one priority. Where is Mullah Omar?"

* * *

When I woke up with a splitting headache, I wondered what had happened the day before, and then I remembered. The telephone was ringing, and I went into the living room of my tiny apartment to answer it. Rachel was sprawled on the couch, fully dressed, starting to come to.

I snatched up the receiver, "Hoffman."

While I waited for the other party to speak, I looked around my tiny abode. I kept a tiny apartment in the center of Peshawar's red-light district, which sure made for an interesting life. But rents weren't cheap, and this was all I could afford. The paint was faded, the furniture needed replacing and the carpets were showing their age, with the occasional bald patch poorly disguised by a small table or a planter. It would have been depressing, except that I spent little time here, and when I did come home, I only had to tumble out of the door to find plenty of entertainment. I had another rat hole of an apartment in Kandahar, which was our main center of operations.

The caller finally spoke. "My name is Walker. You brought me in from Vietnam yesterday."

I remembered him, the spook from the CIA. "Yes, Mr. Walker. I thought you were flying into Afghanistan."

"So did I, but we hit problems, and I'm still in Peshawar. I wondered if you would consider a short term contract to help me out."

I laughed out loud. Rachel sat up and groaned, then looked at me, her eyebrows raised. "The question is academic, Mr. Walker. My airline has gone bust. You'll have to find someone else. Good day to you."

"Wait a moment. I may be able to do something about that," he said quickly, just as I was about to hang up. I laughed again.

"I doubt it. The debt is pretty heavy. For your information, Mr. Walker, it's more than half a million dollars. No short term contract would cover that amount of money."

"This one would."

Rachel was on her feet now, wincing as the weight came on her injured leg. She'd caught the gist of the conversation. I was about to get rid of the man when she grabbed the receiver from me. She held me off with one arm while she spoke to Walker.

"Ok, buddy, what's on offer?"

I pushed the button for speakerphone so that I could

hear.

"Who am I speaking to?"

"Rachel Beckett, I'm the co-pilot who flew you back from Vietnam yesterday."

I was listening now, holding my ear close to the receiver. Our heads touched, and I smelled the delicious odor of her, a combination of last night's fragrance and the succulent aroma of musk. I fought down my desire for her and tried to hear what was being said.

"Are you empowered to discuss business on behalf of Helene Air?"

"I am," she replied firmly. "Fire away, buddy. What are you offering?"

"The company I work for may be prepared to pick up your mortgage. We would then lease back the assets to you, and you can repay us by way of agreed monthly installments which would be covered by work you carry out for us."

I could see her calculating percentages in her brain. "That's very generous of you, Mr. Walker."

"Yes, it is. So what do you say? Do you want your airline back?"

I was shaking my head. I wanted no part of it, no part of their vicious and mostly illegal operations. I'd sooner sell drinks in a bar. In fact, that's probably what I would be doing, for there was precious little work in Pakistan, outside of the arms and drugs trade. And the sex trade, of course, despite their Muslim pretensions.

"Who would we be working for, what's the name of your organization?"

"Double Eagle Security, Miz Beckett."

"An American company?"

"As apple pie, yes."

"Ok, we're interested. Let's meet and talk it through. The Fez Bar, in one hour, will that suit you?"

There was a short silence on the phone, and then I heard him say, "I'll be there."

The Fez Bar was only a short distance away, but we rarely went in there. The drink prices were outrageous, which did at least keep out the riff raff. Except for the drug dealers and brothel owners, who could afford to drink there? Ed Walker was already sat at a table, and we joined him. It did give me a little satisfaction that after witnessing our downfall at the hands of our creditors, he had to ask for their help.

"So what went wrong?" I asked him by way of a hello.

He flushed. "The fucking pilot we hired, he'd been drinking. He swerved off the runway during take-off and put one of the wheels in a drainage ditch. The aircraft is out of action for several weeks until they can fly in replacement parts from the States."

"That's unfortunate," I said drily. "But look on the bright side. He could have messed up in the air, in which case you wouldn't be here to tell the tale."

"Yeah, I guess," he muttered. "But my bosses are not too happy about it. This brings me to you guys. I noticed you had a problem yesterday, so I made enquiries. It seems you ran into some financial difficulties, so I came up with this idea. We can help keep your company afloat if you're prepared to help us."

"You mean fly you and your bunch of mercenaries into Afghanistan?"

"They're not mercenaries, my friend. Every one of them is a licensed security operative."

"Give me a break, Walker. We've been here a while, and we know the score. When you say 'help you', what are you saying?"

"As I said on the phone, we'd pick up your mortgage, and you'd sign a contract to fly our cargos exclusively. You pay us monthly installments out of the fees we pay you for your services."

"How long would this contract last?"

"We'll pay you regular cargo charter rates, so it would last until the debt is paid. We'll allow enough for your expenses, fuel and so on."

I didn't want it, not for any price. Before she died, my grandmother, Helene, had warned me about the CIA. 'For every problem we had with the Vietcong, we had twice as many with the American military, and five times as many with the CIA. Keep away from them, Max. They're poison. Their business is lying, and they're very good at it.'

I glanced aside at Rachel. "What do you think?"

"It's your company, Max. I just work for you."

Walker interrupted. "I gather you're US Air Force, invalided out?"

She nodded. "So what?"

He shrugged. "It's just that if you can't fly for them, I wondered how you could keep going anywhere else."

Her face flushed red. "If you think the US Air Force is so fucking hot, get them to do the job for you. And even if they would do it, which I doubt, I can outfly any ten of those macho fighter jocks."

"Ok, sorry. I just had to ask. What do you think about the deal on the table?"

"It's up to Max, I told you."

"I thought you two were, like, engaged."

So he'd talked to the customs official in Tan Son Nhat about us. These people had a long reach, a very long reach. "No, we're not," she snapped.

Walker turned back to me. "What do you say, Mr. Hoffman?"

I knew I was cornered. He knew it, and Rachel knew it. But I would only go so far. I nodded.

"Very well, here's the deal. We'll go with what you're offering, Mr. Walker. But this is a strictly commercial deal. We want nothing to do with any black operations, no spy missions. Nothing like that, we fly in and out of commercial airfields, period. No midnight landings on isolated fields or country roads. We're not part of the Air Force or CIA. We'll do what we've always done, that's it. We're not about to become a subsidiary of Air America, or whatever you call it these days."

He smiled and held out his hand. "I wouldn't dream of it, Mr. Hoffman. We'll keep it strictly legit, so it's a deal. Miz Beckett."

He shook our hands, and we toasted our agreement with another round of drinks the waiter brought for us in response to Walker's wave. That was it. I realized we were back in business. Even if we had been forced to make a contract with the devil. I recalled that those contracts were always signed in blood, but he didn't ask for it on this occasion. As we parted, Walker told us to report to Peshawar airfield tomorrow afternoon, by which time his lawyers and bankers would have ironed out the contracts. We were to fly out to Kabul in the afternoon. It was a short trip with no stops to refuel, which suited me. Our tanks were less than half full, and we would need to discuss a line of credit to buy aviation gas.

"Our schedule had been put back a day or so, but it's not a serious problem. Just be there tomorrow afternoon. We'll go through the formalities, and we're in business."

"One thing before we go. We have two smaller aircraft in our Kandahar base and three employees. What do we do about them?"

He looked puzzled. "Do? I couldn't give a damn what

you do. That's your affair, between you and the bankers. Just make sure you're ready to fly out tomorrow."

I realized with a sinking heart that I'd have to contact our three part-timers in Kandahar and tell them they were unemployed. In Afghanistan, that often meant the difference between eating and starving. I got through to them eventually and promised to take them back on as soon as we were out of trouble. They knew how things were, as the liquidators had already seized the two aircraft towards the debt. They didn't sound very happy about it all.

But at least we had something to work with. Rachel and I went out to dinner to celebrate. We got a little drunk, and despite my determination to keep romance out of our working lives, we slept together that night. Rachel started it, pulling me to her and kissing me with a passion that was breathtaking. It was wonderful. She was one of the most agile women I'd ever slept with, and I'd been with a few. Asian women were supposed to be amongst the most skilled in the world at the arts of love, Muslim countries excepting, but Rachel could teach them all a thing or two. We kept at it for almost two hours, and by the time we pulled apart to grab some sleep, I was a hollowed out shell, totally spent. But it was worth it. When I awoke in the morning, she was next to me, still asleep and breathing evenly. I studied her face; she was truly beautiful. I wondered which of her eyes the false one was.

They looked identical when she was awake, although now the lids were closed.

"It's the left one."

Her eyes flicked open, and she smiled a long, lazy, satisfied smile. Like a big cat that'd just devoured its prey. I thought about that, was it a reasonable comparison?

"How did you know what I was thinking?"

She grinned. "Men! We always know what you're thinking, so just watch yourself. What time do we have to leave?"

I checked my watch. "It's just after nine. We could go and grab some coffee and breakfast, make it a leisurely morning, see some of the sights. I've got some food here. I'll fix us lunch, and we can leave for the airfield afterwards to sign up with Mr. Ed Walker and his friends. Then I guess we take off for Kabul."

She turned her face towards mine. "Max, do you think he's on the level, Ed Walker?"

I laughed. "Not in a million years. I expect we'll have to fight him every step of the way to get him to honor the contract, but it's our only hope. Don't worry, Rachel, we'll manage."

She nodded uncertainly, then wiped the expression off her face and grinned. "I'm not really hungry yet, Max. Can't we take a late breakfast, there's no need to rush, is there?"

She reached for me, and I couldn't think of a single

reason not to stay in bed for a while longer.

When we reached the airport, Walker was waiting for us, checking his watch.

"If you're all set, we need to finalize the details and get moving," Walker grunted at me.

This time, he'd abandoned the Ralph Lauren and wore a set of beautifully cut combats, trousers and jacket. He had a camo scarf wrapped around his neck and sported a canvas shoulder holster over his jacket, the Ivy League at war. Eight men lounged a short distance away, and they made no effort to conceal their weapons. All of them had assault rifles within easy reach and a variety of handguns strapped to their belts. The Pakistani bankers were waiting for us too. They both looked uneasy in the presence of the small mercenary force. My own banker, Mr. Khan, had a half smile on his face. He was obviously glad that someone was buying the bank's mortgage to save him the trouble of disposing of the assets at an inevitable loss. We signed the documents, and the moneymen disappeared. I now had control of the airline back from the bank, provided that I kept the agreement with the devil; and that they kept their agreement with me.

"We're overdue in Kabul. Can you get the show on the road, Hoffman?"

Walker stared at me, not even trying to disguise his impatience. I noted the lack of a 'Mister' now that we'd signed the documents. Now he was the American overlord, and I was just the bellhop.

"Sure. Do you want me to carry your bags, Sir? Any golf clubs this trip?"

Rachel grinned. Walker gave me a nasty glare. "Just get the fucking plane into the air, Hoffman."

We flew towards the Khyber Pass, the scene of so many battles when this part of the world was ruled by Great Britain. During the journey, I went to check on our passengers. They were huddled in a group talking quietly. When they saw me enter the cabin, they went quiet. Walker stared at me.

"What is it, Hoffman? We're busy."

"I just came to ask if there was anything you wanted. Are you all ok?"

"We're fine. All we need is some peace and quiet."

One of his men grinned broadly at that.

"Very well, but if there is anything, just let me know."

He'd already looked away, and as I entered the cockpit, they started talking between themselves. We left the Khyber Pass behind us, and we were in Afghanistan. We touched down shortly afterwards at Kabul International Airport.

Despite half the country still having failed to crawl out of the middle ages, the airport was modern and busy. The architecture left something to be desired, but that was to be expected. It had been designed and built by the Soviets during their occupation, and the buildings bore the Communist stamp, bland, functional, and depressing. If it hadn't been for the presence of hundreds of heavily armed soldiers everywhere, it may even have looked normal; as much as any Soviet era airport could look. Walker directed us to taxi to a hangar that was signed 'Double Eagle Security'.

"This will be your operating base while you're in country."

I glanced at him. 'In country' was a phrase used by American soldiers when they served in Vietnam. He ignored my look.

"When you've parked the aircraft, or whatever you do with it, instruct my people to get it refueled and checked out. I want you to be ready to fly out tomorrow. We leave at first light."

"What's the destination and load, we'll need…"

"You'll know all that tomorrow," he cut me off. "It's need to know out here, Hoffman. Anything else, don't ask."

I nodded at him and glanced at Rachel. So that's the way it was to be. We were flying truck drivers, no more, no less. She gave me a small, uncertain smile and tried to reassure me.

"At least we'll be flying out of mainstream airfields, Max. No cloak and dagger stuff, that's the agreement. Isn't it?"

I stared at her. "Yes, of course it is. That's what he said.

You're right."

But how good was Ed Walker at keeping his agreements? As I watched his security men walk away, carrying their assault rifles, and the cargo handlers unloading the wooden crates, I felt a lightning bolt slash into my guts. I didn't know why, but something was wrong, very wrong.

* * *

The Kabul-Kandahar Highway was a three hundred mile long road linking Afghanistan's two largest cities, Kabul and Kandahar. The highway was a key portion of Afghanistan's national road system, and more than a third of Afghanistan's population lived within thirty miles of the Kabul to Kandahar road. Rains led the column, conscious that on every yard of road they could encounter the enemy. Who the hell was the enemy? They all looked the same. Some of the men wore that strange hat, the pakul, which looked like a kind of odd-shaped meat pie. It was made famous by Massoud, the charismatic Mujahedeen leader who led his guerrillas against the Soviets so effectively during the eighties; and was later murdered by the Taliban when he led the Northern Alliance against them. Others wore turbans, some black, some were white, and others too filthy to pick out the color. They all wore tribal robes and carried weapons, many of them assault rifles. Most women wore blue burqas, the voluminous robe that made them all but invisible. I'd heard the men call them bluebottles. But who were the terrorists? He'd asked his sergeant, Mason, how to tell them apart.

"Yeah, that's the trick LT, how to tell them apart. It beats me."

So great, he was here to fight an enemy that was indistinguishable from the friendlies. Shit! At any moment, a mine could explode underneath their hull, or a rocket could strike the sides of the vehicle. They were well protected, with steel grilles to intercept a missile before it struck the hull, as well as massive armor protection that were proof against most things the enemy could throw at them. But most things weren't all things, and every man flinched when they struck a bump, or there was an unexpected loud noise. It was unnerving. At one point, Rains opened up the hatch and observed the countryside they were passing through, but after the fifth false alarm, when they'd sighted possible insurgents, he stayed inside, battened down. If they needed to fight, the Protector M151 Remote Weapon Station mounted a .50-cal M2 machine gun, and an Mk-19 automatic grenade launcher. There was no need to expose the crew; all of the weapons could be operated and rearmed from inside the armored hull. Not so the Afghan Army regulars who manned the soft skinned trucks. To a man, they were sullen and defeated, with eyes that were unfocussed, dark pits. They counted themselves already dead, no doubt. Rains had done his best to instill some confidence in them. He'd spoken to the Lieutenant in charge of the M35 two and a half ton cargo trucks. The US military had used them in Iraq, with additional armor to protect them against mines. The Afghan National Army vehicles did not carry such protection, and a fact the Afghans were very conscious of.

"We'll be watching every step of the way," he'd tried to reassure the Lieutenant. Don't worry, my friend, we'll take good care of you."

The Afghan officer was expressionless as he replied. "From inside your armored vehicles, that's easy to say. The insurgents are not fools. They are quite aware of the strength of your new Strykers. That means they'll attack the unarmored vehicles. Do you see my men manning the trucks? There are twenty of us, two for each vehicle, yes."

Rains nodded. "I see them."

"Last year this was a company of more than two hundred men. Most were wiped out in a succession of attacks and ambushes. This is all I have left."

He'd walked away without replying. What was there to say to him? Christ, ninety percent of his outfit, killed! Poor bastards. But he'd do his best to make sure they were protected this time out.

Rains peered out through the periscope. There was no sign of any problem, but that could mean nothing. He leaned across to his weapons specialist, Corporal Delgado.

"Any sign of the enemy?"

They all noticed the nervous edge to his voice.

"Nothing, LT." Delgado's voice was flat, expressionless. But they all knew what he was thinking about the rookie officer. And they all wondered how he'd cope when the shit did hit the fan.

"Ok, keep your eyes skinned, Corporal. I don't want those trucks to get hit if we can avoid it."

Sergeant Vince Mason interrupted. "Ruben Delgado is one of the best, Lieutenant. If there's anything on the screen, he'll see it. Believe me. There's no need to worry about him."

Was that a criticism? Rains was acutely conscious that Mason was a veteran of countless firefights. He was also conscious that if any action started, Mason would be the one the men looked for to lead them.

"Aircraft, five miles, they're coming in low." Delgado's voice was still flat and unemotional.

"Are they ours, Corporal?"

"Sir, LT, the Taliban ain't got any air force, last I heard."

The Lieutenant ignored the quiet sniggers. It wasn't what he'd meant, he was new here, ok, and everyone had to start somewhere. He just wanted information, not constant jibes. He called up the Afghan Lieutenant on the radio. "All ok back there?"

"We're alive, yes. So far."

He decided to keep quiet. Listen and learn. That's what they'd told him at West Point. He just wished they'd told him how to deal with sullen, dispirited native troops and sardonic comments from hard-edged veterans. And he hadn't even tasted combat yet.

CHAPTER FOUR

The US will make no distinction between the terrorists who committed the attacks and those who harbor them.

George W Bush

They waited and watched while the man they had come to hear seemed lost in contemplation. He sat on the rug, cross-legged, his back straight and black-turbaned head held erect. His eye was open, staring into some distant place to which they were not privy. The other eye socket was empty; the eye lost to a Russian shell splinter when the last infidel invaders had dared to set foot on the God-gifted land of Afghanistan. His name was Mullah Mohammed Omar, and he was the highest authority in the Taliban organization. Just the name, Mullah Omar, was enough to inspire respect amongst the legions of fighters who owed him allegiance. And inspire fear and fury amongst the enemies of the faithful who fought to free their country, in the name of the Prophet. Blessed be his name. His gaze focused on the two men who faced him.

"I have word from Kabul, from a friend in the traitor Barzai's government. The Americans have a new plan."

They looked at him intently, waiting to hear the details. Omar continued to pause for a few seconds and then continued. "You have all heard of their Phoenix program in Vietnam?"

Abdul Qadir, the local commander, looked puzzled. "I know nothing of this."

Mullah Abdul Ghani Baradar glanced at him. "It is the name of the tactic the Americans used when they sent assassination teams to murder the leaders of the people's revolution."

Abdul Qadir nodded. "I see. Are they planning to try something similar here? They lost the Vietnam War, so I doubt it will be any more successful in our country."

Mullah Omar looked at him intently. "Do not confuse their tactics with the outcome of the war? They are not fools, and you should remember that in military terms they were successful. As was the Phoenix program. It did a great deal of damage to the North Vietnamese leadership, and they lost a great number of valuable people. And yes, it seems they are planning a similar operation here."

Qadir sneered. "In that case, we will do as we have

always done, and slaughter them as soon as they try to attack us."

Baradar glared at him. "You underestimate them, Commander Qadir. These men will be highly skilled, and trained to attack undetected and melt away afterwards. All you will see is the bodies of their victims the next morning. Perhaps one of them will be yours."

Qadir stared back. His hard gaze meeting the Mullah's. Neither man looked away. "I am not afraid to die, if that's what you think."

"Like a woman, in your bed during the night?" Mullah Omar snapped at him. "Is that the way for a fighter to die?"

Qadir looked down, embarrassed. He shook his head. "It is no way to die. You are right. What do we do to stop them?"

"We use their tactics against them. We shall double our watchers and try to catch them before they are able to mount their attacks. If we are careful, we should be able to stop them. Even better, we can turn the tables and kill these infidel assassins before they get a chance to strike. That is the way we will beat them, to watch and wait and strike them down as soon as they come near our bases."

The other two men nodded. "It shall be as you say, Mullah Omar," Qadir intoned.

"They will regret the day they thought of this unholy plan," Baradar added.

Omar inclined his head. "Make sure it is done. We watch and we wait. They will come to us, and we will kill them. That will teach them a lesson that their war here is a waste of time and lives. The sooner they leave our country the better."

He went silent again and slipped into contemplation. The others took it as a sign that the meeting was over, and they got up and left. They walked away side by side.

"Perhaps we could use something similar," Baradar muttered to Qadir. "If we sent assassination teams to kill them in their beds, it would send a tidal wave of fear through their hearts. They would soon learn to leave us alone."

Qadir stopped and turned to look at him. "You just said it was an unholy tactic, Mullah. Have you changed your mind so quickly?"

Baradar flushed red with anger. "We do God's work here. How can anything that is the will of Allah be unholy?"

The other man turned away to make his way back to his men, who waited a few hundred yards away. It was what they always said, God's work. But didn't the Americans say the same thing? How could they all be right?

* * *

The Double Eagle Security hangar was more spacious and luxurious than we'd been used to. Doubtless funded by the American taxpayer, and no expense had been spared. The building was constructed of reinforced concrete, with huge doors that would allow most transport aircraft to taxi straight in for maintenance, or for loading and unloading operations; at least those operations where it was best not to let the locals know what you were doing. We'd stopped the Twin Otter outside on a concrete stand. I hadn't needed to instruct anyone to refuel. The bowser was already drawn up, and the connecting hose was pumping the tanks full of aviation fuel. The last of the wooden crates was unloaded and stowed inside the hangar, and soon we were left alone. We watched the bowser finish the refueling and stow the long hose. Then it drove away and there was only silence. I checked my watch. It was three in the afternoon, and I was starving hungry. Rachel read my mind.

"We need to get a cab into the city and find a restaurant. I guess we'll need a hotel. God only knows how long we'll be here."

"Let's find a bar first, somewhere that has a dinner menu. We can eat and drink at the same time, and ask the barkeeper where we can find a decent hotel. If there is such a thing in Kabul."

"As long as it has a room with a double bed for me and my fiancé, that's fine by me," she grinned.

So it was like that; it seemed I had a regular girlfriend, but I wasn't complaining. She was an attractive girl and a great lover. But I wished I hadn't started the fiancé thing while we were in Vietnam. Women could get the wrong idea, so very easily. Rachel was using her cellphone to call a cab, and we didn't have to wait more than five minutes before a Mercedes Sedan purred across the tarmac and stopped right by us. It was an International airport, so of course there would be taxis waiting to ply their trade. We got in and instructed the driver to take us into the city center.

Halfway there, he asked for an address.

"We're looking for a bar, can you suggest something? Plenty of good food, a few friendly faces, something like that."

"American bar?"

Rachel nodded eagerly. "That would be good, yeah. I could do with hearing some real American voices again."

"Thanks, Rachel," I murmured drily. She grimaced. "Damn, you know I didn't mean you, Max. It's just that I get a little homesick now and again."

I let it go. I didn't have that problem. I was a bastard child of mixed ancestry, part French, part German, and part American. My name was German, and my grandfather was German, yet I didn't think of myself as anything other than Thai, where I was born. It was the cause of a few strange looks; there weren't many Thai nationals of pure European ancestry. Many saw me as almost a stateless person. I carried a Thai passport, yet didn't fit in, and the French refused on principle to issue any documents to someone related to Jurgen Hoffman. As for the Germans, they were still trying to ignore the fact that people like my grandfather, Waffen-SS Sturmbannführer Jurgen Hoffman, ever existed. I was told he'd been a severe embarrassment to them during the Indochina colonial war. Yet I wasn't Thai, not in looks or parentage. In short, I'd learned to be a kind of chameleon, able to fit in wherever I went. And I spoke English, though with a skewed accent, part French, and part German.

"It's ok, an American bar is fine with me."

We drove through the outskirts of Kabul. The city was depressing. It still bore the scars of the Soviet war, and the constant conflict since had done nothing to improve things. And there was the dust; it was as if the whole of the country was one gigantic dustbowl. We passed building after building that was totally or part destroyed. Guards were everywhere, and most carrying assault rifles; a few carried rocket launchers.

"Jesus Christ, those are Soviet RPGs. I thought only the Taliban carried them!" Rachel exclaimed.

The driver looked over his shoulder and grinned. "They're very common and very cheap in this city. Some of the security men carry them instead of a rifle. They can kill a whole group of fighters in one shot. Bang!" he shouted gleefully. "Very good."

"Great," Rachel muttered.

The first surprise was the bar we stopped outside. It was in a long street that seemed to have more than its fair share of bars, brothels and hourly rate hotels. It was called Abe's. That was it, not 'Abe's bar', just Abe's. Like it could have been a Mom and Pop store, or a shop selling auto parts. The exterior was pre-Soviet occupation, the kind of Afghan style that had a faded grandeur all of its own. We paid the driver and went in. The bar was small inside, maybe twenty tables, and only five were occupied, so we were able to find a quiet table at the rear. I'd been brought up on tales of street bombings, and if the glass started flying, I wanted us to be as far away from it as possible. The front windows were covered in crossed tape stuck to them, to prevent broken glass flying everywhere if a bomb went off. There were no locals in the bar. Outwardly, the Muslim government had a dual approach to booze. It was ok for foreigners, but off limits to the natives; except in their own private homes, where anything went. But the native booze was often cheap, Uzbek vodka or phony Scotch that tasted like gasoline. In fact, it probably was, at least in part. But Abe's was anything but native, so we were reasonably safe. An old guy came out from behind the bar and brought over a menu. I looked at it and discovered the limited choice, steak and French Fries with salad, ice cream for seconds.

"We'll take the steak and French Fries," I said to the guy. He looked American, and when he spoke it was obvious that he was a long way from home.

"A good choice, buddy. It'll take about fifteen minutes, you in any hurry?"

"That'll be fine. Could we have a couple of beers?"

"Sure. This is your first time here, so welcome to Abe's. I'm the owner, Abe Woltz."

He held out his hand and I shook it. "Max Hoffman, this is my colleague, Rachel Beckett."

He studied me for a few moments.

"Where're you from?"

"We're based in Kandahar, occasionally Peshawar."

"No, I mean originally. I knew a guy called Hoffman, a long time ago. In Vietnam." As if that explained everything. And in a way it did.

"My grandfather, Jurgen Hoffman, was in Vietnam."

He nodded. "Jurgen Hoffman, yeah, that was him. Jesus Christ, if that don't beat everything, at least, if it's the same guy, I fought with him back in 'Nam."

I was puzzled at his comment. "I think you must have the wrong man. My grandfather fought in the French Foreign Legion when Vietnam was Indochina, in the late forties and early fifties. He was a pilot when the Americans were there, in the sixties. He ran an airline. In fact, the same airline that we're trying to keep afloat right now, Helene Air."

He grinned. "We're talking about the same guy. Yeah, I guess he did run that crazy airline. But it's not the whole picture. So you're German?"

I shook my head. "Not really. My passport says I'm Thai. But I'm part German, part French, even part American, I guess."

His stare was intense, and I felt uncomfortable. When he spoke, I was astonished.

"Your mother must have been Sophie, Jurgen and Helene's daughter."

My eyes must have telegraphed my surprise that this stranger knew so much about my mother. "That's right," I replied. "So how did you know her, and my grandparents?"

"I was with Jurgen in Vietnam, as well as running an airline he helped bring a Special Forces team out of the north, a rescue mission. I was the unit sniper. He was a great soldier, knew the Vietnamese jungles better than any man alive. He was shot down in seventy five, if I recall, a North Vietnamese Mig?"

I nodded. "Yes, that's right."

"I saw your mother when she was just a child in Thailand," he continued. "Before your grandmother died. Helene was a great lady. What about your mother, Sophie? Where did she wind up?"

"Paris."

He understood the terse reply. "You don't talk to her much, eh?"

"No. She wanted me to leave South East Asia, and I wanted to stay. So we don't see eye to eye on that."

"No, I guess not. Let me get you your food. Would you mind if I join you later? I have to know how things went with Helene and Sophie after I lost touch with them."

"Sure, and I'd like to know more about my grandfather, if that's ok with you."

"It sure is, Max. He was quite a guy."

When the steaks arrived, they were perfect. We sat in silence, devouring the delicious food and swilling down an endless stream of beers that seemed to keep coming over to our table. Afterwards, Abe joined us. He had with him a woman who looked a little older than me, I guessed about forty. I afterwards found out she was in her fifties. There was also a young man, a Eurasian in his early twenties. They were his wife and son, Cam Woltz and Luk. Cam was Afghan, the daughter of the Afghan ambassador to Thailand, which is where she and Abe had met when he was on furlough after the withdrawal from Vietnam.

"You're not based here in Kabul?" Luk asked. Despite his Asian appearance, he had the typical American way of asking a direct question. I didn't mind at all, sometimes the Asian way was a pain. This was the twenty-first century, after all.

"No, we operate out of Kandahar, with a small presence in Peshawar," I replied.

Rachel leaned forward. "We came here with a cargo from Pakistan, a group of security men and some supplies, bound for Double Eagle Security," she continued on my behalf.

He looked at her, then me. "You're CIA?"

I shook my head emphatically. "No way. I own a small airline, and it ran into trouble. These guys at Double Eagle bailed me out so that we could release the aircraft and work off the debt flying contracts here in Afghanistan."

"You know that Double Eagle is a CIA funded company?" Abe put in. "But I guess you had no choice. Who's your contact?"

"Ed Walker."

There was a silence for a few moments.

"What's up?" Rachel asked.

The three Woltz's exchanged glances. It was his wife, Cam Woltz who replied.

"In that case, you're working directly for the Agency. Ed Walker III is the deputy CIA Head of Station here in Kabul," she said. Her voice was soft and seductive. With her looks I could see why Woltz had fallen for her.

I tried to keep the shock out of my face. I knew we'd gone in over our heads, but not quite how deep we'd sunk. "We didn't have much choice. The airline was broke, and it was accepting this work with Walker or nothing."

Abe excused himself and walked over to a group of men who occupied three of the tables. I heard him speaking to them, and they all got up and came over to our table.

"Max, if you don't mind, these guys want to meet you.

They won't have met your grandfather, but his name is kind of a legend to all of them."

We shook hands, and I looked them all over. They were all fit, hard and tough looking. Their faces wore that cold, calculating stare that soldiers the world over displayed to the world. When they came over, they moved with a fluid grace that betrayed their high level of physical readiness. They could only have been Special Forces, or something very similar.

"You're all security people?" I asked.

They burst out laughing. "Hell, no," Abe responded. "That name's a crock of shit to hide the truth. These guys call it as it is. They're mercenaries, every one of them. All of them are American, and most saw service in Iraq."

After we'd been introduced, we chatted for a short while and swapped stories, and then the mercs drifted back to their tables. As Abe had said, my father's name was well known in their circles, and his behind the lines exploits for the French Foreign Legion would have filled a book, even if only half of what they said about him was true. The name of Ed Walker III was just as well known, only it in the opposite sense to my grandfather.

"Let me tell you something about your boss," Abe said to us. "He's CIA royalty, make no mistake. The guy is on his way up to the top floor office, and no one's going to stop him. He'll crawl over a mountain of bodies to get there if it suits him, so watch out for him. His father was

CIA, and his grandfather before him. The other guy you need to watch out for is Joe Ashford; he's the CIA Head of Station here. He's even more ruthless than Ed Walker, as treacherous as a wounded rattlesnake.

"Is Ashford headed for the top floor office too?" Rachel enquired.

"No, not at all. Ed was born rich. Ivy League college, no shortage of money, he had it all laid out for him on a plate. Joe had to fight his way up. He has one interest in this world, and that's money. He's making a mountain of cash from this war, make no mistake."

"How does he make money out of the war?" I asked fascinated.

"He trades anything. Drugs, information, weapons, you name it. And he'll use you to get richer if he can."

Rachel and I both nodded. It was a timely warning. "We'll be careful, don't worry."

We chatted for a while longer. It turned out that Cam had run a business in Thailand after the end of the Vietnam War. She was in fact twenty years older than I'd calculated, one of those women who retain their beauty. Something to do with the genes, I expect. When the war in Afghanistan hotted up, Abe brought Cam back to her home country with Luk, to start again. It was also where the Americans were, so it satisfied some of the homesickness he still felt; the need to hear a friendly, American voice. So they wound up back here in Kabul, the capital of Afghanistan, where she had so many relations and contacts, and Abe could chew the fat about the military with the customers who frequented his bar.

"Do you ever regret coming back here?" I asked them. "I mean, it must be difficult for Cam, seeing how bad things are in the country."

Cam answered. "Once, this was a country to be proud of. We had a civilization, a culture, and a history. Now, all we have is barbarism and cruelty, starvation and war. It is my home, true, but if we did not have this business, we would go elsewhere."

It was a sobering reply. I asked Abe for the name of a decent hotel, and he wrote down the address of one nearby. The mercenaries got up and left shortly after we'd spoken to them. I asked Abe about them. I was that curious.

"What exactly do they do, those guys? I mean, I know roughly, but who do they work for? Who employs those kinds of people?"

"The mercs? They work for the highest bidder, same as it's always been, as long as it's someone friendly to the US, of course. Your own father worked several missions in Vietnam, when the Americans were there."

"He was a mercenary? That's not right, during the American war, he ran a civilian airline."

"That's not the whole truth, Max. Did you know his outfit was known as the 'Devil's Guard' during the French

Indochina war? At least, that's what the Viet Minh called it."

I shook my head. It was news to me.

"Yeah, the Viet Minh changed their name to the Vietcong afterwards, and they sure as hell didn't like Jurgen's outfit. His Foreign Legion guys, they were tough fighters, maybe the only soldiers the Viet Minh ever really respected. In the early days, they were ordinary serving legionnaires, but Jurgen trained them to use tactics that were not what you'd call conventional. They were not unlike those guys that just left the bar. I guess you'd call them the modern Devil's Guard. Those men served in a variety of outfits, mostly Special Forces in Iraq, and one or two other foreign wars the Americans prefer to forget. The insurgents hate them when they go into action. They're not bound by politicians and rules of engagement, and just like in Jurgen's day, they fight to win, by any means necessary." He grinned. "So I guess you could say that Jurgen almost invented that kind of behind-the-lines warfare. Shock and awe, they call it these days, except that his battles took place behind their lines. It frightened the shit out off them, then and now. But enough of that, tell me about this job you've taken for Ed Walker?"

I told him we were due to fly out at dawn with a mixed cargo of security men and cargo.

"You don't know where you're going?"

I shook my head. "He wouldn't tell us, something about

need to know. But we've an agreement. We only fly in and out of established airfields, so we'll avoid any rough field, Special Ops type stuff. We just want to finish the job, pay off the mortgage and carry on running a business."

Abe chuckled. "And you believed that he'd keep to that agreement?"

"Well, yes, I did. We've got it on paper."

"Well I wish you luck if it doesn't turn out the way you planned."

We all looked to the front of the bar just then. There was a loud explosion outside, like a grenade going off; then gunfire, shouts and screams. Abe turned to Luk.

"Time to put up the shutters, son. It looks like we're in for another riot."

"You get many riots around here?"

Luk had run outside and was pulling the heavy wooden shutters across the windows. Abe looked grim. "I don't know how things are in Kandahar, but they hate us, the Afghans. Some of them do, anyway. These Pashtuns, they go crazy for the slightest insult. So when out soldiers hit their people in a friendly fire accident, it's a reason for a permanent vendetta. There've been too many accidents, and too many of them hate us as a result. Riots are a fact of life, I'm afraid. There's always some crazy mullah to wind up these people as well, and they're deeply religious. Then there's the suicide bombers, that's a trick they picked up from the Iraqis. Most of them are not Afghans, though.

There are a lot of foreign fighters who've come in to join the Jihad, and they're the ones most likely to carry out the suicide bombings. Iraqis, Chechens, Saudis, even a few Brits. The Afghans don't see that as productive. They'd sooner live to fight rather than die to fight. We've learned to be pretty careful."

I walked to the door and looked out. Luk had finished fastening the shutters, and we stood watching the nearby crowd, about forty people waving their arms and shouting at a bar that was blazing along the street. I felt Rachel come up behind me and touch my arm.

"What are they doing?" I asked Luk.

He shrugged. "I've no idea. It could be the mullahs getting upset about an Afghan bar selling liquor to Muslims. That's the usual grouse, something crazy like that. Maybe women taking a walk outside without their heads covered too. They go crazy for this Islamic stuff."

Then we ducked because there was another explosion, even bigger. The crowd seemed to split apart like dust in a sandstorm. Luk pushed us both down and led us back on all fours inside the bar. He locked the door securely, and when he turned to us, his face was grim.

"Another bombing, and could be a suicide. The poor devils that got caught in the blast never stood a chance. You need to be careful when you leave, they sometimes have a second bomber to wait for the police and emergency services, that's assuming they turn up. Often they don't even bother to come. I can't blame them. Too many have been killed trying to help the wounded."

We waited for a half hour. There were no more explosions, and a couple of ambulances arrived to carry away the dead and wounded. But the ground was still littered with the debris of the second blast, broken bodies, men, women and children. There were fragments of glass, odd possessions, women's purses, hats, and shoes. Pieces of wood and metal, the flotsam and jetsam of a war that gave no quarter to civilians or soldiers alike. Abe came and joined us.

"If you think this is bad, you wait until you get out into the boonies. They shoot first, and ask questions afterwards there."

I looked at Rachel. "How would you feel about employing some kind of protection? I feel we could be getting in over our heads. I'm not too happy about us being thrown in at the deep end with Ed Walker and his buddies. We know nothing of their kinds of operation they undertake."

She raised an eyebrow. "What do you mean, their kinds of operation?"

"Exactly."

She nodded. "Yeah, I get the point. Maybe that would be a good idea. We'll get caught out like babes in the wood. We know nothing about the CIA, and the games they play. I've heard stories of what they got up to in Vietnam in the old days. Here, who knows?"

I turned to Abe. "Can you suggest anyone that could help us out?"

"My son here, Luk." He looked at the young man. "How about it?"

His son looked enthusiastic. He also looked solid enough, and he had a soft, almost feminine face. He was quite short, so he'd taken after his mother more than his father. But he had the eyes of a marksman, a level, intense stare that never wavered. And he carried himself with a fluid grace that demonstrated a high level of fitness and strength.

"Sure, I'm looking to find work outside of the bar."

Abe looked back at me. "What do you think?"

"Is he any good?" I asked him. "I mean, with weapons, stuff like that."

"He was a champion marksman in the Afghan Army, did military service and joined me in the bar when he'd finished his time. Yeah, he's real good, and I know that the ANA doesn't have a great reputation. And even more important, he knows the country and knows the people. In Afghanistan, that can be the difference between life and death."

Rachel indicated her agreement. I turned back to Luk.

"Ok, then, you're hired. But it would be better if we called you the engineer. I don't want to upset Ed Walker by taking a mercenary with us."

"That's fine by me, Mr. Hoffman."

"It's Max, and Rachel. We're not American Airlines, not yet, anyway."

"We do share one thing with them," Rachel smiled. "I believe they're as broke as we are."

We said our goodbyes and agreed to collect Luk on the way to Kabul International in the morning. In the meantime, Abe directed us to the hotel. He also gave us a card with his contact details.

"I'll give Luk my satphone. He carried it when he was on his military service. It'll mean you can get through to me at any time if you have problems."

"Thanks, Abe, I appreciate it. But I don't think we'll have any problems, I'm sure Luk won't be called upon for anything drastic."

"Maybe not, but hear this. Jurgen, your grandfather, saved my life on more than one occasion. That's a debt that is still outstanding, and I always pay my debts. Any trouble, you get Luk to call me. Hear?"

"I copy that. And thanks."

We left the bar and found the hotel nearby. It wasn't too bad, by Afghan standards. Which meant it was a shithole by any normal standards.

"What do you think?" Rachel asked me.

"Of the hotel?"

"No, of this new deal we've got for ourselves. The whole shebang."

I thought about her words for a few moments. But there was only one honest answer I could give her. "I think it stinks, and I think that Ed Walker will be trouble, and I think I'd like to screw you, right now. You're the only sane thing about this place."

"We're going to share a long and satisfied relationship, Max," she smiled. "We operate along the same lines."

Afterwards, we lay on our backs on the bed, still naked.

"We need to finish this contract as fast as possible and get out of here," Rachel said suddenly. "I smell trouble, and when I say trouble, I mean big trouble. I'm glad we've got Luk coming with us."

I couldn't have agreed with her more.

It was still dark the next morning when we awoke, showered and dressed. We went out to find a taxi and pick up Luk. Abe had one last surprise. He handed each of us a pistol, a military Colt .45 in a canvas shoulder rig. Each of the guns had three pouches with spare clips that were already loaded with bullets. I protested, but he'd have none of it.

"Take them. Without a gun in this place you're not dressed, and you may as well walk around without your pants."

I protested hard. I'd never forget the nightmare of the guy I'd killed. Never be certain whether he was about to shoot or not. Never be sure if I'd be able to kill an enemy if I was faced with one again. But Abe was insistent, and

I gave in. We thanked him and strapped on the weapons. They felt heavy and uncomfortable, but it did give me a certain reassurance. If it ever came to it, maybe the threat of being armed would be enough. Helene, my grandmother, had insisted I learn how to shoot a pistol from a young age in case it was ever needed. After that, I'd had very little weapons training in the Royal Thai Army, until that fateful day. Rachel had learned in the Air Force, of course, so we both had no problem about knowing which end the bullet came out. When we reached Kabul International, the Twin Otter was fueled, loaded and ready to go. The security men were already aboard and Ed Walker looked impatient. This time he was wearing camouflage combat clothes, canvas boots and carried an assault rifle. A man we hadn't seen before accompanied him. I could see Rachel's nose twitching.

"Where've you been, Hoffman? It's late."

"It's the time we agreed, Mr. Walker," I replied.

He grunted. I was looking at the other man, and Walker caught my gaze.

"This is Joe Ashford. He heads up the Afghan operation for Double Eagle Security. Kind of the regional manager," he chuckled.

So this was the Head of Station, the CIA's chief spook. We shook hands, and his grip was cold and hard. He was an immensely strong man, which was obvious from the start. Ashford had the physique of a college footballer. He was both tall and heavy with broad, strong shoulders, but none of it was fat. His huge, hard muscles told of a man who was very strong. He didn't talk, he growled. "Pleased to meet you, Hoffman. Don't let me delay you, the boys are waiting to go."

There was no warmth in his handshake, or his hard, cold tones, and the message was clear. The master had spoken, and the help had better get his shit together and jump to it. His voice was pitched deep, a low thunder, like the sound of an earthquake miles below the surface. He had a broken nose, and his face bore the obvious scars of bruising encounters during his football career. Or perhaps from his career since then, which had clearly been colorful. I noticed his expensive and complicated Swiss watch, no doubt sequestered from an enemy in some previous CIA operation. Both men eyed our pistols, Rachel's and mine. They didn't like them, which pleased me for some crazy reason. Then they looked at Luk.

"Who's this?"

"Oh, yes, this is Luk Woltz. I took him on as our engineer. The facilities can be primitive in some of these places, and it's advisable to carry an engineer in case of any emergencies."

Walker grunted. Joe Ashford stared at him for a few moments, and I could see he didn't believe a word of it. But neither was he pilot-in-command. I was, and he had no choice but to demur to my wishes where aircraft operational safety was concerned. He stared at me.

"It's late, you should get moving."

"Mr. Ashford, I haven't even filed a flight plan yet. Where are we going?"

"It's all taken care of. Ed's coming with you, and he'll let you know when you're in the air. Just take off and fly north west."

It wasn't enough, not nearly enough. It was crazy to take off from a war torn country to an unknown destination with an aircraft crowded with armed mercenaries and a cargo of dark secrets. I wanted to protest, and saw Ashford smiling, waiting for me to ask. He knew he held all the cards, so I didn't give him the satisfaction. I turned to Rachel and Luk.

"Let's get aboard, we'll take off now."

The three of us climbed aboard the Twin Otter. The cargo area was crammed with armed men. They were talking quietly between themselves, and two of them were checking their assault rifles. There was a stack of wooden crates at the rear of the aircraft, and their lack of markings suggested that questions about them would not meet with any kind of an answer.

"Where do I sit?" Luk asked. He was carrying a long, thin, canvas case. As a former champion sniper, I didn't need to ask him what was inside it. It wasn't the most convincing appearance for our new flight engineer. I corrected his ignorance about where an engineer would be stationed.

"In the cockpit, Luk. You're flight crew, remember?" I whispered.

"Oh yeah, right."

Rachel smiled and took his arm to lead him forward to the jump seat in the cockpit, just behind her right hand co-pilot's seat. I was pleased to see that he ignored her limp. She started the engines, and I checked with the tower. We were cleared for immediate taxi and take-off, which was no surprise. Five minutes later, we were climbing to the north west, with the rising sun behind us. It lit up the sky in a kaleidoscope of vivid colors, and Rachel smiled at me.

"We're really back in business, Max. How does it feel?"

"Ask me when it's all over," I called back.

She pulled a face. In truth, I was convinced we were totally screwed. Screwed if we went ahead, screwed if we didn't.

* * *

They'd waited a short while after dawn; time enough for the reconnaissance drones to sweep the Kabul-Kandahar Highway, and for the data to be analyzed. The intelligence guys gave the road a clean bill of health, so they set out for the return journey. The convoy was a reverse of the inbound leg. Rains led the way in his Stryker, with the Afghan M35 trucks strung out behind. Another Stryker was positioned in the center of the column, and the rear was brought up by the third APC. For some reason, the Lieutenant felt more confident. After all, the road had been cleared. Corporal Delgado issued a stream of reports about air activity, and Rains was able to identify several drones that passed overhead. Reconnaissance drones, he assumed. Or maybe they were MQ-9 Reapers, the fearsome attack drones. Rains knew they were controlled remotely by operators stationed at bases such as Creech Air Force Base, near Las Vegas. Thousands of miles away, the operator could control the hunt for targets and observe terrain using a number of sensors, including a thermal imaging camera. The operator's commands only took a fraction over a second to reach the drone via a satellite link. The MQ-9 was fitted with six pylons for ordnance and extra fuel tanks. An MQ-9 with two one thousand pound external fuel tanks and a thousand pounds of munitions had an endurance of forty-two hours; an awful long time to hunt down the bad guys. The weapons load included GBU-12 Paveway II laser-guided bombs, AGM-114 Hellfire II air-to-ground missiles, and the AIM-9 Sidewinder. It all added up to a good feeling of security, and just knowing they were there was quite a comfort.

It was so easy. It was a breeze! Maybe the reports of Taliban activity were macho exaggerations, he considered. They completed the long, uncomfortable journey to Kabul without meeting a single enemy fighter. Every man breathed a sigh of relief, especially when they climbed out of the vehicles to exercise their aching muscles. Traveling on Afghan roads was like being beaten in the ass by baseball bats. At least, it was on the main highway. The secondary roads were worse. Rains decided it was time to relax and get to know his crew.

"You men, if any of you are interested, I'll buy you all a drink when we've checked into Phoenix. I reckon we've earned it."

There were grunts of appreciation. Sergeant Mason nodded at him. "Good idea, LT. That'll give the boys a chance to get to know you. We've hardly had time to get acquainted since the unit was assembled in country."

"They're good troops, and I'm looking forward to relaxing over a few beers," Rains replied, feeling that at last he'd said the right thing. "I'm gonna take a look up top, let some air inside now that we've made the city."

"I'd be careful if I were you, Lieutenant," Sergeant Mason cautioned.

"No worries, Sarge. I need to see the beautiful blue sky again. That was a long trip."

He opened up the hatch and poked his head out. The city of Kabul was bustling. The sidewalks thronged with men in turbans and pakuls, and veiled women. Women in the city wore the traditional blue burqa, just like their counterparts in the countryside. The garment enshrouded them from head to foot, with just a mesh screen in front of their face for them to be able to see out. Christ, how did they manage to swallow a cold drink through that weird contraption! His prevailing impression was dust, rubble and decay. There was little evidence of the billions of dollars that has been spent on infrastructure, at least, not here. He looked casually at a motorcycle that drew alongside the column. The guy steering it wore a turban, and on the pillion seat a blue robed woman sat, her burqa flowing in the slipstream as the bike roared along the road.

"The fucking maniac, he's much too close to the trucks. He'll be under the wheels if he gets any nearer."

"What's that, Lieutenant?" Mason opened the adjacent hatch and poked his head out. He glanced at the motorcycle then ducked down, shouting at Rains.

"Suicide bomber, get inside and shut that fucking hatch!"

The officer heard the words and reacted with the speed that had been drummed into him during basic training. Both hatches clanged shut almost at the same instant, and a split second later there was a huge explosion that rocked the vehicle on its suspension. The soldiers were flung across the interior, and only their Kevlar helmets saved their heads from being dashed against the steel hull. Rains felt a blow to his head and shook it to clear his brain. The tactical screen had gone white as the software automatically went into reboot mode. The soldiers picked themselves up off the floor and felt their limbs for anything broken.

Sergeant Mason was already peering through the optical periscope.

"Those poor bastards," he said, his voice colored by the anger he felt. "They've lost two of the trucks. There's almost nothing left."

Rains waited until the Sergeant ceded the periscope to him. The scene was one of utter devastation, and the two trucks were smoking skeletons of metal and rubber. There was no sign of the crews. Their bodies had been shredded in the blast. He felt a terrible sadness, a sense of failure. They were in his charge, and he'd failed them. Mason looked at him, seeing his despair.

"It's not your fault, Lieutenant. This is normal. Welcome to Afghanistan."

"It happened on my watch, Sergeant. The fuckers, I'd like to make them pay for this."

"I hear you, LT. But they already did. It was a suicide bomb, so they will be a bucket load of little pieces. They've made their payment."

When they returned to Camp Phoenix, it was as if nothing had happened. It didn't make Rains feel any better. Maybe it was normal for this hellhole of a country, but it wasn't normal for him. Next time, he'd make sure he was more alert. Maybe it would make a difference, maybe not. But he'd try. Major Fairchild was sympathetic.

"It's bad luck that it happened on your first mission, Rains. Don't let it worry you. I've got something coming up that you can do for me. They've got an outbreak of disease in Pakistan, some little town over the border. Medecin Sans Frontieres is sending some of their people to go over there and help them out. You can run escort for them. It's a milk run over the Khyber Pass, so you shouldn't hit any problems. I'll let you know when everything's in place for you to go. In the meantime, just take it easy. Relax, have a few beers."

His weapons specialist, Corporal Delgado, was having an equipment malfunction. When he went to check, he found shreds of flesh hanging from his aerial array. The shreds of Afghan Army uniform were still visible, and Delgado took them down.

"Hey, guys, lookee here what I've found."

He proudly showed what he'd found. Rains excused himself and barely made it to the bathroom to throw up.

CHAPTER FIVE

To America I say I swear by God the great... America will never taste security and safety unless we feel security and safety in our lands and in Palestine.

Osama Bin Laden

The messenger rushed into the inner cave. "They are coming, these infidel Americans. The assassins, they're on their way!"

Commander Abdul Qadir ignored him for a few moments. Then he turned to him, not reaching for the piece of paper. "Calm down, Mohammed. We already knew this."

"But, Commander, their plane has already departed. We have no idea where they will strike. They may even be coming here."

"In which case they will die, my young friend. Our preparations are all ready. Now, give me the message."

He scanned the paper and frowned. "It seems there are nine of these American killers. The message does not say exactly where they are planning to attack, so we will just have to keep alert and watchful."

"It will spread our forces very thin, Commander," one of his squad leaders objected. "Even though they are small in number, they will have unlimited resources, air support, drones, reinforcements and artillery."

"Perhaps," Qadir nodded, deep in thought, "but I think not. These killers come alone, so that their government can disown them when they are killed, which they surely will be. Send out word to all of our fighters. They are to be prepared and send word to me here when they see where these infidels land."

The man inclined his head. "It shall be as you say, Commander. We shall slaughter them as soon as they set foot on our soil."

"If God wills it, yes, we will slaughter them," he agreed. But privately, he thought, what if God does not will it? He had no answer for that question.

* * *

We had traveled for almost an hour, and still there was no clue as to our destination. I went back into the cabin to find Ed Walker. He was sat on his own, a few feet from his men, who were stretched out and dozing. I tapped him on the shoulder, and he looked around.

"Yeah, what is it?"

"I need the destination airport, Mr. Walker. Where are we going? You can't keep it to yourself any longer. I have a plane to fly."

"Ok, sure." He handed me a piece of paper. "We're heading there. It's a map reference."

"I can see it's a map reference, but which airport is it?"

"I've no idea, Hoffman. You're the pilot. Look it up," he sneered.

I went back to the cockpit without another word. I keyed the coordinates into our navigation system, and there was no airport within a hundred miles. Nothing. I went back to find Walker. He was waiting for me, wearing a challenging look on his face.

"Where's the airport? I've checked, and there's nothing there."

He nodded. "Then I guess you'll just have to wait and see what they've got ready for us. It'll be usable, whatever it is."

"We had an agreement. I said I would only use regular, mainstream commercial airfields."

He smiled. "Hell, to these people I guess that's what it is."

"I'm going to alter course to the nearest commercial

airfield. I told you. I don't fly into places where I don't know whether I'll be able to get down safely, let alone take off again. The deals off, Mr. Walker, so you'll have to find someone else."

I heard a click behind me. Two of his men stood there; one had cocked his automatic and pointed it at me. It was my turn to smile.

"I doubt even you would be so stupid as to shoot the pilot."

"No, I guess you're right. That's why we'll shoot the co-pilot if you don't cooperate. That would be a pity. She's a pretty little thing, for a cripple."

I made to swing at him, but one of his men twisted my arm behind me and screwed the barrel of his pistol into my neck.

"That'd be a stupid thing to try. Just remember whose paying the bills, Hoffman. Now do we fly with one pilot or two? It's your choice."

We stared at each other for a few moments, and all of Abe's words came flooding back to me, along with my Grandmother Helene's advice about dealing with the CIA. I knew I was beaten, and I backed down.

"Ok, you win. What am I expecting when we land?"

"It's a field. They cleared last year's crop and smoothed over the worst of the bumps and rocks. We'll be fine. If I didn't think so, I wouldn't have gone for it."

I nodded my agreement, and he waved for the guy to

release me. I went back into the cockpit and gave them the bad news. Rachel surprised me with her reaction.

"So we're going into action? This could be interesting."

"It could get us all killed. I wouldn't be so keen if I were you. It will be a rough strip landing, and we've no idea how good the field is. And there is the other matter, we've no idea either who will be waiting for us when we get there."

I glanced at the back of the cockpit. Luk hadn't said a word, but he was quietly unpacking his sniper rifle and assembling it ready to go. Rachel saw the direction of my gaze.

"Luk, what are you doing? We're not going into battle quite yet."

He didn't look up. "Can you guarantee that?"

She shook her head. "I guess not, no. So what do we do now?"

"Do? We do our job. Didn't they used to say, 'keep your faith in God and your powder dry'? I think we should check our pistols and make sure they're ready for use. As for God, he can take care of himself."

"He?"

I chuckled. "Yeah, whatever. The important thing is to keep the engines running when they're unloading so that if there's any trouble, we can make a fast take-off. I'll go and have a word with Walker, and let him know what we're doing. Luk, you and I can make sure that no one stumbles into the propellers. Rachel, you stay at the controls."

He nodded. "I'll take my rifle with me."

Walker barely took any notice of me when I spoke to him. He was busy briefing his men. He looked around when I tapped him on the shoulder and told him what we planned.

"Yeah, that's no problem. We'll be jumping off from the landing field, so you'll be coming back without any passengers. There'll be some more crates, and I want you to take them to Joe Ashford. He'll be waiting for you in Peshawar. Don't land in Afghanistan or anywhere else other than Peshawar."

"What's in these crates we'll be carrying?"

"Need to know, buddy," he grinned. "And you don't need to know."

"I assume it's enough to know that it's something that could cause me a problem if I land inside Afghanistan?"

"Don't even think about it. They'd have your balls if they found out what's in those crates, and if they don't, Joe will. Just follow my instructions, and it'll all be fine."

"Like the pilot of the Cessna Caravan did?"

He grimaced. "Fuck you, Hoffman. The stupid bastard messed up, period. Make sure you do it right."

I left him to his briefing and went back to the cockpit.

"We're twenty minutes out from these coordinates, Max. Do you want me to take her in?"

"You may as well, yes. I'll let the passengers know, and

then I'll stay up front."

I went aft again and told them our ETA, but they barely took any notice. Then I went up front and strapped myself into the left hand seat. We had full daylight, and Rachel had already begun the descent. Mountains surrounded us everywhere we looked. As we drew nearer our landing site, I could see it was a narrow valley with a high mountain, capped by snow on each side. It was no wonder these were such a hardy, tough and savage people. It was that kind of a land where the weak would perish, and the strong would struggle to survive by right of superior strength. It was a medieval concept of society, but these were medieval people.

"Three miles to run," Rachel intoned. "Still no sign of the landing field."

"Ok, reduce speed to ninety knots, thirty degrees of flap. Luk, strap in. This could be bumpy."

I took out my binoculars and looked ahead for the landing field. Then I saw it. It looked like a pocket-handkerchief from three miles out. There were tiny dots around it, and people and vehicles came into focus.

"I see it," Rachel called across to me. "I'll increase the rate of descent. We're nearly there."

She was an expert pilot, and I was happy to let her handle the controls while I surveyed the surrounding area. It seemed peaceful enough. The nightmarish vision of hordes of savage, heavily armed tribesmen waiting in ambush didn't look as if it was going to happen today. The field came nearer, and I could make out the people and vehicles with the naked eye. One of the men down there fired a flare into the air, and we were able to determine the wind direction. Rachel grunted as she worked out the options. The wind blew diagonally across the field, and we were landing in the best direction, slightly into the wind. The men who watched our descent were all in Afghan dress, robes and turbans, and all carried weapons, although they didn't look as if they were about to threaten us. The two vehicles that waited for us were Toyota Land Cruisers, the tough Japanese SUVs that would go to most places closed to ordinary cars. The long wheelbase, crew cab models would be enough to transport the men and equipment that were about to disembark. The field came nearer, nearer.

I automatically checked the instruments, speed eighty knots, and altitude one hundred feet above ground level. Rachel dropped down lower and flared on to the field. The Twin Otter could land in three hundred yards at a pinch, and take off in an even shorter distance. I held my breath. If we didn't make it, it was going to be a long walk home. It was a good landing, just a slight bump, and a number of jars as we hit irregularities on the surface, but none were serious enough to cause any problems. She managed to brake the aircraft just before the end of the field. There was enough room to turn around and head back to face the way we'd landed, into the wind. We stopped right at the head of the landing strip, and Rachel applied the brake, keeping the engines running. I went aft with Luk. Walker's men already had the door open and were jumping down. I wondered if scheduled airlines ever had this problem with controlling their passengers. Maybe I was in the wrong part of the business.

I jumped down. Luk came with me, carrying his rifle.

"Take the port engine, and make sure no idiot runs into the propeller," I shouted to him above the noise of the engines. He nodded and ran off. I heard Walker calling my name, and I went over to him.

"We need about an hour on the ground, so you can switch off if you like."

"An hour? What the hell for? You told me this was a straight in and out job. I don't like the idea of waiting."

He sneered. "Scares you, does it?"

I didn't give him the satisfaction of a reply.

He continued. "Our return cargo hasn't arrived yet, so there's no choice, you just have to wait. The cargo is what pays for this mission, so the two are linked together."

I nodded and went inside the aircraft to let Rachel know. She switched off the engines, and we walked out into the cabin and jumped to the ground to stretch our legs. Luk had taken up a position by the nosewheel leg, and he was surveying the ground around us with his telescopic sight. Walker's men had loaded their equipment into the Land

Cruisers and were sat on the grass waiting. All of them had their assault rifles ready for instant action. I wandered over to Walker.

"What's the arrangement for getting your men back to Kabul?"

He considered his answer for a few moments. "This job should only take us two days. I've got a satphone with me. If everything goes to plan, I'll call you to pick us up here. Make sure you keep the coordinates."

"They're programmed into the aircraft's GPS system," I replied.

"Right. I hope to Christ these guys we're waiting for don't take much longer. You can't leave without the shipment. Joe would go crazy."

So that confirmed it. I was about to become a drug runner, as well as carrying armed mercenaries and their guns and equipment. It was the low point in my career, and one that I could do nothing about. These people had a long reach, and I knew that if I failed to do what they wanted, they'd find me and ruin me. Or worse. I returned to Rachel, and we sat together, not talking. It was a fine morning, cold, but not the harsh cold that can make the interior of this country so forbidding.

"Look, Max, this could be them."

She was pointing to the far corner of the field. A line of donkeys had appeared laden with bulging hessian sacks. They were accompanied by four men, and all of them were carrying shoulder launched RPGs. It was pure Afghanistan; the ancient meets the modern. The scene would have been exactly the same a thousand years before, were it not for the RPGs. I saw Walker striding towards me.

"We're running behind schedule, Hoffman. We'll check the load, and then we need to get moving. See that it's properly stowed in the aircraft, then head for Peshawar. Joe will meet you there. He'll see to the unloading and give you your next instructions. Any questions?"

"I don't want to handle drugs, Mr. Walker. That's not part of the deal."

He laughed out loud. "Sure. Well let me tell you, my friend. The deal has changed. Just get it done and don't fuck with me. And you really don't want to fuck with Joe Ashford, no way. I'll see you back here in two days. I'll call you."

Then he was gone, racing away to round up his men and meet the donkey train. Luk and Rachel joined me, and I explained what was expected of us.

"I don't like that guy," Luk murmured. "Whatever he's up to, it's nothing that's going to be good for us."

"I agree. Keep the rifle handy. Perhaps you could climb up onto the wing and keep a lookout."

The Twin Otter was a high wing aircraft, so it would give him a good observation platform. He climbed up onto the wing, and I felt better with him standing up there, keeping a good watch. The Land Cruisers raced away in a cloud of dust, and we were left in a field in the middle of enemy territory with barely enough room to take off and a donkey train guarded by four Afghan tribesmen, about which I knew nothing. I was watching Luk, but I heard the sound of hoofs behind me and the creak of leather harness. I turned to find the donkey train next to the aircraft. The tribesmen were already unloading the sacks. Rachel pointed up to the cargo door of the Twin Otter. One of the men stared at her and smiled through black and broken teeth. Then he made a rude and filthy gesture. I saw Rachel color, but then she relaxed and came over to me.

"I guess that means we load the stuff ourselves."

"It sure looks that way."

We watched them continue to toss the sacks to the ground. Rachel and I started to carry them to the aircraft and throw them on board. They weighed about fifty or sixty pounds each, not a massive weight, but there were forty of them. I calculated it was about two tons, and by the time we'd tossed them all on board, we were exhausted.

"Let's take a few minutes before we lash them down," I suggested. "I could do with a soda. I'll grab one each for you and Luk."

I climbed aboard and looked out at the donkey train. It was moving away from us, already about two hundred yards distant. I took three sodas out of our cool box, and that's when I heard the first shot. I tossed the sodas down and ran out.

"What going on?"

Rachel was staring into the distance. The shot sounded as if it had come from about three hundred yards away, in the opposite distance to where the donkeys had disappeared. I heard Luk shouting down from the wing.

"How do we know if it's Taliban?"

"They wear black turbans. I think that's the only way."

"There's about ten of them, and they're coming down from the low hill off to the east. I'd guess they're two hundred yards from us."

"What are they wearing?"

"Black turbans."

"Then they're Taliban. Can you slow them down?"

"Sure. I'll see what I can do."

"We'll tie down the load, and we can get airborne. Give us three or four minutes."

"I've got it."

His rifle cracked out, shot after shot. I afterwards found he hit a target about one shot in four. His main object was to stop them getting any closer. The steady rate of fire only stopped when he changed magazines, and the incoming fire was fragmented and wild. The moment our attackers put their heads up for an aimed shot, Luk put a bullet into them. I scrambled to pull the heavy sacks into the center of the aircraft where they would not upset our trim. Rachel came and helped, and we lashed them down. Rachel limped forward to start the engines, and I went to call Luk.

"We're leaving. You need to get inside."

A fusillade of shots came towards us, and two holes appeared in the fuselage.

"Luk! Hurry up."

His rifle cracked several more times. There were several cries of agony in the distance, and then he was in the doorway, sliding down from the wing.

"They'll come now that I've stopped shooting, Max. I hit maybe six of them, but the other four have assault rifles."

"You did well. Time to go."

The whine of the Pratt and Whitney turboprops filled the cabin as Rachel spooled up. I closed the door and went forward. She grinned at me. Her eyes were dilated with the excess of adrenaline that had flooded her system when the shooting started.

"I guess you won't be doing a walkaround check?"

"Maybe next time. Get us out of here, Rachel. We haven't much time before they come closer."

She put the engines to maximum boost, and the aircraft strained against the brakes. Then she released them, and we hurtled forward.

"Max!"

"I see him."

A Taliban shooter had come nearer, and he was about two hundred yards ahead of us, eighty yards off to the port side. He had an RPG rocket in his arms, and it was clear he was waiting for us to take off. Our forward speed would be miniscule when we left the ground. The aircraft would be struggling for height, and we'd be a sitting duck. I turned around and shouted for Luk.

"Your rifle, you need to hit that guy with the rocket. I'll open the port window."

The tiny window next to the left hand seat opened. I slid it aside and let Luk get to it. The aircraft was bumping and jolting on the rough ground as Rachel fought with the controls to keep it in a straight line. Luk fired, but just as he did the aircraft hit a bump, and his shot went wild. I decided that we only had one chance.

"Luk, he won't fire the rocket until we're airborne. These missileers will have done this many times before, so he'll know the best time to fire. As soon as our wheels unstuck, the aircraft will be stable. Hit him then."

He nodded. Rachel looked across at me with her eyebrows raised, but I considered it a risk worth taking. I couldn't take the pilot's seat, so I held onto the seat backs and waited.

Rachel handled the aircraft with her usual aplomb while I watched the instruments.

"V1, fifty-five knots." We needed sixty-five knots to take off, at least with the half load in the cargo area.

"Ok."

"Sixty-five knots, rotate."

She held it steady, accelerating. "Rachel!"

She didn't look at me. "I'm trying to give Luk the best angle for the shot."

She was right. It was difficult to point the rifle out of the window at such a steep angle in the cramped cockpit.

"Try not to leave until we run out of field."

"I'll see what I can do."

I saw her face crease into a smile. We hit seventy knots, and there was a tiny window when Luk had an almost perfect angle on the missileer. It all happened in a fraction of a second. Rachel hauled back on the control column, and the aircraft left the ground, just inches above the rough, stony soil of Afghanistan. Luk fired. I watched the missileer; hit by the heavy rifle bullet that pierced his eye and threw him backwards. He must have had his finger on the firing lever, for the missile hurtled into the sky in a blaze of smoke and sparks. It flew away from us to disappear somewhere in the foothills, a long way away. Its only threat was to a passing goat, perhaps. Rachel climbed for altitude, refusing to swap height for speed. Two more shots pierced the fuselage.

"Rachel, they're shooting!"

"And I've got a bloody mountain in front of me. I can't avoid both of them, Max."

The distant hills had grown alarmingly close, and as

we cleared a low hill, another higher peak appeared in front of us. Two more shots hit. Rachel had both engines straining at maximum power, and slowly we climbed away from the dangers of bullets, missiles and mountains. The danger was over, and Luk moved out of the window. I sat down in my seat and closed it.

"Is everyone ok? Nobody hit?"

"I'm good," Rachel replied.

"No problems," Luk added.

"Good. We need to set a course for Peshawar. I think it's time we had a word with Mr. Joe Ashford."

Halfway through the flight, Luk came into the cockpit. He'd been aft, checking out the cargo to make sure it hadn't moved.

"Max, I think you should come and see this."

I followed him into the cargo space. "What is it?"

"I guess you don't need to know what's inside these sacks."

"No. It's opium, couldn't be anything else."

"That's my feeling too. But they left two of the wooden crates behind, and I don't know why. I checked them out. They were about two feet by two feet square, and about a foot high.

"There's a smaller box over there." Luk had prized off the lid of one of the crates, and there were a number of wrapped parcels inside. I didn't recognize what it was.

"Do you know what it is?"

"It's C4, plastique. Plastic explosive. I came across it in the Afghan Army when I did my training."

"Jesus Christ! Is it dangerous?"

"Not immediately, no. But there is a small crate in the corner of the hold with the detonators inside it. Put the two together, and yes, it's very dangerous."

I tried to think why they'd left such an important consignment on the aircraft. I could only come to one answer. It was a simple oversight. One that I'd prefer people didn't make on my aircraft, not where explosives were concerned. We went forward, and I warned Rachel what we were carrying. Her eyebrows shot up.

"Fuck! The crazy bastards, what are they playing at?"

"It could be an error, who knows? Let's just wait and see. Luk says it's not dangerous."

"Sure, plastic explosive has that reputation."

We droned on through the day towards Peshawar. It was a journey of two and a half hours, and we flew past the awesome grandeur of the Afghan mountains. I took over the controls and watched the soaring, rocky peaks fall behind us; mountains that swooped down into green, often fertile and verdant valleys. Could this ever truly be a country at peace with itself and with the world? It seemed as if it could, placed astride a number of major trading routes, and with some natural resources of its own. So far, Afghanistan had been a place of misery, drought, famine, poverty and death to its population. The poor devils could do with a decent oil strike, if that was possible; something to put enough money in the treasury to pay for the essential infrastructure they so desperately lacked. But would these people spend that kind of sudden wealth wisely, or would it just go to equip the warlords with more weapons to continue their endless fighting between each other; fighting that only ended when they joined forces to attack foreign invaders. Then it was back to their internal squabbles. I'd thought Rachel was dozing.

"They're in the crapper for all time, these people."

I looked at her. She'd been thinking along similar lines.

"You're right. Poverty, disease, war, you name it. Tribal feuds, foreign invasions, and if you're a woman, God help you."

She shuddered. "These women spend their lives in abject poverty and misery. They're cooped up in their houses, and when they go out, they wear those awful blue burqas. It's no wonder so many of them commit suicide. I sure would."

"You'd get out, Rachel. You wouldn't put up with it."

She shook her head. "They're brought up into a culture of no hope. No money, no passports, nothing. No, better to end it all before it becomes unbearable."

"It's a good reason to beat the Taliban. And we're on the side of the good guys, so at least we can take comfort in that when we're bitching about being stuck with this crazy agreement."

"I'm not so sure about that, Max, the CIA, the good guys? I hope so, but that'll be a first."

I thought about that for a while. Did the Agency ever do anyone any good, apart from themselves, that is? They'd missed the fall of the Soviet Union. Then I remembered something else. It was thinking about the Soviet Union while we were flying over Afghanistan. They'd trained and equipped the Taliban with the latest weaponry. I nodded slowly. "I hope you're wrong, but I have a nasty feeling you could be right."

We made final approach to Peshawar. I took her in to land this time. The Pakistani air traffic controller was crisp and professional, with none of the sarcasm of his Vietnamese counterpart. I was not surprised that they were expecting us. Where Joe Ashford and Ed Walker were concerned, there seemed to be no difficulty in smoothing over red tape. By one means or another. I made a comfortable landing and taxied over to the stand we'd been assigned at the far end of the cargo area. A car was parked there, a Chevrolet Suburban, so beloved of the FBI in the USA and obviously other government agencies elsewhere in the world. I switched off the engines and began to shut down the aircraft systems. Rachel and Luk went aft to open the cargo doors, and when I followed them, Ashford was waiting on the tarmac. He wore a lightweight tropical suit in cream linen, well cut to fit over his huge, muscular frame. Obvious bodyguards, almost laughable in their dark glasses and plain khaki baggy combat suits, flanked him. They each carried a stubby Ingram submachine gun and wore shoulder rigs for their pistols, straight out of central casting in Hollywood, USA. I could have told them they were nearer Bollywood than Hollywood, and that something a little more ethnic and colorful may have been more appropriate.

"You're late."

"We were held up on the ground waiting for the cargo you wanted brought back."

"You got it all?"

"We've got what they gave us. Ed Walker was there, so I assume it's all ok."

He didn't acknowledge my words.

"Unload it into the SUV."

"Look, Mr. Ashford, I want a word with you before we go any further. Maybe you could get your men to unload while we talk."

I noticed a fuel bowser heading towards us that he'd clearly organized for us to make a fast turnaround. He looked in our direction at last.

"Fuel up and get back to Kabul. Unload the cargo yourselves. I don't pay my men to fetch and carry. I've got you to do that. I'll catch up with you in Kabul. I'll see you there tomorrow."

"But, we need to talk." I took a step nearer to him, but his bodyguards automatically moved to intercept me before I reached him. He came up to me and stood six inches away, huge and threatening.

"No, we don't need to talk. I need to give the orders. You need to follow them. That's all. Now get unloaded."

"Ed Walker said he'll contact us to pick him up in two days," I finished, trying to keep him talking.

He waved my remark away, as if it was of no consequence. We were left with no choice. We unloaded the sacks into the Suburban and watched as he drove away. I had a sudden thought.

"The explosives, they're still in the aircraft. Should we have unloaded them too?"

It was Luk who answered. "Max, people like that, if they were missing the plastique, they'd be on to us in a second. They clean forgot it, that's all."

Rachel stared, shaking her head in disbelief. "So what the hell do we do with it?"

"If it was me," Luk continued. "I'd save it for a rainy day. You never know, we might have a use for it one day. We could sell it, trade it, whatever, or even blow something up with it."

"Like Joe Ashford and Ed Walker, you mean," I smiled.

He nodded. "There you go, so it could come in mighty handy."

"You're mad, both of you," Rachel exclaimed. "If we get searched in Kabul airport and they find that, we're in deep shit."

"We're flying a plane that effectively is owned by the CIA, flying on CIA business. Who's going to search us?" I pointed out.

"Christ, I don't believe this," she countered, her voice ringing with anger. "It could finish us."

"So what do you want to do, Rachel? Drop it off at the local recycling facility. Tell them we've got some unwanted plastique if they'd care to dispose of it safely?"

"We could drop if over the Afghan mountains," she suggested.

"Great. You're talking about carpet-bombing Afghanistan."

She chuckled then. "Hey, maybe that's not such a bad idea."

We left the plastique where it was. The bowser finished refueling, and we got clearance and took off for the return leg to Kabul.

* * *

Lieutenant Dwight Rains popped his head over the parapet and immediately put it down again as a hail of bullets chipped pieces of stone that whizzed around his position.

"Sergeant Mason, what's the situation back there, are they holding them?"

Vince Mason crawled over to speak to his officer.

Mason was a ten-year veteran. He'd been through Iraq, and this was his second tour in Afghanistan. He had respect for Rains. The officer commanding the third platoon, C Company, 2nd of the 45th, US Infantry, meant well enough, but the guy was just too inexperienced for a situation like this one. They'd set out to travel from Kabul via Jalalabad to a town in Pakistan, outside Islamabad. Theirs was a humanitarian mission to collect a cargo of medical supplies with a group of medics and escort them to the stricken area. There'd been an outbreak of disease that was as yet unidentified, but it needed to be treated and contained as a matter of urgency. It should have been easy; collect the men and supplies, women too, there were two female nurses in the medical squad, and take them to the stricken town.

They'd reached Jalalabad, loaded up their vehicles and helped the medics to board their APCs. Their transport should have been using the latest Strykers, heavily armored APCs, fast and effective against most IEDs and incoming rifle fire. There'd been a change of plans. The Allied force was under heavy attack, and instead, they'd been issued with M113s. The vehicles had been good, once up on a time. But they were Vietnam era, and fighting against the Vietcong they'd been very effective. But here in Afghanistan, they were only used for local transport. They were, in effect, a light transport truck. Out in the countryside, in the badlands, they were deathtraps.

The Major had had a serious expression on his face, so why did Lieutenant Rains feel the man was sneering at him?

"I'm sorry, Lieutenant, but every single one of our Strykers is being readied to roll out to search and destroy the fuckers who attacked us. It's like fucking Tet out there, and I guess you know what happened back in Vietnam. I can't spare a single one, so it's the M113 or nothing, I'm afraid. They should function perfectly well as ambulances, and it's not as if you're going into combat, is it?"

He left the 'like real soldiers' bit out, but Rains knew what he meant. He also knew there was no choice but to carry out his orders. They'd loaded up and moved out with the medics huddled in the lightly armored hulls, grateful for the comforting feeling of the steel that surrounded them. And the infantrymen, who knew better, tensed their bodies, waiting for the roar of the explosion that would rip into them or the heavy machine gun rounds that would perforate the hull, turning their vehicle into a blazing, corpse-filled coffin. And they muttered the infantryman's prayer, 'please, let it not be me'.

The explosion, on the lower approaches to the Khyber Pass, had ripped apart the last vehicle in the column. They'd leapt out of their APCs, herding the medics to the relative safety of a nearby stone building, apparently a long abandoned police checkpoint. They'd left behind the bodies of eight of their comrades. The rest of them, thirty-one infantrymen, two doctors and six nurses were pinned down. Their transports were all smoking wrecks out on the road, destroyed by the withering fire the Afghans poured into them. Worst of all, the radios were in the vehicles, or had been before they were destroyed. So they kept the Taliban at bay, but for how long was anybody's guess. And Mason could see that his officer hadn't a clue about how to handle the situation. They were pinned down from both sides with no means of escape.

"There's no immediate threat, Lieutenant, but they could come at any time, who knows?"

"In that case we'll have to hold them," the officer snapped at his sergeant. "Make sure that everyone is ready for the next attack."

"Oh, they're ready, LT, they're ready all right. And if the ragheads don't attack, what then?"

He waited for a reply. That was the problem. If they just sat and waited, sooner or later the Americans would have to come out. They'd be short of food and water; the Taliban were not fools. And when they came out, they'd be waiting to fall on them like a pack of dogs. "So what do you want us to do, Lieutenant?"

Rains shook his head in misery. "I don't know, Sergeant. I haven't a fucking clue."

A soldier shouted suddenly. "Hey, Sarge, look, up there! A drone."

Every man in earshot looked up. Sure enough, a drone

was slowly crossing the sky from south to north. It flew at a height of about five thousand feet, and low enough to have seen them if the operator was sharp and observant.

"Do you think he saw us?" another man shouted.

Rains and Mason glanced at each other, and both shared the same thought. "I sure as fuck hope so," Rains muttered.

"Amen to that," his sergeant added.

* * *

Eight thousand miles away Master Sergeant Carol Wendelski sat down in front of her screen to start her shift. She was a wannabe fighter pilot, and when they'd turned her down for the flight crew, she'd volunteered for this assignment instead. At least it meant she had free time at home, to pursue her hobbies of writing a history of the gambling industry in Las Vegas, and even occasionally going to Sin City itself to play the tables. She grinned. What was the point of writing the book if you couldn't sample some of what you were writing about at the same time? The operator she was relieving stood up and relinquished the chair. Corporal Vernon Munch gave her a nod of welcome. "It's all yours, Carol. Try not to crash it."

"Yeah, yeah," she acknowledged. She'd heard it all before, the cracks about women drivers. And pilots. "Anything doing?"

"There could be, yeah. A group of our people is under attack up near the Pakistan frontier. I saw the action when the drone flew over. They know about it in Kabul, so I guess they'll take care of it in good time, but they've got their own problems. The Taliban are attacking the major cities. It's a major battle over there."

"Ok, what's the state of our ordnance?"

"We're unarmed, sadly. In their wisdom, they decided to send her out with maximum fuel, which means no missiles. All we can do is to watch the fun. I guess you'll see the coordinates in the nav computer when she flies past on the next leg."

"Ok, I'll keep an eye on it," she told him. Munch left the Ground Control Station, and she settled down to the long, monotonous task of looking down on a barren country eight thousand miles away.

CHAPTER SIX

The revival of certain industries, the revival of agriculture, schools and hospitals... there is really no area in which Afghanistan does not require assistance.

Hamid Karzai

The President had pulled out of the meeting at the last moment, citing an emergency meeting with Treasury. General Mann wondered sometimes if they shouldn't link the Treasury Department with FEMA these days. The economy was perpetually in crisis, and it seemed that never a day went by without total panic gripping the nation. He stood up as the Secretary of State walked into the room.

"Ma'am," he inclined his head.

She gave him a frosty glance. "General, I'm getting reports from Afghanistan, and I don't like what I'm hearing."

And good day to you, Ma'am, he thought. So there aren't going to be any niceties today.

"Which reports would they be?"

"First off, your new policy of taking out the leaders. How's it going? So far, I have no indications that there's been any progress. None whatsoever."

"It's early days yet. Give it time, Madame Secretary."

"Time we don't have. You know that the President, indeed the whole country, wants out of that manure pile by the end of next year."

"We're doing our best, Ma'am. We have to tread carefully. Lives are in danger here."

"General, every day you delay, lives are being lost, not merely in danger. You pressed for this action, so I suggest you see it through. No more delays."

He nodded. "I'll get onto it as soon as I get back to the Pentagon, and I'll tell them to accelerate the program."

"You do that. Keep me informed. The President is anxious to be certain that we don't have another total fuckup on our hands."

"Ma'am, the political and military realities don't always come together, we…"

"In the President's case, General, they do. He is also your Commander in Chief. Now, the next piece of bad news coming out of Afghanistan. My State Department tells me there are stories of drugs being shipped from

Afghanistan to other parts of Asia and even to the US, coming in on military flights. What do you know?"

He shrugged. "It's the first I've heard. Drugs are always a problem. You know that. We can't search every returning soldier to pat him down for drugs."

"General, I'm not talking about a couple of joints. This is a wholesale, multi-million dollar operation."

"Christ!" He was shaken. It was the stuff of nightmares, and the kind of story you often heard about the Vietnam War but assumed was a thing of the past. It was the kind of story that could destroy a soldier's career, and he wasn't without enemies in Washington, he knew that. "I know nothing of that, but believe me, I'll get an investigation mounted right away. Do you have any ideas who's behind it?"

"I'm told our friends in Langley know more than they care to admit."

"CIA?"

She nodded. "The CIA. I've no idea how true it is, but I want you to find out. Whoever is responsible, the President will want them hung out to dry for this. No exceptions. There's a cell waiting for them in a Federal prison in some isolated part of the US."

Mann whistled. "It could be someone high level, and someone who could throw a lot of dirt."

"Not from twenty years in solitary confinement."

"So he means business."

"He does, yes. Find the bastard and bring him in, General."

"I don't have full authority over the CIA, Ma'am," he objected.

"You do now, General. The President has issued a special order, giving you full powers to resolve this matter. The documents will go straight to your office."

He nodded. "I'll do my best."

"You'll do better than that, General. You'll find out who is responsible and bring them to justice. The war on drugs is every bit as big as the war on terror. The President sees the distinct possibility of losing both of them."

"We're not losing the war in Afghanistan. We've made some major gains," he objected.

She gave him a tired smile. "Yeah, I've looked at the military bulletins out of Vietnam during the late sixties, and they said exactly the same thing. I don't know about the Taliban, but you can win this problem with the drugs shipments. See that you do. The President would even go as far as to find someone who could do the job if you fail."

He glared at her. "You don't need to threaten me. I'll get the job done."

She smiled a sweet, friendly smile. "I never doubted you, General. Now, the military situation, I'm getting reports of a Taliban build up. Some intelligence analysts predict a big Taliban push against some of our areas, particularly the main cities. What do you know?"

He shrugged his shoulders. "It's news to me. But I'll check on it."

"Let me know what you find, General," was her parting shot as she got up and left. "And let me know when you locate Mullah Omar."

He winced. "Yeah, you want me to carry your bags, Ma'am," he muttered to her retreating back.

* * *

This time we were directed to the military terminal after we landed. The stands were crowded with aircraft, helicopters, transports, light armored APCs, troops doubling across the tarmac, Afghan civilians and military mingling with the chaos. A ground controller waved us to a stand next to a hangar. It was painted khaki like the others, but there were no unit designations, and nothing to indicate its purpose or who it belonged to. It didn't take much imagination to work it out. We shut down the aircraft and made it secure, then dropped down the ladder. Luk carried his rifle. It was still assembled ready for use, and we all carried pistols in holsters. Somehow, it didn't seem out of place here. In fact, there were no Europeans or Americans who didn't carry a weapon of some sort. A tired looking guy came out of the hangar and approached. He held out his hand.

"Hi, I'm Roy Waverley. I'm the manager of this operation. Welcome to Loonytown."

I grinned and held out my hand. He shook hands with all three of us, and I gave him our names.

"So you work for Joe Ashford?"

He grimaced. "Yeah, that about sums it up. Joe called earlier. You're to fly a cargo out to Islamabad in the morning, so I guess you guys may as well get some shut-eye in the meantime. I gather you've been pretty busy."

"We've run around the place, yeah. So what is this, another dawn departure?"

He looked slightly embarrassed. "Actually, I'd like you to get underway before then. Kind of get into the air before the place starts to wake up. Can you be here for four in the morning and wheels up by five?"

I hesitated. Why did he look so strange? "Sure, we can do that, but I'd like to know the reason why. What's so important about leaving in the dark?"

He fiddled with some change in his pocket, kicked up some dust and looked around. He finally came to a decision. "Look, Joe sends these cargoes all over the place, and he has a kind of understanding. We earn three times the pay of anyone else doing similar work. In return, we don't ask any questions. I'm not saying there's anything illegal going on, of course."

We all smiled. "Of course not," Rachel replied. "But we need to have an idea what we're carrying. It's our asses after all. Is it drugs, locally grown opium?"

His embarrassment turned to fear. "For Christ's sake,

don't say stuff like that, not if you want to get out of here in one piece. Just let it go."

I glanced at Luk and Rachel. They both nodded.

"Ok, Roy, we'll be here at four."

"I'll put the coffee on." He grinned, trying to ease the tension that we all felt. Running drugs was a passport to hell, and something I'd avoided up till now. The involvement of the CIA should have made me feel easier about it, but it didn't. It made me feel worse. We were about to leave to make out way to the hotel when all hell broke loose.

The explosions were the first surprise. Roy Waverley was just going back inside the hangar. He turned and shouted to us, "Mortars! Get yourselves under cover!"

We looked across the airfield. A mortar shell had scored a direct hit on a helicopter, and there was just a blazing ruin where seconds before there had been a functional flying machine. I couldn't see what kind of shelter we could head for that would keep us safe from the incoming mortars. Another shell landed, and this time if just missed a huge C5 Lockheed Galaxy transport aircraft. Already, a pall of smoke was spreading across the airfield, but I could still see the crew huddling behind an aircraft tractor. For some reason, I thought how useless and pointless their action was, when their vast, multi-million dollar aircraft lay at the mercy of the Taliban attack. There was the sound of keening in the air, shouts and warlike screams, and I focused on an area about half a mile away. The perimeter fence had been breached, and a horde of black-turbaned men was pouring through it, firing as they ran. The Galaxy crew saw them and started to run, but one of them fell, brought down by a burst of fire from an enemy assault rifle. I swiveled around to see how the Americans were responding. It looked patchy, and a group of MPs were hurtling towards the enemy. Their jeep-mounted machine gun was already blazing away, scything through the attackers. But they were too few, and too late. The Taliban attackers were growing numbers, and they started to fan out across the airfield for what looked like an intended head-on attack. It struck me that I was stood immobile, doing nothing while the battle built up in momentum. Already, US private security men, infantry and Afghan National Army sentries were starting to rush out and take up defensive positions. The air was filled with the whine of helicopter engines starting to spool up, and it occurred to me that our precious Twin Otter was in a position of maximum danger. I turned to Rachel and Luk.

"The aircraft, we're getting out of here. Get aboard!"

I was already running and almost vaulted up into the cabin. Rachel followed, and Luk came last, pulling up the ladder. Rachel helped him close the cargo door while I ran forward and began the engine start procedure. The port engine started to spool up, caught and idled. I started the starboard engine and saw Rachel slide into the seat beside me.

"You'd better tell them what we're planning," I shouted at her above the noise of the engines warming up. "We don't want them to think the insurgents have taken control of the aircraft."

She called up the tower.

"Can any of them fly, do you think, these people?"

"They managed it on 911."

She nodded grimly. The tower had replied and gave us emergency clearance. The controller sounded frantic. I guessed he was undecided about evacuating the control tower, a prime target, or staying on duty to help some of the aircraft escape.

"Keep your eyes open, Helene Air. There's a lot of unauthorized aircraft movement out there today."

Rachel and I exchanged smiles, but I thanked him for the warning. Half a dozen helicopters floated into the air about a quarter of a mile in front of us, and one of them was immediately brought down by a missile or rocket. The others screamed away into the distance, out of immediate danger. Luk watched them, wide eyed.

"The cowards, they should stop and fight."

"They may be unarmed, Luk," I pointed out. "They could be here for maintenance and repairs."

He nodded. "I guess so."

Rachel was taxiing out to the main runway, and I was scanning the instruments to assess our ability to take off. Everything looked ok, so I shouted at Luk to strap in, then made a final check. We were as ready as we could be. I turned to Rachel.

"Take her straight out, and try to steer clear of the fighting."

"No worries, I had the exact same thought," she said grimly.

She hit the throttles forward, and the aircraft leapt ahead. We were unladen and only needed three hundred yards, maybe less, to get off the ground. Except that the wind was in the wrong direction.

"Max, we need to turn at the end of the runway and take off into wind!" she shouted.

I glanced at the windsock. Sure enough, the wind had changed. We could take off with the wind, but we'd need a much longer take-off roll, and maybe more than could be accommodated, especially, as we'd be under fire for every yard of the way. The aircraft was rushing towards the end of the runway, and I made the decision.

"Make the turn, we have to do this properly, otherwise we'll be a target for every Taliban shooter within half a mile."

She started to slow as we neared the downwind end of the runway. A pair of Stryker APCs rushed past us, heading straight for the enemy. No troops were visible as they were all tucked safely inside the hull. But the top mounted M2 .50 caliber machine gun was traversing, seeking its target.

"They're remote controlled, those things," Luk pointed

out. "The crew are safe inside the vehicle, and they're controlling the .50 cal from inside there. They're almost unstoppable, those things."

Almost, but not quite, and two missiles slammed into the lead Stryker in quick succession. The remarkable armor prevented any damage to the crew, but obviously some of the drive components were damaged when the missiles hit. Smoke was rising from the hull. The door slammed open, and the crew burst out. The other Stryker had stopped, and its own door opened to admit the men from the first damaged vehicle. Then it accelerated away again towards the source of the missileer who had just hit them. Now the gunner inside the armored hull had located the nearest insurgents, and he locked the .50 caliber heavy machine gun onto its target.

The stream of bullets smashed into a group of about fifty Taliban who were racing forwards. It was like a First World War battle; a line of screaming and heavily armed men running into the attack, only to be cut down by machine gun fire. They were decimated by the unremitting gunfire that tore them to pieces. A few survivors ran for cover or flung themselves down, but for most of them their most pressing need was a decent burial. The Stryker bumped over several bodies that lay on the ground as it pressed forward, searching for the next target. The invisible gunner found it; a second group that had smashed through the perimeter fence and were circling around to the south side of the airfield. The .50 opened up, and bodies were tossed into the air and thrown to the ground like wheat before a farmer's thresher. But they didn't have it all their own way. Another missileer, a survivor from the first group of fifty, had hidden in a shallow fold in the ground. Abruptly, he stood up and took aim. The gunner saw him at once, and the .50 caliber barrel began to traverse. They both locked on at the same moment. A stream of heavy shells flew towards the missile shooter, and he disappeared in a ragged mess of shredded flesh, but he'd done his work well. His missile flew away directly towards the Stryker. It struck just forward of the center of the vehicle, low on the port side. Two of the vehicle's eight wheels flew high into the air, but incredibly the APC kept going. But only just, the steering gear had obviously been damaged, and the driver was forced to stop, and the crew began to abandon.

"Max!"

I turned to see what the problem was. Rachel had spotted two fighters on the runway, four hundred yards ahead of us. They were lying prone, firing at the defenders as the private security men, infantry and Afghan regulars tried to regroup and deploy for an assault that would sweep the attackers back the way they'd come.

"Keep going. We don't have a choice."

"But they'll see us in a few seconds, and they'll start shooting up the aircraft."

"Ignore them, just get us off the ground."

I heard her mutter something about, 'at this rate we'll never get off the fucking ground', but I ignored it. We were in an exposed place, stationary at the end of the runway ready to depart. Sooner or later someone was going to start shooting at us, and I calculated our only option was to go straight ahead. Maybe we'd strike lucky and run the two fighters down with our landing wheels. Or they'd get lucky and shatter the cockpit with salvos of bullets fired from their rifles.

"Luk, is there any way you can get a shot at them?"

"No way, that side window is the wrong angle entirely. I'm sorry, Max."

"Get the rifle ready to fire, and poke the barrel out of the side window. I'll try and get you an angle on them."

"Er, Max, you're in the way."

"Then lean across me," I shouted. "Just do it, Luk. Rachel, I'm taking over the controls."

"It's all yours," she replied, glancing over to make sure I had my hands on the control column. Her expression changed to one of horror.

"Max, you can't take off with Luk draped across you! What the hell are you doing?"

"I can do it, just leave me alone," I snapped with irritation. I looked forward again, working out the angles. Rachel automatically took up the role of co-pilot.

"Ground speed fifty knots, instruments are all good.

Ten degrees of flap."

"Roger. How far until we hit the shooters?"

"About a hundred and fifty yards."

"Ok. Flaps up, we'll manage without them."

There was a brief silence. Then, "Flaps going up. About a hundred yards to the shooters."

The air in front of us was like a Fourth of July fireworks display. The dark night was lit by thousands of flashes from small arms fire, punctuated by explosions from heavier ordnance fired by both sides. The thick fog of war already covered the airfield, and smoke and debris swirled everywhere making it difficult to see who was fighting where. Then I kicked on the rudder and swerved the aircraft over to starboard, exposing the shooters to the port window where Luk waited. I didn't need to tell him. He fired, once, twice, and then the whole clip was emptied. But he'd only knocked down one of them, and the other leveled his assault rifle and began to shoot at our cockpit.

Three shots struck the side of the nose of the aircraft, and one hit the sliding window, punching a hole clean through. Rachel screamed. I shouted at Luk.

"For Christ's sake, hit the bastard! I have to turn back onto the runway in a couple of seconds."

There was no reply. I realized that his body was resting on me, but it was a dead weight, and not that of a man who was active and moving. I didn't have time to speculate. I peered over his lifeless form and looked out of the windshield. We were running out of room. I kicked the rudder again the opposite side, and the aircraft lurched back towards the runway. When the wheels were stable on the tarmac, I corrected our heading and continued on our take-off roll. Two more shots hit the nose, but fortunately none damaged the windshield. I couldn't worry about Luk or the shooter, or anything other than getting airborne.

"Call it, Rachel!"

A fraction of a second's hesitation, then, "Fifty-five knots, V1."

Where was the shooter? I had a brief glimpse of a turbaned man frantically loading a fresh clip into his assault rifle, but then he disappeared, and there was a 'bump' as our wheels went over him.

"Sixty-five knots, rotate!"

I hauled back on the column and felt the Twin Otter straining to get into the sky. I'd not used flaps, so it meant that we'd have a fast, shallow ascent, rather than a slow, steep ascent that would leave us at the mercy of the shooters on the ground. We screamed over the airfield, narrowly scraping over the roof of the control tower, the highest point, and then we were airborne and away. A few rounds followed us as the attackers tried to prevent our leaving, but no more shots hit us, at least, none that we felt or could see.

We climbed to three thousand feet, at which height I

felt reasonably safe and circled the airfield. The battle was at its peak. Broken aircraft burned, and they sent plumes of smoke high into the sky. A few hundred yards away a squadron of Apache Longbow helicopters had formed up and was swooping down to attack. The Boeing AH-64Ds were equipped with a chain gun mounted under the chin, and I knew that within seconds their targets would be shredded to little more than matchsticks, if they could identify them. Their opponents weren't fools, and they wasted no time in infiltrating the Allied positions. It was going to be difficult for the brutal helicopters to wreak their terror on the attackers below. In which case, they would need to be eliminated one by one on the ground. It was going to be a slow, bloody and painful process. A pair of Apache Longbows loomed in front of us, and I threw the control column over sharply to keep out of their way. They were concentrating on the ground, not the sky. But a collision would be as deadly as a Taliban rocket. I turned to speak to Rachel and felt the heavy weight that pressed down on me. Luk!

"Rachel, get Luk off me and see how he is."

"What happened to him?" she cried in alarm.

"He was hit by that shooter on the runway."

She was already pulling him off me. "He looks bad, Max. I don't even know if he's breathing."

I felt my guts churning. I was already working out what to say to his father, Abe Woltz, the man who'd been with my grandfather during the dark days of Vietnam. And now this, no!

"Rachel, do whatever's necessary. You have to keep him alive. I'll find somewhere to land near a hospital."

"I think that would be a good idea, Max. I can feel a faint pulse now, but he needs a medic, and fast. An army medic might be best in this country."

"You can forget Kabul. They've got their hands full, and I doubt they'd even let us land."

"Jalalabad?"

"Sounds good," she replied. "I'd call them up on the radio."

The reply was prompt. "Don't even think about coming here. We've got our hands full sending out reinforcements to Kabul International. The airport is shut down for non-military operations. Try Kandahar."

I punched in the coordinates. It was two hundred miles away.

"I have a casualty, and he won't live that long. I must land at Jalalabad."

"That a negative, Helene Air. You come here, and you'll circle the city until you run out of fuel. Your best bet is Kandahar. Try and keep him alive, good luck, buddy."

"Yeah."

I told Rachel.

"You're not serious? How long will it take us to reach Kandahar?"

"About an hour and a half."

"Fuck it. You'll have to go for it, Max. I'll try and keep him alive."

That was when the next blow hit us, in a message that came over the radio.

"Helene Air, this is Walker. We're ready for the pickup."

I hit the transmit button. "That's a negative, Walker. We have a casualty on board. He needs urgent medical treatment, and we're heading for Kandahar."

The radio went silent for half a minute. Then Walker came back on.

"Hoffman, I don't think you understand whose paying the bills. Your job is to get your ass here fast and pick us up. We've just finished a successful fire mission, and we don't want to wait around for the ragheads to get their shit together and come after us with all guns blazing. We blew those fuckers apart, and they never knew what hit them." He sounded exultant, as if he was on some kind of a drug high. Or perhaps it was the way men behave when they'd just bathed in their enemy's blood. He cleared his throat and continued. "You can forget Kandahar. A group of our people is overdue on the border near Tora Bora. They're a mixed group, a military escort with civilian medics who were making the crossing through the Khyber into Pakistan, some kind of aid mission. We've been tasked to locate them and get them out of trouble. It's not going to wait. They're pinned down under fire, so your guy will have to hang in there."

I felt my anger begin to boil over. "Look, we're taking our guy to Kandahar for treatment. We'll come and…"

That was as far as I got.

"Hear this, Hoffman. I'm about to relay an order for Kandahar airfield to be closed to your aircraft. You try it, and they'll shoot you out of the sky. Now get that fucking plane here and pick us up. I won't tell you again!"

The radio went dead. The conversation was over, and I knew we had no choice. I turned to look at Rachel. She was kneeling over Luk, applying a pressure bandage to stop the blood loss. "You heard?"

She nodded. "Yeah, I heard. The bastard."

"Can he hold out for long enough to make the pick up?"

"He'll have to," she growled, her voice bitter and angry.

"Anything I can do, Rachel?"

"No, you fly the aircraft. I've had elementary battlefield first aid training in the Air Force. I'll do my best for him. I've found Luk's satphone. I'm going to find a signal and call his father, Abe Woltz. How long before we pick up Walker's team?"

I made a rough calculation in my head. "About an hour, maybe a bit more. I'll punch in the coordinates and get a better idea. Walker's people may have a medic that could help Luk."

"Only a battlefield medic, and they won't be any more

effective than me. But didn't he say something about going on to pick up civilian medics? That could mean a doctor, which would give Luk a much better chance."

"Ok, I'll be more cooperative with Walker."

She laughed. "I wouldn't bother. The only way he'll ever help anyone is at gunpoint."

"I guess so."

I hit the coordinates for the landing field into the navigational computer. The aircraft swung onto the new heading, and we settled down for the flight across the bleak, harsh grandeur of the Afghan landscape. The flight seemed long, very long. And all the time I thought of Rachel, working to keep Luk alive as he lay on the cockpit floor; his bed a pool of drying blood. At one point she shouted to me over the roar of the engines.

"I got through to Abe Woltz. He knows some people in Peshawar. He said he'd get them standing by to help if they're needed."

"Help? What can they do? Are they doctors or medics of some kind?"

"I've no idea. He just said they'd be there to help us if necessary."

I dismissed it from my mind. I couldn't see any kind of a scenario where Abe Woltz's contacts could help out. I flew on, willing the time to pass quicker.

* * *

Vince Mason crawled back across the hard packed earth to where Lieutenant Rains was huddled behind a low stone wall. They'd suffered two more casualties, a private and a corporal, and the medics were working on them. He glanced up at the soaring heights of the pass. They should have been over the other side by now. Surely someone would realize they were overdue and send a chopper or a reconnaissance aircraft to check them out. If Rains had held out for Strykers, it would only have cost them an extra day or two, and they wouldn't be in this position. Neither would they have lost eight dead and two wounded. Let alone be faced with losing the whole platoon. Rains stared at him as he crawled behind the wall.

"What's the situation, Sergeant?"

"The two casualties are out of danger, LT. Those medics are doing a good job of patching them up, but we can't stay here much longer. They'll pick us off one by one until we're all dead. There's been no sign of that reconnaissance drone coming back, so we may be on our own."

"So you've worked that one out? In case you hadn't noticed, Sergeant, we've lost our vehicles. How do you suggest we get out of here?"

"We've got a tradition in the infantry, as I recall. We walk."

Rains reddened. "Cut the sarcasm, Sergeant Mason!

I've considered getting of here on foot. The problem is we'll be under fire for every step of the way."

"Not if they can't see us. We've a couple of mortars, the boys brought with them when we bailed out. They've got eight smoke bombs amongst the ordnance. If we lay down a pattern of smoke, we should be able to break out and get up into the hills."

Both men looked up at the distant Khyber Pass. It soared three and a half thousand feet above them, winding through a cut in the mountains. They could clearly see the snaking road that was the only way of getting through from Afghanistan to Pakistan.

"It's a long way to go on foot and a hard climb," Rains mused. "I'm not sure we can get our wounded up there. What about the road back to Jalalabad?"

Mason shook his head. "No chance. The Taliban main force is set up across that road, and they're expecting us to try it. The road through the Khyber Pass has only a few defenders. They're not expecting us there."

"Because it's crazy?"

"I guess, yeah, it's crazy. It's also the only way. Either that or wait for help to arrive. And with the Taliban attacking all over, everything is buttoned down, and nothing's moving. We may be spotted by a passing aircraft or drone, but it's a maybe."

Rains sighed. Whatever he decided, it was going to be bad. He nodded at Mason.

"Get them together, Sergeant. We'll go forward, through the Khyber Pass. And God help us all."

"I hear you, LT. I kind of assumed you'd go for it. The mortar crews are set up ready. The medics have the casualties strapped to the gurneys, and they'll carry them while the platoon keeps everyone covered."

"Good, I guess you've got it all worked out. I appreciate it, Sergeant."

"I'm just trying to live a bit longer, Sir. I guess we all are."

"Yeah, let's do it. Start the smoke barrage."

* * *

In Creech Air Force Base, Master Sergeant Carol Wendelski checked her gauges and discovered they were running low on fuel. She'd have like to have taken another pass over the position of those troops who were under fire, but it was impossible without landing for more fuel. She expertly guided the Predator back to Kabul; a long, slow flight, during which she had to keep flexing her muscles to stop them going numb. Finally, the video display and nav computer showed her the airfield dead ahead. She called up the tower.

"This is Creech Control Center. I need urgent clearance to land a Predator. The bird's low on fuel."

Less than two seconds later, the reply came in.

"Clearance to go straight in, Creech. Be careful when you taxi. They're prepping some new birds that just arrived from the States. Do you want me to alert your ground crew?"

"Nah, I'll call them, thanks Kabul."

"You're welcome."

Carol called up her ground crew on the secure communications system.

"We're all ready for you, Master Sergeant. Just bring her in, nice and easy."

"Roger that." She dropped the tiny aircraft onto the runway and taxied over to where a group of USAF personnel waited. Using her comm. link, she spoke to the Sergeant in charge.

"Sarge, some of our people are in trouble, and I need to get the bird back in the air as fast as possible. Can you fuel her up straight away and get her aloft?"

"Sure thing, we're ready and waiting. Give us a half hour, and we'll have you flying again. Have you located him yet?"

She was already thinking of her next task. She turned her attention back to the voice from eight thousand miles away.

"What?"

"Mullah Omar, did you locate him?"

"Maybe this time," she chuckled. She thanked them and checked the clock. It was time for her lunch, so she went to the canteen and ate a salad. It was vital to watch your weight in her job. There was no physical activity, and the excess of adrenalin that the tense operations generated meant that it would be easy to become obese. She'd avoided it so far, and intended to keep her slim figure. She checked the clock again. She'd give herself twenty minutes and then start preparing flight operations again.

CHAPTER SEVEN

We told our community that we are not afraid of Bush's and America's threats. We are continuing jihad against America and all the invaders. We reassure Muslims everywhere that we are abiding by the pledge, and that victory is coming.

Mullah Mohammad Omar

Mullah Omar came out of his trance and gazed at Abdul Qadir. "Commander, perhaps you would tell us what happened. You had sufficient warning, yet still you managed to lose at least ten of your men, including six of your local commanders. You were lucky to escape with your life."

Qadir stared at him. "Mullah Omar, my men fought like lions, but the Americans attacked us from behind. They seemed to come out of nowhere. I've no doubt we were betrayed."

"Perhaps you should have taken that into account when you made your preparations, Commander," Mullah Baradar said quietly. "Your failure has cost our movement dear."

"My failure?" Qadir swiveled to fix the man with a hard gaze. "The area the Americans came from was under your control, Mullah. Are you suggesting that I should take the time to watch over your responsibilities as well as mine?"

Baradar's expression darkened, and he was about to spit and angry reply, but Omar's voice cut through them like a scalpel, sharp and precise.

"This is not a time to argue about whose failure allowed these Americans to kill our commanders. I have already decided how we will go forward."

They leaned towards him, waiting to hear their fate.

"One of our units has pinned down a small American formation, a group of infantry escorting doctors and nurses on a relief mission to a town in Pakistan stricken with plague. They were attempting the journey on the road through the Khyber Pass. It is unfortunate for them that they departed just as our major attacks had begun. The road through the pass is undefended as a consequence, and we were able to make our attack without hindrance from the normal road and air patrols. However, our forces are not strong enough to finish them off. I want you to take your men and join the attack, Commander Qadir. The next phase of our operation is about to begin, a series of suicide attacks on targets in the cities of Kabul, Jalalabad and Kandahar. I want that American group wiped out to add to our victories. I believe it will be enough to persuade the Americans that there is no advantage to them in staying here."

Mullah Baradar bared his teeth in a ferocious smile. "This truly will be a blow from which the Americans will never recover. An entire contingent of their people wiped out, against a backdrop of our attacks and suicide bombers, how can they possibly resist? I have read of the Tet offensive during their Vietnam War, when the American's enemies came out in a similar series of coordinated attacks. It was a glorious time for the Vietnamese people, and a dark time for the Americans."

Omar nodded. "Quite so. Now you understand how important this is. We have to encourage our forces to press their attacks hard and our suicide bombers to make the ultimate sacrifice for the cause. This could be the beginning of the end for the Americans, and we will be able to cleanse our country of the infidels, and once more have control of our destinies."

"Allah be praised!" Baradar and Qadir both exclaimed with varying degrees of enthusiasm.

Qadir was concerned that his leaders could be so blind. Did they not know that Tet was a major defeat for the Vietcong and North Vietnamese regulars who took part in the battle? The military losses were so terrible that the attacks had to be called off early. Yes, politically it had helped the Vietcong; there was no doubt. But militarily, whole units were obliterated. What was more, his men were well aware of that famous military engagement. If they found that their leaders planned on a repeat, how much enthusiasm could he expect from his troops, knowing they were going to their deaths?

There was another problem. Could there be any honor in making deliberate attacks on medical personnel, doctors and nurses? Some said that these people were a legitimate target for the Taliban. But he didn't agree, and neither did many others. It was all very well for Mullah Baradar to show enthusiasm, but he wouldn't be in the front line, leading men to their deaths and slaughtering unarmed doctors and nurses. Perhaps there was no option. He could understand that. But it was not a time for joyous celebration.

"Commander Qadir, you do not seem to be enthusiastic, is something wrong?"

He looked at Mullah Omar, seeing the cold, dark depths of the single eye staring at him. "Nothing at all, Mullah. I was merely contemplating my good fortune in being on the front line of this glorious battle."

"I am pleased you feel so. Tell me, Commander, you have sons. Have you considered putting them forward for martyrdom?"

Qadir shivered inwardly. But outwardly he was calm, as he'd trained himself to be when facing the maximum danger.

"I have not, Mullah. They are training to be fighters and leaders, like their father."

"Good, good. Do you have any daughters?"

He thanked God he did not. "I have no daughters, no."

"So be it. I wish you success in your venture."

"Thank you, Mullah." But for a long time he struggled to keep the image of his sons wearing the canvas suicide belts out of his mind.

* * *

When I was on final approach for the landing ground with Ed Walker, I called him up.

"This is Helene Air, ETA in about ten minutes, Mr. Walker. Are you ready to leave?"

"Just get your ass down here, Hoffman. There's a group of Americans waiting for us to haul their asses out of the fire, so hurry it up. Out."

He sounded drunk, and I couldn't work it out. Surely they weren't drinking booze out in the field. But it wasn't the normal voice of a drunk. No, it was different. I couldn't be sure why.

"We'll be landing in a few minutes, is Luk ok?"

"Make it as gentle as possible, Max. He's pretty weak."

"Roger. Stand by."

They saw me coming in and popped a smoke flare. The wind was blowing towards us, perfect for a landing. It was very light, and I estimated ten knots. I lined up the nose and began to descend through the last few hundred feet. It was an easy landing, and yet the hardest I'd ever made. It had to be gentle, so light, that the wounded man lying a few feet beside me didn't even feel the jolt as our wheels touched down. I thought I'd made it, but the first jolt was when the port wheel went into a pothole that was outside of my control. I braked before I overshot the field and ran into a heap of rocks, spun the aircraft around and taxied back. I turned through one hundred and eighty degrees and put the brakes on; we were ready to leave. I got up to attend to the cargo door, but Walker's men were already opening it. He was first up, charging through the fuselage and into the cockpit, almost dragging me behind him.

"Fuck!" he shouted. Exulted would be more accurate. "Jesus H Christ, we rammed it down their fucking throats. We must have killed twenty of them, Hoffman, and leaders, all of them. Fuck!"

So that was the way it was. It wasn't war. It was blood lust. He rammed a cigar into his mouth and dug into his pocket for a lighter. When his hand came out, something dropped onto the floor. He bent down and picked it up. It looked to me like a bloody rag, and he saw the direction of my gaze.

"It's a souvenir, Hoffman. Something to show the boys when I get back home."

"What is it?"

"What is it? It's a scalp, of course. Shit, you should see those bodies when we'd finished with them. Like a fucking butcher's shop."

My mind went numb for a few moments, but I managed to recover a degree of calm.

"We're going straight out, Mr. Walker, would you make sure your men know."

His smile was manic, like a schizophrenic who hadn't taken his medication. The eyes were glazed, and the skin had that bone-white quality, like stained porcelain.

"Too violent for you, eh? I didn't peg you for a squeamish type. I'll warn the men. I wouldn't want to put you off your food."

He left the cabin with a braying laugh. He hadn't even noticed Rachel, still trying to keep Luk alive on the cockpit floor. They were lying in a heap of bloodied blankets.

"As soon as we're set on course, I'll put her on autopilot. I'm going aft to see if any of Walker's men have experience with battlefield injuries."

She smiled, a tired, frightened smile. Frightened for the man she was trying to save. "It won't put you off your dinner if they're playing with their trophies?"

"It's not the trophies that puts me off, Rachel. It's the kind of men that would take them."

I pushed the throttles all the way forward and let off the brakes. We picked up speed and bumped our way back along the field. Every time we hit a pothole or small mound the aircraft jarred, and Luk groaned. Finally, I reached take-off speed, and I pulled back. We lifted off; immediately the bumping stopped, and Luk went quiet. I throttled back when we'd gained some height, turning to Rachel now that the engine noise was quieter.

"That sounded bad, I'm sorry. I couldn't do anything about the bumping. How is he?"

She didn't reply at first. When she did speak, I could hear the desperation in her voice.

"The take-off opened his wound, Max. He's bleeding again. I'm afraid he's dying."

"Keep him going, Rachel. His father was vital to my grandfather's survival in Indochina. We can't let him die."

The aircraft settled on course for the coordinates Walker had given me, the frontier between Afghanistan and Pakistan. I locked in the autopilot and went back to speak to Walker. He was dozing on a canvas jump seat and looked up at me as I approached. The manic expression had largely faded, and he looked tired, perhaps even depressed.

"What's up, Hoffman. Don't tell me you have a problem."

"One of our people, Luk, he was shot when took off from Kabul. He's pretty bad. Are any of your men experience with battlefield injuries?"

He shook his head. "No, not that I'm aware of. Their job's to kill the enemy, that's all. I'm sorry I can't help you. These people we're hoping to bring back, they're medics. They should be able to help."

"Right. What kind of a landing field are we talking about here? Is it flat, or a proper airfield, perhaps?"

"We haven't got an airfield. This is a scratch operation, so we just have to make do."

I guess he knew what effect his words would have on me. I gaped at him, and he smiled back.

"How do you expect me to land an aircraft like this without an airfield?"

He shrugged. "You'll find a way, Hoffman. They do it all the time in these backwoods countries. Just find a nice tarmac road and put her down."

"Is there a tarmac road where we're going?"

"It's possible, yes. But one way or the other, you get her down on the ground."

"How many people are down there?"

About forty is my best guess."

I couldn't help it, but I could feel my mouth gape open again. "You know that the capacity of this aircraft is twenty passengers maximum? How the hell do you expect to get them all out?"

"Who said anything about getting them out? We're going in to nail the suckers who've got them surrounded.

We're going to kick ass, Hoffman." He stared at me, and I could see that his adrenalin was running high again. I wondered what he was on. "And don't forget, there're medics down there, so if you want to save your guy…"

He paused and stared at me. "GET US THE FUCK DOWN THERE! YOU HEAR!"

I remember saying coldly, "I'll get you down, don't worry," before I returned to the cockpit. Rachel was holding Luk gently, talking to him softly. He'd regained consciousness, and he looked up at me as I crouched down.

"How are you feeling?"

I was trying to put a brave face on it. He looked ghastly, chalk-white, and his skin stretched tight over the bones as he fought to control his agony.

"I've felt better," he whispered. He tried to grin, failed, and then lapsed into unconsciousness again.

"Rachel, I need his satphone."

"What for, who are you planning to call?"

"Abe Woltz. He said to call if we needed anything. I figure that time is now."

"What do we need?"

"A miracle."

I punched in the fast dial, and within seconds the satphone had connected direct to a satellite in low earth orbit, then down to Abe Woltz. It was like talking to a guy across town. The line was that clear.

"Woltz."

"It's Max. You said to call if we had problems. I believe that time has come."

I outlined our difficulties. Luk badly injured; and a group of mercenaries in the cargo space led by a crazed career CIA officer who seemed to have learned his ideas from a Boy's Own comic book.

"I don't know if you can help, Abe, but we need something. If we're lucky enough to make the landing, Luk is seriously wounded. Believe me, it's touch and go. Yet all Walker wants is to start a new war with a large group of insurgents down there. We need to get Luk away from here and take him to a hospital, but I don't know how to get away from Walker before he kills us all."

He was silent for a few moments. Then he fired off a series of questions. He wanted coordinates, strengths of friend and foe as much as I knew, armaments, fuel situation, radio frequencies and a load more. It was like being interrogated by an expert, which I assumed was indeed the case. Then something occurred to me. "Abe, have you ever encountered the CIA before, I mean, have you ever had problems with them?"

"Yes."

"So you know what kind of situation we're in here. I tell you, the guy's crazy."

"I doubt he's that crazy, Max. People like him. They play the odds. One thing you can be sure of, when the dead bodies have all stacked up, the Ed Walkers of this world always seem to walk away."

I could believe that. "Can you help at all, Abe?"

"Sure, I'll see what I can put together. Call me back and tell me how things are going."

I ended the call and went to check our heading. I estimated we had just over half an hour to run. I left the aircraft on autopilot and went back to Luk. He was still unconscious. I looked at Rachel.

"Any change?"

She shook her head. "He's no different, but I'd guess he won't last much longer. We have to pray that we can get those medics to help him."

"Rachel, it's not that simple," I reminded her gently. "They're pinned down under enemy fire, and so far there's no sign of a place to land."

"You'll manage it, Max. I know you will."

"Thanks for your faith in me, but there's a lot depending on chance. Too much."

"You'll get us down, if anyone can, I know you will."

I nodded and went back to the pilot's seat. We had a few hours of daylight left, which was the only factor we had on our side. The mountains of the Pakistan border appeared in the distance, and I went to call Abe.

"We're not far away now, I'd estimate fifteen minutes or so."

"Right. I've been pretty busy, and with any luck I'll

have someone come out there to help you. As far as I can gather, those coordinates put you at the foot of the Khyber Pass."

"That's my assessment too," I agreed.

"Ok, the problem is that all hell is breaking loose in Afghanistan. It's like the Tet offensive during the Vietnam War. What it means is that the military has its hands full fighting off the insurgents. My people tell me there are some heavy pitched battles being fought right now. There's no help available for these people trapped at the bottom of the Khyber until they've contained the situation, and that could be several days. I guess that's why they sent that maniac Walker to take care of it."

"That all makes sense, Abe, but what you can do?"

"Right. You know anything about Peshawar?"

"No, Yes, it's a city in Pakistan, close to the border."

"Yeah, that's true, but it's a center for weaponry and mercenaries, has been for centuries. I've been in touch with my contacts there. There's nothing's moving inside Afghanistan, so you need help from outside the country. I'm sending in the Devil's Guard."

I felt a shiver down my spine as I remembered the stories and legends I'd been brought up with. My immediate thought was that the ghost of my grandfather was about to materialize. "Mercenaries, Abe?"

"They're tough fighters, every single man," he corrected me. "They've seen their share of the world's trouble spots, I can assure you. They've been in and out of more firefights than you could imagine. They're heading up to the Pass right now from Peshawar, and they'll move down to meet up with you as fast as they can. Do you think you can land that plane?"

I heard the anxiety in his voice. His son was dying a few feet back from the cockpit, and we had no designated landing field even if we could link up with the besieged medics. But that was my job. "I'll land the aircraft, Abe. That's a promise."

I signed off and started looking through the charts to see if there was anything that resembled a flat strip close to where we were headed.

* * *

Master Sergeant Carol Wendelski approached her console to start the next shift. As usual, Vernon Munch ran his eyes over her figure and made a macho remark, but this time it was different.

"There ain't much going on over there. The stupid bastard's screwed up the electronics package on the bird. When they went to pick up a spare board from the QM, they found they'd forgotten to order them in. Our baby is sat in the hangar doing nothing, just waiting for the next supply flight to come from Stateside."

"Christ, Vernon, there're people down there in trouble.

The whole place is going up like a torch, and we're blind."

Munch shrugged. "There's nothing we can do about it."

"What about a spare bird, don't they have anything else that can fly?"

He sniggered. "Oh yeah, they can put a Reaper up in the air, but I'm not cleared on that particular drone, so I had to say no."

A thrill went through her as she thought about the fearsome Reaper. Operators here at Creech Air Force Base could hunt for targets using a number of advanced sensors, including a thermal camera. But best of all was the extensive weaponry the drone carried, Hellfire II air-to-ground missiles, the Sidewinders and the latest the GBU-38. So when those fuckers tried to mess with her people, she could take direct action and blast their asses. She smiled at Corporal Munch. "I'll get back to them and tell them. I'm cleared for the Reaper."

* * *

"What the fuck's going on, Roy?"

The cargo operations manager looked up from the manifest he'd been examining as Joe Ashford stormed into his office. He sighed. When Joe was in that kind of a mood, everyone got his ass kicked, and the atmosphere in the CIA's Kabul International cargo hangar would be soured for days.

"What do you mean?"

"I've got a cargo waiting for shipment. Yet both the aircraft and my people are somewhere else. I want them back here, now!"

"But Joe, we had orders from ISAF, routed through Langley, to bail out those medics who were ambushed near the Khyber Pass. I passed on the orders to Ed Walker. I had no choice."

"Fuck Langley and fuck ISAF. How am I supposed to get the cargo out if my transport disappears on some wild rescue mission? There must be someone else can do it."

"There's no one else, Joe. You know the whole country is going up in flames. They were caught on the back foot. Until they've straightened this out, they don't have any spare people."

Ashford sighed heavily. "What's their current status?"

"They're still on the way. Once they get there, they've got to join up with the medics and fight their way out. There isn't room in the aircraft for all of them, so I guess they'll take the civilians on to their destination in Pakistan, and then return for Ed Walker and his people."

"No!" Ashford's huge fist crashed down on the desk. "I want them back here. I've got customers waiting for product, and if they don't get it, they'll be mighty unhappy. As soon as they've pulled them out of the ambush, they're to get back in that plane and get straight back here to

Kabul. You hear?"

"How will the civilian medics get out of there without support?"

"I don't give a shit, Roy. They can walk out on their own for all I care," he laughed. "That should do it. Just get my plane back here on the ground and get it loaded."

"And if Langley call up wanting to know what's going on?"

"Tell 'em the plane's got engine trouble or something like that. Maybe the pilot's got the flu. I don't care. I need that plane!"

"Why is it so important? We've got regular transport aircraft we can use."

"Because it's off the books. I organized it so that it doesn't appear on any paperwork. You don't need to know any more."

"Ok, Joe, I'll tell them."

"Yeah, be sure you do."

Ashford stormed out of the office. Once outside, he tried to assemble his thoughts. He needed a way to get through his current problems. Running drug cargos made money, lots of money, bucket loads of money, but it had to go somewhere. He'd made massive investments in real estate back in the States, millions of dollars to buy prime land in Florida for leisure development. It still hadn't been enough, so he'd borrowed millions more. It was easy enough to pay back, and just a matter of time before a few more drug shipments raked in the money, and his new golf course and leisure park was completed. The sale of the condos alone would bring in twice as much as he'd laid out. At least, that was the plan. Then came the property crash. Half the apartments weren't finished, and most of the ones that were stood empty, their values falling like water down a drain. And if that wasn't bad enough, his creditors wanted their money back. The debt currently stood at over two hundred million dollars and rising, and the interest calculated at loan shark rates. They could do that, these people. After all, who was going to argue with them?

It was only after borrowing the money that he'd discovered who the lender was; one of the Mexican drug cartels using him as a conduit to launder their money. That would have been funny, his development to put his drug money to use, part funded my laundered drug money. Yeah, it would have been funny if it hadn't been for the threats; either make the overdue loan payments that were increasing at a crazy rate every day, or wait for the shot in the back of the head. He remembered the spic that had flown out to Afghanistan to speak to him.

"It's just business, Mr. Ashford. The Jefe insists on his money. You do understand that he can't have people failing to pay?" The guy had laughed. "That's a bad way to do business, no? If people don't pay their bills, the Jefe has a simple solution, a permanent solution."

"If he kills me, he won't get any of his money back," Ashford had snarled.

But the man smiled even wider. "That is true, but you see, it encourages the others to make their payments. It's simple mathematics, a long-term business strategy. You must see that."

"Yeah, maybe. Where did you learn business?"

"Princeton, Senor. A fine American university."

He had to have that fucking aircraft. His superiors were starting to look at his operations with a critical eye. The only way he had to fulfill his part of the deal was to use that plane so that no one was any the wiser. Otherwise he was dead.

* * *

I dropped down to five hundred feet and searched for a flat strip for a landing. On the ground I could see the extent of the ambush. It was some kind of a ruined village, probably abandoned. The American troops were sheltering behind the broken stone walls, while two hundred yards in front of them a large force of Taliban had them pinned down. As I looked down, several of the turbaned heads looked up, and I saw their rifles point towards the aircraft. Puffs of smoke showed where they tried shooting at the Twin Otter, but none of their shots struck the aircraft. Between the village and the Taliban position, the wreckage of the American vehicles lay, still smoking. There was only one possible landing strip, the road. I couldn't leave the controls to alert the passengers in the back, so I forgot about them and circled while I assessed the size of the road. It was going to be close, too close, but I didn't have a whole lot of choices. I banked slightly and went round again to put the aircraft on final approach.

"Rachel, we're about to land, how is Luk?"

"The same."

She sounded tired, dulled, resigned, perhaps, to the inevitable. To losing the man she'd nursed for so many hours.

"We're going to make it, hang in there. Tell Luk we'll have medical help, just a few minutes more."

"He's unconscious."

I didn't reply. There was nothing to add. I banked again and completed the turn, ahead of me the long, ribbon of road. It wasn't long enough, not wide enough, but I was determined that we'd get down. I brushed over a low mound, and the startled face of a Taliban scout, or sniper, glanced up at me. Then I was leveling out to put down on the road. The ground came up to meet us, and the wheels touched. I flared slightly, then pushed the column forward and slammed her down hard. It was the only way. There just wasn't enough road to make a normal landing. Immediately, I felt all three wheels on the ground, and I slammed on the brakes and chopped the throttles. We were bouncing and swerving towards a low stone wall, some kind of a boundary marker, and I applied maximum brakes. The aircraft slowed. It was a near thing as the wall rushed towards us, but ten feet before the port wing tip was about to ram into it, we stopped. There were a pair of grain stores just off the road, or I assumed that's what they were. I taxied off the road and across the ground, parked the aircraft in the space between them and cut the engines. It was the best I could do, and at least the plane was partially hidden from direct view of the road. The door to the rear opened, and Ed Walker barged into the cockpit.

"That was a bumpy landing, couldn't you have warned us?"

I ignored him and turned to Rachel. "How's Luk?"

"Same."

I looked out of the cockpit window. The stone buildings shielded us from the besiegers. It meant that we could get Luk out and across to the medics that were sheltering in the village. I turned to Walker.

"We need someone to help carry Luk out to the medics. Can you ask a couple of your men to lend a hand?"

He sneered at me. "Fuck that, Hoffman, we're not here to offer first aid. As soon as we climb out of this aircraft, we're going to rip through those ragheads and send them back to Tora Bora. Can't you get one of the docs to come here?"

"Mr. Walker, I'm no soldier, but I would have thought the aircraft will be a target for every rocket and mortar crew within five miles."

"Yeah, you could be right. Except that we have to have this plane."

"In that case, you'd better get out there and deal with them. Now if you'll excuse me, Rachel and I need to carry Luk across to the medics."

He shrugged. "Whatever. Tell 'em we'll be moving in right away to clear out those insurgents. So they can stay out of our way." He left the cockpit, I heard him shout, "Let's go get those motherfuckers. I need a few more scalps."

We carried Luk as gently as we could out of the Twin Otter and managed to get him on the ground. They were watching from the village, and a doctor and two soldiers ran over to us with a gurney. The doc put out his hand, "I'm Doctor Yves St Roulemont, Medecin Sans Frontieres. My nurses are back there, setting up a makeshift treatment room. We saw you unloading a casualty and came out to help."

We shook hands. "Max Hoffman, this is Rachel Beckett. The guy on the ground is Luk Woltz, gunshot wound, and he's lost a lot of blood."

The doctor nodded and bent down to check out Luk. After a few minutes, he shouted to the two soldiers with the gurney.

"We need to get this man under cover right away. He needs urgent attention."

They lifted him onto the canvas gurney, and we each took a corner. The doctor walked alongside Luk and continued the diagnosis. When we reached the village, they led us to a semi-ruined house. Inside, the roof was still partially intact, and a group of four nurses waited for us. Doctor Roulemont began issuing orders, and Luk disappeared behind a scrum of nurses and doctors. From behind me a man cleared his throat.

"I'm Lieutenant Rains."

I looked around. An American officer, and he appeared haggard and frightened. I made the introductions and then asked him how things were.

"As bad as you can imagine. We lost our vehicles and means of communication. We've been completely cut off and unable to escape. The Taliban have a heavy blocking force in place. What happened to those men who just got off your plane?"

"They've gone to tangle with the Taliban. Their leader said he would clear them out."

He looked dumbfounded. "With just twelve men? Their leader must be insane. There are around fifty insurgents just waiting out there for us to try something like that."

I didn't think it would help to tell him that he was perfectly correct. Walker was without doubt an insane, blood-crazed psychopath.

"I don't know, but maybe they've got a plan."

He shook his head. "That'll be some plan. Tell me, can you take off from that road?"

"That's the idea, yes. My first priority is to get Luk out of danger. If Walker's men manage to clear the ambush, I'll try and organize a take-off. But it'll be dangerous if they're still in the area. As soon as we start the engines, they'll try to hit us with everything they've got. The landing surprised them, a take-off won't."

"What's the capacity of your aircraft?" the officer asked. "It doesn't look very big."

When I told him, his face fell. "That won't even take half of us out of here. How do they plan to handle evacuating the rest of us?"

"You'd better ask Ed Walker when he gets back," I replied grimly. "This is his operation."

He looked bewildered. When he saw us land, he would have thought that a rescue was about to happen; instead of the arrival of a gung ho psychopath and a plane that was too small to carry them out.

We walked around and looked at Rains' position. He had a couple of dozen troops and the civilian medics. It was a pity that Walker hadn't waited. If he'd added these men to his own, it would have been a useful force. I shook hands with a tough looking sergeant, Vince Mason. He'd already made the calculations.

"You won't get us all out on that," he glanced across at

the Twin Otter.

"No, I'm sorry."

"Do the people in Kabul have some plan for getting us out?"

"I don't know. Look, I'm sorry, Sergeant, but it's Ed Walker's show. He's the guy who's leading the attack against those Taliban."

"Is he regular army? Special Forces?"

"He's CIA, with mercenaries."

He grimaced. "I hope he knows his business."

I nodded. "Me too. If they're still here, the Taliban, they'll hear the moment I start engines and have plenty of warning to start shooting at us."

"I reckon so, yeah. Maybe they'll send an armored column to get us out. We could do with some Strykers here."

"I doubt you'll get them. The whole country is ablaze, and they've got their back to the wall. It'll be several days before they push back the enemy."

"Right, in that case, we won't make preparations to leave anytime soon."

I walked around, looking at their positions. It wasn't good, and if Walker failed to clear the enemy, all they had to do was wait for reinforcements and sweep over us. I had to make a decision if that happened, whether to try for the plane or leave on foot. A fusillade of shots rang out a few hundred yards away, obviously Walker engaging the enemy. Rains was shouting orders at his men to be alert. He was crouched behind a low wall, but I didn't think they needed any telling. They were all hiding behind cover, and their rifles leveled ready for use. I'd seen enough, so I walked back to the building where they were treating Luk. Rachel came out to meet me.

"They think he'll survive, and they're giving him massive blood transfusions. Thank God they were able to do that."

"That's good. Listen, I we need to make an alternative plan to get out of here."

"So you think the aircraft won't get out?"

"I'm not sure, but help won't be coming anytime soon. It's all up to us."

In fact, we weren't going anywhere. The light started to fade, and we had little choice but to settle in for the night. We could still hear desultory fire coming from the nearby hills. We had no idea how the firefight was going, until just after nightfall, Ed Walker stumbled into the village with two of his men. One of them was wounded in the upper arm, and all three of them looked all in. I was outside the stone hut where Luk was being treated, talking to Rachel. He loomed up out of the darkness, muttering curses.

"Motherfuckers, they were lying in wait for us. Jesus Christ, we were lucky to get away!"

"Where are the rest of your men?" I asked him.

"The others? Fuck knows. Dead, I guess. One thing's for sure, they ain't coming back. If they're prisoners of the

Taliban, they'll wish they were dead before long."

I was aghast. "So you abandoned them?"

"Too right, useless bastards. They walked slap bang into an ambush, and they were shot to pieces."

"I thought you were leading them, so doesn't that make you responsible?"

I shouldn't have said it, but it was too late. He glared at me, and I could see the fear in his face.

"Not for fools like that, no. We all have to take out own chances. You'd better get the aircraft ready, we're leaving."

I felt my anger glowing red hot. This callous fool was planning on abandoning these people. "The hell we are. I'm waiting until Luc has been treated, and we have a proper evacuation plan for the rest of them."

"I call the shots, Hoffman. If I say we're leaving, we're leaving."

"You're wrong. I call the shots around here."

We all whirled. Lieutenant Rains had appeared silently from behind the building. He was with Sergeant Mason and two of his infantrymen who both carried M-16s.

"Who the fuck are you?" Walker snapped.

"Lieutenant Rains, US Infantry. And I decide when and if we leave."

"That's my aircraft, Rains, and this is a CIA operation, so you'd better not interfere."

They squared off against each other, Walker's men with stubby M4A1 carbines, Rains' men with their assault rifles, and us waiting to the side, forgotten. Rachel looked at me and raised her eyebrows. It was a pissing contest, which was for sure, one between heavily armed men, and outside the hut where Luk lay desperately ill, fighting for his life. I felt it was time to do something positive before these macho idiots started shooting.

"You're both wrong," I interjected, moving to stand close to them, but not in their line of fire. They stared at me. I'd broken the spell, but now I needed to concoct another.

"As pilot in command of the Twin Otter, technically, that leaves me in command of the decision as to when and if it leaves. And that decision will be taken by me, and not by either of you."

"Bullshit!" Walker snarled. But before he could say anymore, Rains cut in.

"That sounds fair to me. You've got to fly it, and so you call the shots."

It struck me that he was relieved to have someone to take over the responsibility of command for him. Some officer, and even his sergeant looked surprised.

"That's crap!" Walker continued.

"Mr. Hoffman, any trouble with these people, and I'll have them restrained. What do you want us to do?"

"Sir, is this the correct…?" his sergeant murmured.

"This is the way we'll handle it, Sergeant Mason. Now, Mr. Hoffman, what's the plan?"

* * *

Master Sergeant Wendelski flexed her fingers and put them on the control stick for the MQ-9 Reaper attack drone. She felt excited. At last she would get the chance to kick some ass. Except that it was nightfall in Afghanistan. She'd called up her commander and offer to fly a night operation.

"Sir, those birds are equipped with thermal imaging. There's plenty to see even at night."

"Yeah, I'm sure you're right. Isn't this your first time out with one of these birds?"

"Well, yes, but I've had dozens of hours on the simulator."

"That's what I thought. Go home and get some sleep, Master Sergeant. Report here in ten hours time, and get yourself ready for daylight operations. You know that you'll need clearance before you can launch any of those missiles, at least until you've got some flying hours under your belt."

"Yes, Sir, but there are people out there that…"

"Go home, Master Sergeant. That's an order."

"Yes, Sir."

She hung up the phone. Maybe he was right, and at least in daylight she'd be able to see everything. And with any luck, she'd be able to file an after mission report with a list of her kills. Now that was really something!"

CHAPTER EIGHT

The Taliban are not demoralized. Despair is a sin. The Taliban are united. We are giving the US and the coalition forces a tough time. We are hunting them down like pigs.

Mullah Omar

Marine General Daniel Westwood, the ISAF commander for Afghanistan, emerged from his bathroom, his face still dripping with cold water while he dried it with a hand towel. Both officers noticed the tiredness in his eyes, but it didn't show anywhere else in his face. All three officers were wearing Universal Camouflage Pattern fatigues, but there was no doubt about who was in charge. General Westwood, shorter than the other two men and slight in build, crackled with a ferocious energy that seemed to constantly seek for an escape, like high pressure in a steam engine. Westwood was an old school marine, hard as hickory, and he expected his men to display the same qualities of energy and toughness. They'd been up for an hour, and it was still only three in the morning. He glanced at Lieutenant Colonel Brooks, his intelligence officer.

"How are we looking Charlie, are we holding them?"

"We are, General, but we're stretched to the limit. We need a few more days before the emergency is over, and we can start taking the offensive again."

"General, my men are ready to go now," Lieutenant Colonel Vance Everard protested. "These tribesmen will just fade away into the mountains if we don't hit them hard. They did the same when the Russians were here."

"I'm with you there, Vance, but we don't have the men to protect our people, look after our Afghan allies, and go after the bad guys. Not yet, anyway. Give it a few more days."

Everard grimaced. "It'll be too late, as usual. They'll get clean away."

Westwood glanced at him and smiled. "Maybe, but if we go off half cocked, we could lose a lot of the advantages we've won so far. Our allies need help, Vance, and they need our protection. If we charge out with our battle flags fluttering in the breeze, and the Taliban come in behind us and murder the people we left behind, how much good will that do us?"

Everard said nothing. General Westwood seemed

satisfied that he'd made his point and shifted his gaze to his intelligence officer.

"Charlie, what about those infantrymen who were escorting the French medics?"

"Medecin Sans Frontieres," Brooks reminded him. "We lost touch with them. One of our drones from Creech had a sighting yesterday, and we're hoping to regain contact today. They had some technical trouble with a Predator, but they're putting up a Reaper instead."

Westwood grunted. "That should be helpful if they're in any kind of trouble."

"The first drone sighting showed their vehicles destroyed, and the group is sheltering in a village near the border."

"Are they in trouble?"

Brooks nodded. "Big trouble, a strong force of Taliban was nearby. Maybe it had them pinned down, we're not sure. Until this emergency is over, there's not a lot we can do. The morning overflight should tell us more."

"Ok, now listen. I know that the Rules of Engagement are for those Reaper drivers at Creech. But they are for normal operating conditions. It's anything but normal at present, so you can advise whoever is flying that bird that they are to make a unilateral decision on any fire missions. Will you pass that on to Creech?"

"Is that wise, General?" Brooks looked anxious. "We've had more than our share of friendly fire problems."

"Wise or not, those are my orders. If that party is in trouble, it's the least we can do to have someone able to help them without filling in a truckload of forms in triplicate. Is there anything else?"

Both colonels shook their heads.

"Good. Colonel Everard, be ready to move as soon as we're over the immediate danger. Then you're cleared to go and find the enemy. Search them out and destroy them wherever you find them. Until then, you wait."

"Yes, Sir."

"Unless, of course, you uncover our number one target. If that happens, all bets are off."

Everard nodded. Yeah, that was the big question, the one they all wanted answered. "Where is Mullah Omar?"

* * *

It was a bad night. The enemy constantly fired into the village. Their aim was wild, but it was clear their object was to keep them from getting any sleep. The tactic succeeded, and they were all bleary-eyed and tired. While it was still dark, I enlisted the help of six of Rains' infantrymen to help unload the aircraft. We had two cases of C4 explosive on board still, and the Twin Otter was a sitting target. If it was hit, I didn't want to add to the damage by leaving plastic explosive on board. We carried the cases back to the village, together with the satphone and the sniper rifle. I checked my watch. It was four in the morning. To my astonishment, Luk appeared. He was using a stick to support himself.

"What the hell are you doing, Luk? You're supposed to be at death's door."

"They packed me full of fresh blood and stitched up the wounds. Apparently, it wasn't as bad as they thought. You brought my rifle, I see. That could be useful."

The doctor appeared in the doorway. "I told him to rest, but he wouldn't listen. Perhaps you can persuade him?"

"I'll do my best, Doctor."

He smiled. "It's Yves. I don't think that kind of formality serves any purpose in places like this."

He was a good looking man, typically French, with that Gallic élan and flair for style that the whole nation seemed to possess. Even in his camouflaged combat trousers and white jacket, with a T-shirt underneath, he managed to look good. He was young, maybe twenty-five or so, and his unruly hair was a rumpled mess. It could have been from all he'd been through lately, or perhaps it was just the style that young people wore these days on the Champs Elysses. It wasn't difficult to imagine him with a beautiful and chic Parisienne on his arm, strolling through the bistros of the Left Bank.

"Ok, Yves. Thanks for what you've done."

He winked. "I'll send you a bill when I get home. If I get home."

"You will, Yves, and that's a promise."

He stared at me. "You know, I believe you. Get me home in one piece, and I'll tear up the bill."

I chuckled as he walked back into his treatment room. When I looked around, Luk had taken hold of his sniper rifle. I pulled it away from him. "No way, not until Yves pronounces you fit, and that isn't going to be for a while."

He looked very tired, and he didn't put up a fight. "Fair enough. What about the plastique? Can't we do something with that?"

It hadn't occurred to me to do anything, other than make it safe so that it didn't do any more damage. But that was civilian thinking. I was now in command of both civilians and soldiers, which was my understanding.

"I'll think about it. You go and get some rest."

Rachel helped him back inside the stone hut. The medics had just noticed he'd gone missing in the darkness and were already looking for him; like a naughty schoolboy. Rachel and I both laughed. Then the mortar barrage started. Apparently, the Taliban had decided they'd waited long enough for us to come out, so now they were piling on the pressure. I ran around to the stone wall where Rains was crouched down with his sergeant and two soldiers.

"I think we can assume this barrage is the preliminary to an attack, Lieutenant. Is everything ready?"

He looked at Sergeant Mason, who replied. "We're as ready as we can be. We've put machine guns to cover the approaches to the village. That should hold them when they come. There are two mortars ready to use as well, but we need a target for those. The boys are ready, Mr. Hoffman, don't worry."

"It's Max," I reminded him.

He nodded absently, just as one of his men dashed over and slid down beside us.

"They're coming, loads of them. We can hardly make them out in the darkness, but they're there all right."

Mason gave me a cynical glance. I knew what he meant, 'you're supposed to be running this show, you decide'. So I did.

"Are they attacking in a rush or slowly, keeping in cover?"

"They're coming mighty slow, Sir, keeping those turbans well down, so we can't shoot them the hell off."

"Ok, do your best to keep them away. I'll see if I can rig a surprise for them. Sergeant, would you come with me?"

He looked surprised, but Rains nodded, and he followed me to the stack of C4.

"Would you start taking the blocks of explosive out of the crates. I'll go and find someone that knows how to fix the detonators."

"I can do that, Sir."

I noticed the Sir. At least I had one good man on my side.

"Very well, let's do it. I want the explosive stacked

against that defensive wall where your officer is hiding. Then we'll get them to pull back. I guess you know the rest."

He grinned. "That's good enough for me."

We started to assemble the charges, and Mason called two of his men over to start carrying them to the stone wall. When Rains discovered I was leading the enemy onto the wall to destroy it, and them with it, he protested.

"This wall offers good cover, Hoffman. The last thing we want is to destroy it."

I laughed at him. "Rains, they'll charge straight over this wall. You need to pull back into the village and establish a new defensive position."

"I do?" He looked totally lost now, and his men looked worried at his forlorn expression.

"You do, yes. Right now."

"Ok, I'll do it. Corporal Delgado, come with me, and we'll set up a new position."

They left the shelter of the wall. There were several men waiting for orders, and Mason detailed them to bury the explosives under blocks of stone. He made a final check on the wiring, and then we pulled back with the remote detonator. We found a new position almost a hundred yards away, inside some kind of a stonecutter's yard.

"Sergeant, do you think you ought to check how the battle's going?"

"Yeah, I guess so. They've gone a bit quiet."

"Planning a final rush, maybe?"

"Probably. You're all ready, Sir?"

"I am."

He doubled away, and Rachel slipped in beside me.

"How are things going, Max? What's happening?"

I explained as best I could. She looked horrified.

"So you're leading them into the village?"

"The outskirts, yes. Then we blow the charges."

"It's a hell of a risk."

I stared at her. "It's called war, Rachel. You were an Air Force officer, so you should know."

"Yeah."

She waited with me, and Sergeant Mason returned with two of his men.

"We're all set. We just need to wait for the bastards to come nearer."

It didn't take long. The first rays of dawn started to dilute the darkness, and there was a roaring shout as they charged forward. There were at least fifty of them, counting the muzzle flashes as they fired their assault rifles. When they realized we'd pulled back, they came straight over the low wall, and Mason detonated the charges. There was a huge explosion, the ground shook and the wall disappeared in a show of small stone fragments, along with the attackers. A massive sheet of flame lit up the sky, ripping away the darkness. And in that violent light, we saw the second wave of Taliban advancing, another forty or fifty of them, about two hundred yards back.

"Oh, shit," Mason breathed.

"Call up the machine guns. We need to try and hold them off."

"I reckon we do."

He rushed back, shouting orders for them to resite the machine guns. They started their monotonous chatter, and the attackers dived for cover, but they crawled forward. It was obvious it would only be a matter of time before they overran us. They reached the wreckage of the stone wall and the devastation that was all that remained of their first attacking wave. They stopped there and started shooting up the village, and then their mortars started again. Rachel tugged at my sleeve. I hadn't realized she'd been shouting for my attention.

"Max, we could try and get the Twin Otter out of here with the casualties and some of the medics."

I looked across the wide gap to the road where the aircraft sat waiting and shook my head.

"We'd be a sitting target just getting across the open ground, and they wouldn't let us take off. As soon as we start the engines, they'd rip us apart with machine gun and rocket fire. I'm afraid we have to forget the plane for the time being. What about Luk?"

"He's trying to get Yves to allow him to get to his sniper rifle. They're almost having to hold him down," she smiled.

"At least that means he's recovering well. Are you armed?"

She held out her Colt .45. I nodded. "You'd better warn Yves and his people to stay inside the stone hut. It's the best cover in the village." She ran off.

They crawled nearer and nearer, and their fire was so intense that it was all we could do to keep our heads down and stay out of the withering gunfire. Sergeant Mason doubled over to us.

"Any suggestions? I don't think we can hold out much longer. We're running low on ammunition."

I shook my head. "None. Except the obvious."

"Surrender?"

I nodded. "I can't think of any other options."

"The Taliban don't have much of a reputation for looking after their prisoners."

"At least we'd be alive, Sergeant."

"At first, yeah."

I looked around at the battle that was raging around the small village. It was growing even lighter, but the flashes of gunfire and exploding mortar shells still lit up the sky. There were three times as many flashes from the incoming fire than from our defense, and the conclusion was obvious.

"We'll just have to hope for the best. They're not all animals, and maybe this lot are not so bad."

He gave me a skeptical look.

"If you say so. How are we going to play this? I mean. Do we use a white flag, or something?"

"I think so, that's the universal signal, I believe. Warn the men first."

He nodded and crawled away. I turned to look at Rachel.

"I'm sorry, but I can't think of any way out of this."

"It wasn't you that got us into it, Max. I just hope I live long enough to put a bullet through that psycho Ed Walker's brain."

"I think you'll find there's a queue."

I looked up as the incoming fire intensified even more. It was obvious they were building up for the final assault. I looked around for something white to wave at them.

"Max, there's more firing coming from the east of them."

I looked up, and sure enough, more muzzle flashes lit up the sky. Then I realized that they weren't coming at us, they were aimed at the Taliban. The Devil's Guard had arrived.

The enemy didn't stand a chance. There were fifteen men in the group who fell on the larger force from behind, but it was as if they were being attacked by a pack of wild dogs. The newcomers were armed with a variety of automatic weapons, and it was clear that each man was an expert in the use of those weapons. They moved as one, deadly precision ballet. Like experts, they found the best natural cover the terrain offered, cover that would get them to their objective in the quickest way to wreak the maximum damage. They unerringly found their targets, and the turbaned Afghans didn't even have time to turn and aim before they were torn to piece in a hail of automatic fire. Grenades rained down on their ranks, fired from the assault rifles of the attackers. It was as if some kind of demonic vacuum cleaner had arrived to sweep up every single crumb of the attackers. We kept our heads down, occasionally popping up to choose a fleeing Taliban fighter and send him to his God. Then it was all over. They came cautiously into the village, a band of tough, battle-hardened warriors. It wasn't that they were big men, as such, but they looked huge. They all wore camouflage uniforms, of an unusual pattern. They were festooned with more weapons, grenades and miscellaneous equipment than I would have thought it possible for one man to carry. Their leader came in first, and I went out to greet him.

"I'm Art Schramm, and I lead these men. A friend said that you were in need of some help, Abe Woltz."

We shook hands, and I introduced Rachel and myself.

"That's the understatement of the year. Thanks for coming, and thanks for what you've done."

I stared at him. He was short and powerfully built. Underneath the weapons and webbing festooned over him, he wore a sweat-soaked camouflage shirt that failed to hide the hard muscles it contained. He had khaki pants in a different camouflage pattern and lightweight, sand colored combat boots coated with dust. His hair was thick and hung to his shoulders, held in place by a thong leather headband. He looked like the kind of warrior he was, wild and unconventional.

He nodded. "You're welcome, but we're not clear yet. As we were descending the Pass, we could see another group of insurgents heading this way. About two hundred of them."

I could see our group looking at me in despair. Their hopes had been raised by the arrival of these tough fighters, only to have them dashed as the enemy brought in reinforcements. Luk was a few yards away, making strange gestures that I recognized as sign language. The girl he communicated with looked to be about twenty years old, a slim, pretty Afghan girl in Western clothes and a headscarf. He saw me watching and limped over. Before he could speak, I looked at him critically and asked how come he was up and about.

"They patched me up, and I feel much better. I want you to meet Najela."

I felt irritated. It wasn't the time or place to meet a new girlfriend, and I pulled a face.

"I'll talk to her later, Luk. Right now, we've got problems. The enemy is bringing up reinforcements."

"That's just it, you see. Najela knows a way out of here."

"I'm sure she does, but there are a few hundred nasties that are waiting to kill us the moment we make a move. I'll talk to you later, but I need to get back to the soldiers and work out a solution to this problem."

"No, you don't understand. There's hidden path that leads away from here, and it goes through to her home village, where we can hide."

"This Afghan girl, Najela. She told you this?"

He nodded. "Sure. Well, she signed it. She can't speak, so we used sign language."

"I didn't know you could do that?"

"I learned while I was doing my stint in the army. There was a big push on opportunities. They said if I learned sign language, it would help with my promotion."

I smiled at the absurd image of a modern army using sign language to communicate.

"Did it?"

"Did it what?"

"Help with your promotion."

"No."

I nodded. I guessed armies never changed, a sniper with sign language. He saw my expression.

"They had some idea of using sign language for clandestine missions as well. A way of keeping absolute silence in the field for the Afghan Special Forces."

"I didn't think there were any Afghan Special Forces."

"Not now there isn't, no. In the old days things were different, very different."

"You mean when the Soviets were here?"

He grimaced. "Something like that."

"Surely the sign language was a problem at night?"

He grinned. "Maybe that's why I didn't get my promotion."

Using him as an interpreter, I questioned the girl at length. This village was abandoned long ago, during the Soviet occupation. She lived in the village that was about ten miles away, in a straight line, anyway. What was really interesting was that it was on the other side of a mountain, or at least part of one; a massive spur of rock that slanted down from the heights of the Hindu Kush to sweep down into Afghanistan. It was a journey of almost fifty miles to reach the village if you went the long way around, but there was a narrow path the led to a tunnel in the rock, and all the way through to the village. She signed energetically, and I waited for Luk to translate.

"She says it was used during the Soviet times, and the fighters used to shelter inside it. The Russians eventually found it and brought down the roof with explosives. When they left, some of the men cleared it to make a way through from their village to the road over the Khyber Pass. Otherwise, it is a long journey to reach Pakistan when they wish to go there."

"What's this village called?"

"It is called Yaluk."

I mulled over what she'd said. It sounded hopeful as a way of escape, but even so, there was an old maxim. If something is too good to be true, it usually is.

"Ask her if the Taliban know of this village."

There was another flurry of signing.

"She says yes, they do, but they leave it alone. They do not know the tunnel has been cleared."

"Why do they leave it alone?"

He signed again, and I noticed a hesitation on the part of the girl to reply. Then there was more signing that went on for a long time. Luk looked surprised, but he translated.

"She says because of the magic."

I grimaced. "Luk, she must have said more than that. Tell me the rest."

He explained it all to me then, and the picture became clearer. Not that I believed it. It seemed the village was home to a long tradition of healers. I guess they would be like the old native herbalists who were part of all ancient cultures. But these people had taken their skills to new heights, using the knowledge passed down to them over generations, and a number of unique varieties of plants and herbs that only grew at the very highest levels of the Hindu Kush.

"They have a problem, the Taliban. On the one hand, this kind of practice is supposed to be un-Islamic, because of the suspicions of witchcraft about some of their reported healings. On the other hand, they have wives, parents, children, who all need medical help at some time. They sneak into Yaluk to get what they need and sneak out, and the mullahs turn a blind eye. It's kind of live and let live, so the place is like a neutral zone."

"So she thinks we could hide out there?"

"Yes, for a few days, at least."

"I'll talk to the others. Thank her anyway for coming up with the idea."

He smiled and looked at the girl, and I saw it then in his face. He was totally hooked on her. It was like he'd been struck with a lightning bolt. Of all the places for it to happen, it had to be here. I left them to it. Inside, I knew that their chances were almost non-existent. We were trapped inside a war zone, an injured man recovering from a bullet wound and a deaf Afghan girl. It could have been worse, but not much. I rejoined the group of soldiers and mercenaries who were sat on the ground. Some of them had lit cigarettes, and I noticed that the new arrivals, the mercenaries, were cleaning their weapons and making preparations for the next fight. They were not men to be taken by surprise.

Their leader, Art Schramm, nodded at me in a friendly enough way, and he was talking to one of his mercenaries, a huge, muscled bull of a man.

"This is my second in command, Max. Trip Wennerstrom, meet Max Hoffman."

We shook hands, and I explained to both men what Najela had told me. They looked skeptical.

"Do you believe her?" Art replied. "More importantly,

do you trust her?"

"It sounds on the level, so yes, I trust her. I don't think she'd betray us."

"Why not?" Trip asked.

I pointed over to where Najela was helping Luk to sit on the ground. When she got him comfortable, she sat with him, kissed him on the cheek, and he slipped his arm around her. Both men nodded. "Yeah, understood. It could be interesting, so what are you going to do?"

"Me? I thought you were running things now."

Art pulled a face. "Me? No way, I reckon it's time to see if you're as tough as your grandfather."

"I never knew him, you know."

"Yeah, that was a shame," he replied. "But it's time to put another Hoffman in the saddle, so you can call the shots from here on in, Max. If anything doesn't look right, we'll deal with it. The boys all know what your grandfather stood for."

"But, Art, I don't…"

"Max, listen. I won't be doing this much longer. These men need someone like you to take over."

I briefly wondered what he meant, that he wouldn't be doing it much longer. Was he ill? Or was he prescient? Many soldiers were a complex mass of superstition and dark premonitions. I tried again.

"But I'm not really a soldier, Art. I'm a pilot. My military service was years ago, in the Royal Thai Army."

"Don't worry about that, you're doing fine so far. So what's our next move, Boss?"

I winced. But he was adamant, so I decided to make the best of it.

The first step was to assemble the men and women in a group to explain to them what we had planned. When I told them we were heading away from the Khyber Pass, further into Afghanistan, there was a lot of disquiet. Especially from Ed Walker.

"Who the fuck do you think you are, Hoffman? That plane is bought and paid for, and you are, too. I want you to fly us out of here, right now. We'll make arrangements to come back for the others."

I sighed. "I already told you, Walker. The second we start engines they'll blast that aircraft to pieces. This is our only chance, and we're heading for Yaluk. I want everyone to get ready to leave before it's too light."

"Says who?" he sneered. "I've got two armed guards with me that say we're taking that plane out of here."

His men looked uncomfortable, and they didn't meet my gaze. But Art Schramm squared up to Walker. "Says my fifteen armed men, you little shit."

Before Walker could reply, Rains walked up to stand beside Schramm. "My men are with Max. I reckon you're badly outnumbered, buddy."

Walker stared at both men for a few moments, then shook his head and stalked away. Art turned to me.

"Max, it's your call."

"Get everyone ready to leave. We're heading out in fifteen minutes."

* * *

Carol Wendelski checked in with the guards who allowed authorized personnel to enter the Ground Control Station, and arrested unauthorized personnel who tried to get in. She knew one of them slightly, She'd been on a date with him once, but it hadn't worked out when she didn't share his love of baseball, and him not hers for all things technical. But they'd stayed friends.

"Give 'em hell, Carol," he winked. He knew she flew reconnaissance drones over Afghanistan, but he didn't know that today it would be different.

"Yeah, I'll do that, never fear."

Corporal Munch handed over the console to her. He'd been running through the training package for the MQ-9, but he was not cleared for flight operations.

"Hi, Carol. There's a message from headquarters. You're to call this number."

He handed her a message slip. She was to call a Colonel Brooks, ISAF Chief of Intelligence in Afghanistan. She raised her eyebrows.

"Jesus, what have I done?"

He shrugged. "No idea, but you're to call him the

moment you come in, so I'd do it now if I were you."

It took almost half a minute to route the call through the secure military channels to ISAF HQ Afghanistan. The voice that answered sounded as if he'd just got out of bed.

"Brooks."

"This is Master Sergeant Wendelski, calling as ordered from Creech."

"Oh, yeah. Thanks for calling, Master Sergeant. You're flying the MQ-9 today, I understand."

"That's correct, Sir."

"Right, there's been a change of Rules of Engagement, and this is from the top."

Her spirits plummeted. So they were going to prevent her from any live firing, she could see it coming. They were terrified of friendly fire incidents, but even so, she knew what she was doing. It wasn't fair. She dimly realized the Colonel was speaking again.

"I'm sorry, Sir. What did you say?"

"I said you'll be flying weapons free, Master Sergeant. If you see a target, you are cleared to make your own decision whether to engage or not."

Oh, fuck! Was he for real?

"Yes, Sir. Just so I'm clear, I'm flying the MQ-9 today, weapons free, complete clearance to engage on my own authority."

"Correct. Any questions?"

"No, Sir. Thank you, Sir."

But he'd already hung up. Oh, my God, it was for real!

"What is it?" Munch asked. "Bad news?"

"No. I'm weapons free on the Reaper."

"Jesus Christ!"

CHAPTER NINE

Bush said: 'It is better to fight them on their ground than they fighting us on our ground.' In response to these fallacies, I say: The war in Iraq is raging, and the operations in Afghanistan are on the rise in our favor, praise be to God.

Osama Bin Laden

"You wanted to see me, General?"

"That's correct, Mr. President. I'm happy to report the situation in Afghanistan is being brought back under our control. Another three or four days, and we'll be comfortable again."

"Comfortable?" Barrani looked up. "Is that what we're there for, General, to be comfortable? I thought we were there to win."

"That's true, yes, but the situation is rather complex. It's not as simple as that."

Mrs. Chalmers glared at him. "I don't see what isn't simple, General. Al Qaeda destroyed the World Trade Center, and then they tried to hole up in Afghanistan. In the process of hiding, they allied themselves with the Taliban. Ergo, we need to destroy them. Or are you saying that they shouldn't pay for what they did? The greatest crime of the twenty first century, for God's sake."

Mann felt as if he'd been set upon by a pack of wild dogs. For a moment he had the idea of telling them to stop being so stupid, and then walking out of there. Years of experience and self-control stopped him from destroying his career.

"No, Ma'am, of course not. What I'm saying is the situation over there is highly unstable, both the politics and the military. We're doing our best to…"

"Doing your best?" The President looked up and stared at him. "The last time you were here you persuaded us that so-called Black-ops would make all the difference. Tell me, General, how many operations have you mounted so far?"

Mann hesitated, but he knew the truth would come out. This was Washington. It was no longer the Nixon years, when the truth was so often buried. Or the Kennedy years, when even the President himself could embark on illicit affairs, and the newspapers would keep silent. Things had changed, as Bill Clinton discovered during a very uncomfortable two terms in office.

"One, Sir."

"One! And what was the result of this single operation?"

"We took out more than a dozen of their local leaders."

"You mean killed?"

"Yes, we killed them, Mr. President."

"I see. Why have you not sent this team back in to dispose of some more of these bastards that are killing our men? Or was one mission what you had in mind when you proposed this particular course?"

"Mr. President, the team hasn't reported back yet." He took a deep breath. "Our intelligence suggests that they were ambushed on the border and lost most of their men. Since then, we've lost contact with the team leader. He's a CIA operative."

He heard the Secretary of State breathe, "Jesus Christ", behind him. The President was silent at first. Then he spoke slowly, barely concealing the anger in his voice.

"Would you have us believe that this operation is about to shorten the war?"

The General shook his head. "No, Sir."

"No. Now listen, General. Your plan was a good one, but the implementation stinks. If you want to take out their leaders, that's fine. But strike at the top and cut off the head. Not a ragtag bunch of local tribal leaders, and then leave your men exposed to be ambushed and killed. Who's their top man over there? The Taliban leader."

"You mean Mullah Omar, Mr. President?"

"Yes, he's who I mean. If he was captured or killed, that would hit them hard, surely? I doubt they'd recover from that."

"Well, no, but…"

"Find him, General. No more half-cocked operations. Send in your experts, and either kill or kidnap this guy. Let me know how you get on. I'll authorize CIA to lend a hand. That's all, General."

He got up, and the Chief of Staff was left dazed and astonished. As he left the room, the Secretary of State gave him a sweet smile. "Good luck, General. I'd advise you not to screw up this one."

He ignored her. How the hell could he get Mullah Omar? It had taken them many years to hunt down and kill Bin-Laden, the Al Qaeda head and architect of 911. Now they wanted him to get Omar in just a few days. Shit! As he left the situation room, he had another thought. What he needed wasn't Mullah Omar, which was virtually impossible. No, he needed a scapegoat. It wasn't in his nature to play the political game, but it was the game he'd been placed in. Now who would fit the bill?

* * *

The journey was not easy, especially for Luk, but Najela helped him limp along. She'd found a wooden stick that he leaned on to make the going a little easier. But still, I asked Yves to stay close to him with one of his nurses, and several times they called a halt to check the state of his wound. I'd sent Rains on ahead with his men, and posted Art Schramm to bring up the rear. When the insurgents found we'd left, it was possible they'd find our trail and pursue us. If they caught up, I wanted the mercenaries to be there to deal with them. I had little doubt that they'd give the Afghans a hard time if they came near. I walked with Rachel, and we had a little time to talk.

"What are we going to do about the aircraft, Max?" she asked me with a worried tone.

"I've no idea. What I do know is that it's the least of our worries. The first priority is to get these people to safety."

"You're taking it all seriously, aren't you?"

"What?"

"Leading the group. You know they all look to you to get them back."

I shrugged. "I don't know. I think Art would manage quite well with his own men."

"Maybe, but Rains wouldn't. Have you noticed how he's changed since you took command?"

I thought about it. She was right. He had become more confident, and there was less fear and uncertainty in the way he led his platoon. "Yes, he's not so timid."

"That's because he looks to you to make the decisions so that he can handle his men. He's ok, but he's no officer.

A good sergeant, maybe, but that's all."

"I'll tell the US Army what you said."

She laughed. "By all means, but remember this. When we hit trouble, you're the one they'll rely on to get them out of it."

"Rachel, I'm a pilot, not a military commander," I protested.

"Maybe your ticket says you're just a pilot, but all the same you're not flying an aircraft now. You're leading a group of soldiers and civilians through bandit country. And they're all looking to you to make the right choices, remember that."

I didn't reply. We'd covered almost eight miles and were approaching the entrance to a narrow cave, where Rains had halted his men. I stopped and Najela came forward with Luk to interpret. The path ran into the cave and cut all the way through the mountain. In front of us, the sheer cliff face soared a thousand feet into the foothills of the Hindu Kush. It had a bleak grandeur that was perhaps a clue to the Afghan psyche, cold and forbidding. The dark cave entrance was almost invisible, and without Najela, we wouldn't have found it. I understood the tunnel was almost two miles long.

"Would you ask her if there's headroom in there?" I asked Luk.

He signed the question and answered me. "No, Najela says we'll need to crawl through some of the way."

"Can you make it?"

He nodded. "I'll make it, don't worry. It's that or the Taliban. I'll crawl through ten miles of cave if necessary."

They'd gathered in a group, so I told them what was ahead of us. Art Schramm offered to detail a machine gun crew; two men to set up out of sight to guard the entrance until we were through. "I'll set some grenades inside too, and I'll give them long fuses. If the gunners get into trouble, they can start the detonators as they come past, and it'll bring the roof down."

"Right. You'd better not tell Najela that part. I gather they spent an age clearing the last roof fall."

"They won't need to worry about using the tunnel again if they're dead," he said grimly.

"That's true. We need to get moving. Lieutenant Rains, would you lead off into the tunnel."

"Sure. Form up, men. Let's move out."

The first part was easy, and part of the way we were able to walk upright, single file. Then the roof got lower, and we had to crouch down to keep going. The roof lowered again, and we had to get to our knees to keep going forward, pushing and pulling our packs and supplies along with us. It was backbreaking and soul destroying. The bare rock was uneven, and all of us constantly cut our arms and legs as we snagged on the sharper edges of unseen obstacles. We crawled for over an hour until finally the roof started to get higher, and we were able to get to our feet and walk again. Two hours after we entered the tunnel, we emerged the other side into a sunlit morning. Rains and his men had already emerged and were standing and staring into the distance. When I got out into the sunlight, I realized why. There was a village nestling in the foothills of the mountain range. But incredibly for this country, it was undamaged. Rachel caught her breath.

"It's beautiful, Max."

It wasn't beautiful at all. It was a primitive collection of stone huts. There were two lines of them with a main street running between them. I counted about thirty dwellings, and all of them in good repair. A few of them even had glass in the windows, a minor miracle outside of the main cities. Even there many houses had lost their glass in the unending series of wars that had beset the country in the past three decades.

"Let's go and find out if the natives are friendly," I smiled by way of a reply.

Rains took up the lead, and we walked into the main, and only, street. People came out of their stone huts to gaze at us, but there was no fear. Finally, we stopped, and a man stood in the street ten paces from us. Najela recognized him and ran forward to greet him. The man signed a reply to her and both their arms moved swiftly as they conversed. Then she came to Rachel and me and signed. Luk came up to translate.

"She says this is her father, Ban. He is the village

headman."

I shook hands with him. Rachel stood back, as was the custom here.

"Would you ask her to enquire whether we may shelter here for a few days," I said to Luk. "We'll pay, of course."

The signing took a minute or so, but Luk turned to me.

"It's no problem. There are some empty houses and a couple of barns too. You're welcome to any of them. There's no need for payment. Most of their needs are met by trading, a local barter system."

There was a shout from the cave entrance, and Art's machine gun crew emerged. They gave a cheery wave, and it was clear that we weren't being pursued. I waved back and continued the halting conversation.

"Tell him we'll do our best not to get in anyone's way, and thank him for allowing us to stay. We'd like to see our quarters now. We've been without sleep for some time, and we need to catch up."

A guide led us to the houses we'd been allocated. I went into a tiny, two roomed hut with Rachel, Luk and Najela.

"Do they expect the girls to sleep in one room and the men the other?" I asked Luk.

He signed to Najela again. She smiled at me and shook her head. Maybe Afghanistan wasn't so bad after all. The door opened, and Art came in without knocking.

"I've set up a defensive perimeter. The other machine gun crew can cover the approaches to the village, and a sentry is hidden on the opposite side. No one can come up on us without we know about it."

He stared at me, expressionless. I should have set that up before we came to find out where we'd be sleeping. I nodded to him. "Thanks, Art. I should have done that myself."

"Yeah. Don't sweat it, get some sleep."

He turned to walk back out through the door.

"Art, before you go."

"Yes?"

"We'll be here for a couple of days at least, maybe more. Can you run me through some of this stuff in the morning?"

"Sure."

They all smiled when he left, and even Najela had picked it up. But I didn't see the funny side of it.

"Rachel, if I mess up, people will get killed. It's not a joke."

"Art will look after things, don't worry."

"And when he's gone back, what then? He won't stay here forever."

"You're right, but can we discuss it later. I'm exhausted. What are we going to do about food?"

Damn, I'd forgotten that too! "Get yourself some rest. I'll be back later."

She went to say something, but I was already walking out through the door. I found Ban, and by using a number of universal hand signals conveyed that we were very hungry. He smiled and led me to a stone hut that housed the village ovens. There was also a huge cauldron that was bubbling merrily, issuing a smell so good that I nearly put my hand in and scooped out some of the stew that lay inside. He raised his eyebrows and pointed at me, then pantomimed my people. Did we want the food? Dear God, did we? I nodded enthusiastically. He smiled and pointed at a pile of wooden bowls. I got the message and went out to round everyone up. Sergeant Mason came over to me.

"What's up?"

"Chow's what is up, Sergeant. Would you get everyone here, and we'll get something to eat."

"You betcha! I was thinking about turning cannibal."

I laughed as he walked away. Then I went to the house we'd borrowed and gave Rachel a call, as well as Luk and Najela. But the two were otherwise occupied. The door to their room was closed, and Rachel gave a small shake of her head.

"They're busy, Max. I think they'd prefer to be left alone."

"Right."

The word had spread, and almost the entire party was crowded around the cooking hut. Rains' infantrymen, Art Schramm's mercenaries, Doctor Yves St Roulemont and his nurses, and a little to one side Ed Walker with his two surviving bodyguards. I got into line and helped myself to stew from the cauldron, together with a chunk of bread that we all just ripped from an enormous loaf.

"You did well, getting this organized so quickly," Rains said to me as he came up, his face covered in stew with breadcrumbs sticking to it. I looked around and saw that we were all the same. Some of them were sat on the ground, others standing and chatting, but the hot food had worked a miracle. What had Najela said about this village, something about magic? If this was it, I'd take it anytime over the Christian church. I just nodded to the Lieutenant. There was no need to tell him that it had little to do with my efforts. He needed a leader. I could see that now. And I needed him, or at least the firepower his troops carried. Art came to join me with his huge sidekick, Trip. Then Yves wandered over with his nurses, and the conversation became animated. They were all grateful to me, and I felt like Jesus feeding the five thousand. I realized Art was speaking to me.

"I'm sorry, Art. What was that?"

"I said what weapons have you had training with?"

"Only the Colt .45 automatic, I'm afraid. My grandmother made sure I knew how to use a pistol if I ever needed to."

"In that case, I'll start you off in the morning with an M-16. One of my guys carries an AK47 too, so you can familiarize yourself with that one."

"Thanks, that'll be appreciated. What I really need is a

fast primer on strategy and tactics."

"Yep, I'll get to that. But what it really boils down to is hit the bastards hard when they least expect it."

"That's all?"

"It's won more battles than could fill a library full of books. Keep that in mind, and you won't go wrong."

But as I finished the food and went back to our stone hut, I thought about the real battle I'd have to fight. With Ed Walker and his boss, Joe Ashford. They thought they'd bought me - lock, stock and barrel. Maybe it was true, but that made no difference. They'd want me to carry out our bargain, one that I'd entered without knowing the consequences. I wondered how I could adapt Art's strategy to that particular fight. How could I hit them hard when their guard was down? That would take some thinking about. Rachel had gone back ahead of me, and the reason became obvious when I walked into the hut. Despite the cold, she'd stripped off naked and was lying beneath a pile of bedding. Actually, it was old sacks and a couple of Russian greatcoats. I wondered what had happened to their owners. Afghanistan was not a forgiving place.

"Come in, Max, it's cold out there."

I started to rip off my clothes. Before I got into bed, I wedged a chair against the door. It wouldn't hold against much of a push, but at least it would tell anyone we wanted some privacy. An Afghan version of the 'do not disturb sign'. Then I climbed in with Rachel and felt the soft, firm, smooth skin of her body. It had an instant effect on me.

"I can see you're feeling randy already, Mr. Hoffman," she chuckled.

"Is that a problem?"

"Quite the opposite. I was hoping you wouldn't be too tired."

"Good. What are Luk and Najela doing?"

"The same as us, I guess. Now shut up and fuck me, Max. I can't wait another second. It must be this country, you never know if it could be your last."

"Last what?"

"Last fuck, of course," she muttered. "Tomorrow we could all be dead."

"We won't be dead. I won't let that happen."

"No, I know you won't. Now be quiet and screw me."

So I did.

I was still in bed the following morning when someone hammered on the door. It was Art Schramm.

"What's up?" I checked my watch. It was almost six o'clock.

"Weapons training. I thought you'd want to make an early start. We've got a lot of ground to cover."

"Sure, I'll be right out."

It took me a few minutes to throw my clothes on, and the temperature outside was barely above freezing. Then we set out to a piece of open ground where he'd set up some targets, pieces of rock stood on end. He handed me an assault rifle.

"This is an M-16, the standard weapon of the US infantry. It means they're very common, and there's no problem finding ammo." He took it back off me. "This is how you strip it."

It took him less than a minute to take the gun apart, and then he re-assembled it.

"Now you try."

Five minutes later, I had a tangled mess of components that looked as if they would never go together to make a rifle. He showed me how it all worked, and I tried again, and again. Until I had it, and the gun was in one piece.

"That's good, Max. All you need now is to know how to use it."

"Point and pull the trigger?"

He nodded. "It's a start. Our M-16s can select semi-automatic, three shot burst or full auto. They're pretty tough and reliable, just don't get carried away and fire off a full clip, unless it's absolutely necessary. This gadget fitted under the barrel is an M203 grenade launcher. It gives the weapon a lot more firepower. Here, you try it."

I spent the next hour destroying the peace of the village, firing clip after clip until Art pronounced himself satisfied.

"That's good, you got it. Let's finish off with the grenade launcher. Give it a try. There's a grenade ready to fire."

I pulled the extra trigger, and the small bomb launched and flew towards the broken rocks I'd been shooting at. Art dragged me down while it was still in the air.

"Get down! That's a grenade you just launched."

I lay flat on the rocky ground and felt it shake as the grenade went off. Fragments zinged off the rocks and rattled around us. I'd have been shredded if I'd been standing. We got up, and Art grinned.

"See what I mean? When you fire one of those babies, you don't stick around to watch."

"I'll bear it in mind," I replied, a little shakily.

"Good, that'll do for now. After lunch, we'll cover strategy and tactics."

When I got back to our hut, Ed Walker was there arguing with Rachel. They stopped when I arrived.

"What's up?"

"Your fucking bitch is accusing me of theft, that's what's up!"

I hit him then, and just totally lost it. He went flying back to land on the ground. I stood over him, and he looked up at me.

"Christ, you nearly broke my jaw!"

"The next time you insult Rachel, I'll rip you to pieces, Walker. Just watch your mouth. Now what's the problem?"

"Luk's satellite phone, it's been stolen. There's only one person who would have taken it, and that's him."

I stared at Walker. "Did you take it? I can easily get Art

Schramm's men to search your gear."

"No, I fucking did not, and I resent that question."

"I don't care what you resent. Now get out of here, Walker. I've got things to do."

He got to his feet. "Don't you forget who's the boss and who pays the bills, when we get out of here, you'll need me."

"I hope not. I sincerely hope not. Now get out of here!"

He stalked away without another word. I grinned at Rachel. "That's seen him off, shall we get some food?"

We walked towards the cooking hut, where people were already starting to gather as the smell of the stew wafted around the village.

"You're going to have trouble with that guy," Rachel warned.

"You're probably right, but we're stuck with him for the time being. It's a pity about the satphone. Do you think he took it?"

"Yes, who else would steal it?"

"It could have been anybody. There're a lot of people here, Rains' infantry, Schramm's men, the Medecin sans Frontieres people, Ed Walker's two bodyguards and of course the villagers."

"It was Walker, I'm sure of it. Or he got one of his men to do it, that's more his style."

"Probably, but I doubt we'll get it back. Does Luk know?"

"He was the one that told me it was missing."

"Ok, there's nothing we can do now. With any luck, we'll be out of here before much longer. I'll ask Art Schramm if he has a satphone. We could at least get a message out."

I kicked myself for not thinking of it before now. Although the military was stymied until the Taliban had been kicked back to their caves, it would have been useful to let them know where we were and what was our situation. They could, of course, know already, at least where we were, from their drone overflights, but there was no guarantee.

In the event, Art didn't carry a satphone when I asked him after we'd eaten.

"I've got no use for 'em, not in the field, anyway."

"I don't understand, surely it would mean your principals could get in touch with you, in case anything changed."

"Not my way of doing business, Max. Have you heard of the Brit admiral, who deliberately ignored an order?"

I shook my head. "They didn't teach me that one in Thailand, no."

"Horatio Nelson was a famous British Admiral, during the eighteenth and nineteenth centuries, when they had Napoleon to contend with. He was a vice admiral when he sailed into the Battle of Copenhagen. His superior, Admiral Hyde Parker, who Nelson didn't think much of, signaled the British fleet to retreat. Nelson, convinced he could win, put his telescope to his blind eye and said, 'I really do not see the signal.' So the expression 'turning a blind eye' entered the English language."

"Did he win, when he ignored that order?" I had to know.

He grinned. "Oh yeah, he won alright, and they made him a viscount, some kind of English aristocrat. No satphone, see. If he'd carried one, they could have called him up and screwed around with him."

I nodded. "I'll bear it in mind, thanks Art."

"You do that. You're worried about letting people know we're here?"

"I think it would be useful, yes. Sooner or later, they'll come and get us."

"No, they won't, because we'll be leaving. Give it a couple more days for that Taliban force to move off, and then we'll head back to the Khyber Pass. Now let's get on with your military training, strategy and tactics."

We spent the rest of the afternoon working on the complexities of moving troops to their best advantage. By the end of the day, he was satisfied with my progress.

"You're a natural, you know. Jurgen, your grandfather, would have been proud of you. We'll work on leadership skills tomorrow, but you're doing fine. Just remember, don't let them know what you're up to, then hit them hard when they're least expecting it. The rest is easy. And don't forget Nelson. Don't listen to bullshit."

We spent two more days in that village, during which

time we saw no sign of the enemy. The real surprise came when we found the French medical team spending a lot of time with the Afghan healers. Yves was ecstatic.

"These people have skills and knowledge that amaze me. Ailments that we have complicated drugs and treatment regimes for, they just issue a simple remedy, and the patient seems to recover. Sometimes, they just sit with them, and they get better. It's uncanny."

"I'd get their recipes if I were you, Yves. You could make a fortune when we get back."

"I already have a fortune," he replied in a severe tone. "I inherited a chateau and a number of farms and vineyards in France. It means I never have to worry about money. The remedies would change people's lives if I could find out more about them, but the villagers are keen to keep them under wraps."

"Why?"

He shrugged. "They flatly refused to tell me anything. It's their tradition to keep it to themselves. Maybe it's something to do with the plants and herbs they use. If they're very rare, and only local to this part of the Hindu Kush, any increase in demand could destroy their resources."

"They could always be synthesized, surely?"

"I'm not sure they could. It could take away that special something that makes them unique. It's a pity, but they said I could take some preparations away with me, so perhaps I can look into it when I get back to France."

"I wish you luck with it, Yves. You never know, you could be the next Pasteur."

"He was one of my ancestors, Louis Pasteur."

I walked away. I had a feeling it would be something like that. I thought about the people who were very rich and very clever. They always seemed to be one step ahead of you. And despite my being one quarter French, they were the worst. The following day I sent scouts out to reconnoiter the route back to the foot of the Khyber Pass. They came back and reported it was clear, so we made preparations to leave. I thanked Ban, the headman. He refused to take anything in return. All he asked was that we looked after Najela. Luk assured him that he would protect her with his life. He was almost recovered now, and able to walk with only a slight trace of a limp. We set off as before, Rains' men took the point, the Devil's Guard the rear, and the rest of us fell in between them. Walker slunk along near the back with his men, talking to no one. And no one talked to him. Since I'd punched him after the incident with Rachel, he hadn't spoken to me or anyone else. He was morose and sullen, so I had little doubt that he was planning something unpleasant.

We'd had one strange encounter in a remote hut set off to a far corner of the village. I was walking with Rachel late one evening and noticed Najela's father Ban coming out of the hut. The door was fully open as Ban bowed to the man who sat inside on the floor. A shaft of bright moonlight lit up the interior, and we could both see the man as clear as if it was full daylight. He looked old, very old. He wore a black turban, which could have made him Taliban, and a patch dominated his ancient face over one eye. The other eye seemed to shine, like a miniature searchlight, its beam flashing across the distance between us until I felt myself caught in some kind of powerful and invisible force. He stared straight at me for a few moments, and I felt the power of the man reach out to me. He wore the traditional tribal robes of the Afghans, except that they were in better repair than most I'd seen. Their cut was more severe, complimenting the severity of his face. Then two tough looking men looked out, saw me, and one of them glared and pulled the door shut. Ban rushed up to us, and he looked distressed.

"You should not be here. This area is private."

"Who is he?" I asked Ban. "Is he some kind of holy man, your mullah, perhaps?"

"He is holy man, yes. Not be here. You go."

We got the message and left. But for the rest of the evening, I wondered about that mysterious man in the hut. The village of Yaluk was famous all over Afghanistan for its skilled natural healers. Was that guy a kind of master, or was he himself a patient? And that face, the sheer, raw power that I'd glimpsed. He was no ordinary man, which was for sure.

* * *

Master Sergeant Carol Wendelski took over the console from Vernon Munch. He'd been sat doing nothing, as he wasn't cleared for the Reaper. He'd spent his shift playing a multi-million dollar computer game, the Reaper simulator. It was a lot of fun, but after the first few hours as boring as hell.

"I envy you, Sarge, getting your hands on that baby. You gonna launch any of those missiles today?"

She smiled, but she was looking at the console, waiting to sit down and get her hands on the controls. To give the orders to launch, and then look down on her domain like a God of all she surveyed, with the power of life or death over it. Munch finally got up and left, and she sat down and called up her flight crew in Kabul.

"This is Creech calling Kabul. I'm all ready to go here. What's the status of the bird?"

"All ready for the preflight checks, Master Sergeant."

"Ok, let's get this show on the road."

Fifteen minutes later, she was airborne, watching the fearsome landscape roll past from five thousand feet. Now where were those infantry guys, and what happened to them?

CHAPTER TEN

The enemy will have to quit the region with humiliation and disgrace. Afghans have a history of expelling their enemies as no enemy and invader has quit Afghanistan willingly.

Mullah Omar

Joe Ashford put down the telephone and sat thinking for several long minutes. So they were on their way out. How the hell had they managed to get their hands on a satphone? Still, it made no difference. It meant that the game was still in play, if he could put the whole package together. There were still problems. If the Taliban got their hands on that aircraft, they would certainly destroy it. And there was the question of continuing supplies of product. He bought much of his stock direct from the local growers, and once again that meant Taliban. If he was going to pull this off, he needed to ensure that the aircraft stayed intact, and his suppliers were given protection from the constant threats they faced. That meant ISAF forces destroying the poppy fields, Taliban and local militias extorting massive bribes to allow the growers to continue, and Afghan Army and Police units who demanded their share of the cut. It was complicated, especially now that he had no room for maneuver. He needed someone to help him out, and as far as he knew, there was only one man in Afghanistan who could offer the kind of help he needed. He was Taliban, sure, and he would demand a high price for fixing up any kind of a deal, but it would be worth it. Thank Christ everyone had their price.

What would he want? Money, sure, but the big catch of course would be weapons. These people loved nothing more than a shiny new assault rifle, grenade launcher or fragmentation mine. Yeah, he could arrange plenty of that stuff. Here in Kabul International, there were warehouses full of it. All it needed was a few dollars spread around, maybe some faked CIA paperwork, and he could fill a dozen trucks with ordnance. Money, guns and drugs, they were the currency of Afghanistan. Guns were easy. Afghanistan was full of them. Drugs, no problem. The hard part was moving it around so it could be turned into money.

He took a cellphone out of his safe. It was Agency equipment, and secure from interception by any communications satellites that may be nosing around the skies above this part of the world. In the safe there was also a small notebook, written in a code that only he would understand. He found the number he wanted and called. After five seconds, there was an answer.

"Yes?"

"I need to speak to him."

"No one speaks to him, not ever. You know that."

"This is different. It's more valuable than even he could imagine."

"I doubt it. What do you want?"

"We have the product fixed up, as you know. But I need protection. I have to ensure that nothing goes wrong. This is life or death."

"Everything is life or death, here in God's chosen country."

"Yeah. There's an aircraft on the ground. I need it to get my shipments out, including some of the stuff that was bought from your people. I want his people to protect it."

The man laughed. It was an eerie sound, and almost mechanical, like a malfunctioning engine.

"His people have better things to do than protect an infidel aircraft."

"Without it, there'd be nothing to take out your shipments. How much are you losing on the old routes through Iran?"

"There have been losses, that's true. But still, protecting your aircraft, it sounds absurd. Besides, there is already one of our bands on the way to destroy it."

The fuck there was! "You can stop them, surely?"

"Perhaps."

The line was quiet. Both men knew that the price had yet to be mentioned, and it would be the deciding factor.

"How does three tons of ordnance sound, that's a total price for the product and the protection? I'll give you assault rifles, grenades, handguns. A couple of light machine guns, maybe."

There was another silence. He knew he'd won. There was no grating laugh in reply to his words this time.

"Five tons, perhaps. That might persuade him."

Gotcha! "Four tons, no more. Any more than that, and I'll call in some mercenary pals of mine."

This time the reply was immediate. "There will be no need to involve others. He has agreed. We will attempt to contact our fighters, and tell them to keep away from the vicinity of the aircraft. I will have the crates ready. Be sure you bring the weapons."

So his boss was there, listening to the conversation. Like tens of thousands of others, he wondered exactly where Mullah Omar was in hiding.

* * *

The journey through the tunnel was easier now that we'd had some rest. We didn't meet any opposition and emerged into the Afghan morning, our eyes blinking to accustom to the sunlight. Once again, the vast grandeur of this cruel but spectacular country was opened up to us. The peaks of the mountains that were the border with Pakistan, the distant hills and peaks, connected by patches of rocky ground, covered with sharp rocks to make cross country journeys painful and hard. The only way to travel was to stay on the main tracks; even these were uncomfortable, and we frequently stumbled on the rugged, pot-holed surface. At last we reached the village at the foot of the road that led up to the Khyber Pass. We were all astonished to see the de Havilland Twin Otter sat between the two warehouse-like buildings, apparently untouched.

"Can you get her off the ground?" Walker asked.

"Maybe, but it's not that simple. There are too many of us, and I'm not planning on leaving a score of people on the ground to be butchered by the Taliban."

"I still own the charter papers on her," he persisted.

"Yes, and I'm running this show, Walker. So you can forget any ideas about taking off and leaving people behind."

"Max, that may not be such a bad idea," Art Schramm interrupted. "These medics need to get out of here and on their journey to Pakistan. There are still people there that need them. I'm sure Lieutenant Rains can take his men out without any problems. Our two groups can team up until we meet some ISAF forces."

Rains nodded. "That sounds good to me. The current emergency must end soon, and there'll be plenty of vehicles moving around again. They'll pick us up."

"If you're sure." I was doubtful, but it made a lot of sense. The medics were needed elsewhere, and the only quick way to get them out was by air.

They all nodded. "We'll come with you, Hoffman," Ed Walker put in. "I'd like to see the medics safely back. It was my mission after all."

We all grinned. "Right. Before we make any plans, I need to check out the aircraft. Rachel, shall we take a look at her?"

We walked to the ladder and climbed up to the cargo door. I moved the lever to open it and climbed into the dark, cold and silent interior. Rachel followed. We went straight through to the cockpit, and we both started bringing the aircraft's systems online. There was no immediate problem, so I left Rachel going through the pre-flight checks while I got out and conducted my walkaround check. If it was ever necessary, it was now, when this aircraft had been left unattended in enemy territory for several days. But no one had stolen any parts from the fuselage, and everything looked intact. I watched Rachel checking the operation of the ailerons and flaps. It all looked fine, and so I called over the medical team.

"You may as well get aboard while we prepare for take-off. We should be able to leave in fifteen minutes or so if everything is working."

"We'll get aboard too. Come on, men."

Walker signaled to his two bodyguards to accompany him, and they waited impatiently at the foot of the ladder while the medics boarded. Rains and Art Schramm were together, discussing the best route back. I went over to say goodbye to them both, especially to Art.

"You just get that thing flying, Max. We'll be seeing you again. Maybe we can meet up for a beer," he grinned.

"Where are you headed when you get out of here?"

He smiled. "That's need to know, I'm afraid. But it won't be a million miles away from here. You'll be operating out of Kabul International?"

"Yeah, that's certain, until we can unravel this CIA nonsense."

"I wish you luck then. We'll be in and out of Kabul, so we'll pick up with you there."

I shook hands with him and then Rains. The American lieutenant did look different to when I'd first encountered him. In the space of a few days, he'd become less hesitant. It was as if the mercenaries had exerted an influence on him in some way. Perhaps he realized that their shocking and brutal style of combat had something to commend it. It wasn't new, the current American doctrine of 'shock and awe', hitting the enemy hard and fast in overwhelming force, proved effective. But until he'd met Schramm's men, he hadn't grasped the way of applying the tactic at platoon level. He'd seen combat now, had been bloodied by the enemy, and then helped to turn the tables and inflict heavy losses on the same enemy. He was a different man.

"Good luck, Lieutenant, I'll see you in Kabul too, no doubt."

"Yeah, I owe you a beer, that's a promise. When we…"

He didn't finish. A line of shots stitched holes in the ground less than a foot away from where we stood. Art reacted first.

"Take cover!"

Everyone hit the ground and started to crawl for the nearest cover, except me. I only had one place to go, the aircraft. I started to run, and behind me, I heard Schramm's men and Rains' troops start to return fire. Walker was framed in the doorway to the cargo hold, and he'd climbed aboard, but when the shots started to whistle around us, he unslung his M4-A1 and started to shoot in the direction of the enemy. I reached the door, took a flying leap inside and shouted to him.

"Walker, get inside. We need to get the door closed and get airborne!"

"The fuck I will. They need all the firepower they can get. Hey, you two," he shouted at his men. They were sat on the floor, trying to ignore the pandemonium that had erupted around them. "Get the fuck out here and start shooting!"

We could take off with the door open. If he fell out, it was his choice. I left him and ran into the cockpit. Rachel was beginning the start up procedure. She turned a white face towards me.

"I didn't have time for the pre-flight checks. It's anyone's guess if she's ok to fly."

"Just start the engines. If we don't move now, there won't be anything left to get off the ground."

As she went through the engine start procedure, an almost automatic series of actions, I looked out of the window. From the slightly elevated position of the cockpit, I could see more clearly what was going on. A band of insurgents had arrived, black turbaned Taliban. But instead of preparing an ambush, they had no choice but to fall on the soldiers that they encountered on the ground. And the soldiers fought back hard. A lieutenant, who had discovered what it meant to lead men into battle, led the American infantry, and Art Schramm's mercenaries were capable of giving a Taliban force much larger than this one a severe headache. Bullets struck the fuselage, and I reflected that we'd have more than our share of repairs to make, patching up the holes, when we got back. Bursts of gunfire echoed from the cargo space where Walker and his men were lending their support to the men on the ground. I heard a scream, someone shouted, and one of

Walker's men ran into the cockpit.

"It's Ed, he's been hit. You need to get this motherfucker of the ground."

"Is he bad?"

"Bad enough, there's blood everywhere. He needs a hospital. That doctor is looking at him now, but he's going to need blood, that's for sure. I don't think he's got long."

The guy looked concerned, which surprised me. Ed Walker's men were not the kind to be worried about the fate of their fellow man. Then it came to me. Ed Walker was the meal ticket. Without him, their well-paid employment may come to a premature end.

The engines roared to life, and I turned my attention back to getting the Twin Otter off the ground. As we taxied towards the ribbon of the tarmac road, I could see the mercenaries going forwards in short rushes, from cover to cover. As they ducked out of sight of the enemy, they proceeded to lay down a curtain of fire to cover their comrades coming in from behind them. At the rear, Rains' men laid down further fire that served to make it all but impossible for the insurgents to look out from behind cover without receiving a bullet in the head for their pains. It was like watching a well-oiled machine going forward, and I had little doubt that the end of the Taliban warband was imminent.

"Max, the road, it's blocked!"

I looked forward as Rachel shouted. It explained why

we hadn't seen them before; the insurgents had been busy building a roadblock to prevent take-off. It was out of sight of the area where the aircraft had been parked on the ground. They'd piled rocks onto the road, several tons of them. It had all been done so swiftly and silently that we had no idea it was there.

"I'll take the controls," I snapped at Rachel.

She took her hands off the column, and I steered the aircraft slowly towards and then around the obstruction. As I bumped back onto the tarmac road, Rachel turned urgently to speak to me.

"You won't be able to take off, Max. There's not enough room to clear those rocks."

"Except that it slopes uphill just before their roadblock."

"What do you mean?"

"I mean like the ski-jump they use on aircraft carriers. We might be able to use the same principle. Didn't you see that kind of thing when you flew military?"

"I was USAF, not Navy. We didn't have aircraft carriers."

"Right. Well, that's the principle anyway. It was a British invention, an alternative to the catapult system. The ski-jump ramp at the end of a runway or flight deck allows an aircraft to make a running start to transition a portion of its forward momentum into upward motion. The idea is that the additional altitude and upward angled flight path from the jump provides extra time, until the forward airspeed generated by the engine thrust is high enough to maintain level flight."

"You're not serious? Making it work on this roadway may be a little different, of course."

"You don't say."

I ignored her sarcastic rejoinder and concentrated on steering the aircraft. We reached the end of the tarmac road at the point where it disappeared into a sharp bend between two low hills, and which were too close together for the aircraft wings to fit between them. I spun her through one hundred and eighty degrees and looked ahead.

"It's awfully short, Max."

I nodded. "It's all we have."

The brakes were full on. I pushed the throttles forward, the twin turboprops built up speed, and the airframe started to shake as it strained against the leash of the wheelbrakes.

"For God's sake, Max, she'll tear herself apart."

But it was the only way. "Nearly there. My grandmother told me that my grandfather used to shout 'Hals und Beinbruch', break a neck and a leg, as they went into the area of maximum danger. Kind of a German good luck thing."

"Max!"

I let the brakes off, and the Twin Otter leapt forward. It was all we could do to keep it on the narrow ribbon of tarmac. Rachel was right, the rocks were awfully close, but

I figured we had to try it. There could be another Taliban force on their way to reinforce the first group, and we may find ourselves under mortar or machine gun fire to add to the difficulties of the roadblock. The rocks came nearer, nearer still. To her credit, Rachel didn't close her eyes even though she must have been tempted.

"Are we full out?" I shouted at her. "Can you increase power at all?"

"You're right forward on the stops, Max. There's nothing else."

"Ok, hang on."

Then we were on it, and I felt the nosewheel start to rise as it ran onto the slope, then the rear wheels. It was now or never, so I heaved on the control column just as the aircraft hit a bump. That bump in the ground saved us. It was enough to nudge the aircraft upwards, and I felt the propellers biting as they screamed against the wind, clawing for a hold, battling for some kind of altitude. There was another bump from the undercarriage as the tires hit the rocks a glancing blow. I refused to sacrifice speed for height, and for several hundred yards we flew only a few feet of the ground. Then I pulled back gently, and we started to climb. We'd made it.

"I feel sick."

I looked across at her and grinned. "Maybe it was a little close."

"Close! Jesus Christ, we brought half that roadblock

with us. I'll bet we find pieces of rock tangled in the undercarriage."

"Souvenirs. Rachel, would you go back and see how Ed Walker is. He got hit badly before we left. Shit, hang on!"

The vast curtain of the Hindu Kush loomed in front of us, and we were about two thousand feet too low to clear it. The terrifying rock face loomed towards us, filling the cockpit windshield.

"Rachel! Hard to starboard, we'll need to fly adjacent to the mountain range until we've got enough height to cross."

I heaved on the control column, kicked on the rudder and fed in as much right aileron as I could manage to drop the right wing. The de Havilland almost dropped perpendicular on the starboard wing as it came around, slowly. The rocks were near, too near!"

"Bank her harder, it's our only chance."

"I'm doing my best."

"Rachel, this isn't a test, pull!"

We both put all of our effort into turning away from the rocks that waited to end our flight almost before it began. There were shouts from the back of the aircraft as the passengers were tossed around, but I didn't have time to worry. Inch by inch we clawed our way free of the mountain range. At last we could see clear sky in front of windshield. When I was satisfied we'd averted disaster, I asked Rachel to check on Ed Walker. She came back a few minutes later, her face grave.

"He's dying. He said he needs to talk to you, and it's urgent. I'll take her from here."

"What does he want?"

"I don't know. Why don't you go and see?"

I handed over, and she continued climbing to clear the mountains. I went aft to where he lay on an old tarpaulin. His lifeblood had drained into it so that the canvas had taken on the sheen of a wet oil slick, but this was a blood slick. He was white, struggling to speak. I bent nearer and put my ear close to his mouth.

"Tell them to give me some room. This is for your ears only," he whispered.

The medics and bodyguards heard him and went further down the cabin. As Yves walked away, he caught my eyes and shook his head.

"How do you feel?" I asked Walker.

It was a stupid question to ask a dying man with multiple bullet wounds. His lips bared in the ghastly parody of a smile.

"I've been better."

"We'll get you to Peshawar very soon. There's a good hospital there."

"Yeah, fuck you, Hoffman. I'm finished, and you all know it. There's something I need to tell you."

"Ed, it's ok. Why don't you try and rest."

"No time," he whispered, his voice even fainter. "Your

satphone, you'll find it in my pack. I told Kyle to give it back to you."

"Ok."

"Joe Ashford, he…"

He bucked then as the agony hit him hard. I waited for a few minutes until the spasm had died away. He tried to speak again, but it was barely audible.

"What? What is it about Joe Ashford?"

"He's…deal…" I waited again.

"Mullah Omar."

"Mullah Omar? The leader of the Taliban?"

"Yeah. Weird, ain't it? But listen, he…"

Another spasm, and I waited to hear the rest of it.

"It's a double-cross. They think he's on their side, but…"

Then he died. A fountain of blood spurted from his mouth, and I leapt aside to avoid it. Yves was watching and rushed over, but it was too late. Something internal had ruptured from the bullet wounds, and it had pushed his body beyond the limit at which it could survive. His men came over and looked down at their boss.

"He's dead." I looked up and stared at them, but there was no reaction.

"He told me about the satphone, would you let me have it later and cover the body. We'll bury him when we land."

One of the men folded the bloody canvas over the body. The other lit a cigarette and sat down, smoking quietly. He saw me watching him. "Stupid bastard, he led us into that trap and got most of the men killed. Good riddance."

I nodded. "Some epitaph."

Back in the cockpit, I told Rachel what he'd said. She looked puzzled.

"But, who thinks he's on their side? And who is he double-crossing?"

I shook my head. "It beats me. The Taliban, I assume."

"But that makes no sense. They wouldn't trust an American CIA man, so how could he double-cross them?"

She had a point there.

"So maybe it's the Americans, ISAF, the CIA, even the Afghan government."

"But why?"

A new voice called out a reply. "Drugs."

It was one of Walker's men, the one who'd covered Walker's body. I still didn't know his name. He was short, thin and wiry, probably for Special Forces; like so many mercenaries and security contractors I'd come across, especially lately. He saw my raised eyebrows.

"I guess it's time we were introduced. I'm Saul Madden, and the other guy back there is Kyle McDonald."

It was the most words I'd heard him speak. I nodded.

"Ok, well, I guess you know who I am."

He grinned. "Yeah, the guy whose gonna get us back safe."

"I hope so. What's this drugs business?"

"I wasn't gonna say anything, but I've about had enough. The cause of all this trouble is Joe Ashford. The guy's a fucking lunatic."

"The drugs?" I prompted.

"Yeah, I guess you know why he's here in Afghanistan. He's building up a bank balance, something to retire back to the States with."

"I doubt he's the only one doing that, Saul."

"Maybe not, but he's probably the only one whose sacrificing his own people to do it. It was Ashford who put Ed Walker in command of the team, when he knew the guy didn't know squat about military operations."

"But why?"

"Yeah, good question. The only people we can figure out who got any benefit were the Taliban."

"He's working for the enemy?"

Saul shook his head. "I wouldn't go that far, but it's possible. I think it's more likely he deals drugs from these Taliban people, buying them direct and shipping them out Stateside. And in the process, he wouldn't want to put anyone too experienced in command, in case it upset his business contacts. He sends us people out into the field, and we have the occasional success, but not against the big guys. It's always the little ones, like the last mission. A few local leaders, that's about it. The time before we destroyed a bombmaking shop. Only trouble was there wasn't enough material there to make a Fourth of July rocket."

"So how does he run his operation?"

"Like I say, he does just enough to convince the brass that he's serious. On the side he makes his drug deals."

"The bastard," I murmured. "So he's giving the Taliban the money to buy weapons to use against his own people."

"Money? I didn't say anything about money," Saul exclaimed.

"No? If not money, what does he give them in exchange?"

It was a puzzle, and Saul supplied the answer I was least expecting.

"Guns."

The enormity of the double-cross astonished me. So that's what Walker meant. He was selling US military equipment to the Taliban for them to use against US troops. Not actually selling it, exchanging it for drugs with which to destroy the nation's youth.

"We have to do something about it. The guy sounds completely out of control."

"Hey, buddy, a word of advice. Don't fuck with Joe Ashford. Don't even think about it. He's more poisonous than a hungry rattler, and a thousand times meaner. He's got contacts all over the country, back in the US too. Not just CIA, either, he's pretty tight with the drug people."

"So what the hell do I do?"

"Same as me, my friend. Nothing. There's nothing you

can do, not if you want to live."

"What about your comrade, Kyle? How does he feel?"

Saul shrugged. "He's in it for the money. If he's got any conscience, I haven't seen it yet. I don't talk to him about it."

Shortly after, I had to help Rachel navigate to Peshawar. Saul returned to the cargo hold, and Luk came forward with Najela.

"You don't mind her sitting up front with me?"

He looked better, much better. Still pale, obviously recovering, but he was doing better than any of us had expected. And as for Najela, anything that helped him recover had to be a good thing. I grinned.

"I'm always in favor of some extra company up front, especially someone as pretty as Najela."

He signed what I'd said to her, and she looked away, not used to compliments from male strangers. If, as I suspected, Luk intended taking her home to Thailand, she'd have to get used to them. And enjoy them, if she was like most women.

* * *

Joe Ashford finished the brief conversation that had come in from Kyle McDonald on the aircraft. So Ed Walker was dead. That was too bad, he'd have to find a replacement, and maybe bring out some snot-nosed youngster from

Langley. He'd lost most of his men, so he wouldn't be able to blame anyone else for his shortcomings. He'd have to remember to keep his promise to reward Kyle McDonald for giving him the heads up. What he'd said could be serious. Kyle suspected that Walker had blabbed to that fucking pilot, Max Hoffman, before he'd died. What had he told him? He'd have to assume the worst, and that he'd told him everything about his operations. It was too bad, but Ashford couldn't allow that kind of info to get back to his masters in Washington. That meant Hoffman would have to be dealt with very soon. How could he organize that? Oh yeah, Mullah Omar. He'd help, in return for a favor. Ashford knew that Omar operated a base in Pakistan, guarded by the Pakistani Secret Police.

The Inter-Services Intelligence, ISI, was Pakistan's premier intelligence agency, and responsible for providing critical intelligence assessment to the Government of Pakistan. Its work had included supporting the Mujahedeen in Afghanistan against the Soviets in the 1980s and the Taliban against the Indian and Iranian-backed Northern Alliance in the Afghanistan Civil War in the 1990s. The connection to the Taliban had withstood the American backed invasion, and they made certain that the Taliban facilities were safely guarded well away from the American spy drones. Omar's base was near the stricken village. All he'd need to do would be to order Hoffman to fly into the nearby airfield to get aid into the village as fast as possible.

Then make sure that Omar's fighters took him out. In return for the favor, they'd be welcome to help themselves to the medical supplies. What was it Joseph Stalin had said? 'Death solves all problems - no man, no problem'. It was neat, and it would work.

CHAPTER ELEVEN

What we need to do is to correct some of the ways we operated in the past. We need to show the kind of resolve and the imagination in some cases to do this smarter and to do it right.

General Stanley McChrystal

"Let's have it, Charlie, what's the current situation?"

Marine General Daniel Westwood stared at his intelligence officer, Lieutenant Colonel Charlie Brooks. The atmosphere in the room had changed from the last time they'd met here. Then, the whole country was in crisis. But after several days of fierce fighting, they were regaining the upper hand. The other officer present, Lieutenant Colonel Vance Everard, was about to be let off the leash. Defensive operations were almost over, and his new mission was to seek out and destroy the enemy, wherever he could find them. Westwood went to the wallmap and used a pointer to illustrate his talk.

"We've got 'em beat, Sir, no matter where you look. They've been given a bloody nose, here, here and here. Even Helmand Province is back under our control. The time is ripe to counterattack and give them a real bloody nose."

"Good. Vance, are you ready to go?"

"I am, General. The boys are getting cabin fever, stuck behind the defensive lines. They're waiting to go out and finish these bastards. You heard about my infantry, Sir?"

Westwood nodded. "I did, it's good news. A pity about their losses, but they shouldn't have been ordered to go out in those M113s. When this is over, I want that bastard hung, drawn and quartered. Make sure you deal with it, Vance."

"I hear you, General. He'll answer for what he did, don't worry about it."

"Good. Those mercs who helped them out of there, does anyone know where they're at?"

"They're still here, General. We brought them in and gave them facilities to clean up, some hot food and a good night's sleep. Last I heard, they were checking out their weapons ready to make their way back to Peshawar."

Westwood grunted. "Damn, I'd like to thank them personally. And that pilot, Hoffman, wasn't it?"

"Yeah, he did good work. He's in Peshawar, working on

a CIA backed contract."

"Peshawar, eh? Pity, he sounds like a resourceful guy. Let me know if he's ever up for grabs, we need contractors like him in country. He's wasted with the CIA." He turned to his intelligence officer. "You get any more leads on Mullah Omar? The President is anxious to see that guy taken down. Wasn't he supposed to be somewhere near Peshawar? I guess that after discovering Bin Laden's hidey hole, we can assume that our Pakistani intelligence friends are offering him the same cozy hospitality?"

Colonel Brooks nodded. "I've no doubt, Sir. He's sure to stay close to the border, Tora Bora, the Khyber Pass. It's easy to slip away in bandit country."

"Keep on it, I'd like to catch up with that character. Fix up for me to meet those mercs. I mean it. They're not leaving here without a handshake. And good luck, Vance, ace those suckers."

"Yes, Sir."

Both colonels saluted and left. One of them to get his wish and go out on the warpath; the other to continue his patient tracking of the important Taliban targets, and one target more important than any of the others.

* * *

We landed in Peshawar, in an airfield that was dominated by Pakistani military aircraft and helicopters. The airfield was surrounded by rolls of barbed wire, and with sandbagged machine gun emplacements at regular interviews. Not exactly a fun holiday destination. I taxied over to the Double Eagle hangar and switched off. Joe Ashford waited outside to greet us next to a pair of white painted SUVs. While the medics helped unload the body of Ed Walker, I climbed down to meet him. He stared at the lifeless form of his subordinate.

"How'd it happen, Hoffman?"

I explained how we'd been hit by a last minute Taliban attack just as we were preparing to leave. He looked angry, which I guess was to be expected.

"There was nothing anyone could do?"

I shook my head. "Nothing, just bad luck."

He grunted. "That's too bad. I asked for a replacement officer to be sent out from Langley, and he should be here in a few days."

"Replacement? How did you know he was dead? I thought you only just found out."

"Oh, yeah. But he was about to be promoted, so the new guy was already lined up for the job."

It sounded a bit lame to me, but I couldn't work out any possible way he could have known, except the satphone. Of course, I hadn't recovered Luk's satphone. So maybe one of his men had contacted Ashford direct, but who? Kyle Macdonald, probably, but it could have been either of them. I made a mental note to ask for the return of the phone. It belonged to Luk, or his father Abe. The medics had cleared the aircraft, and a gang of cargo handlers was loading a number of wooden crates.

"What's going on, Mr. Ashford? No one said anything about another cargo to me. She's shot full of holes. We need time to repair the damage and make sure there's nothing badly damaged."

He leered at me. He was so huge, I felt as if I was facing a hungry bear. "As I recall, your contract is to run cargos, not hide in a maintenance hangar. This one can't wait. It's a humanitarian mission."

"I prefer that to running guns and mercenaries."

"I couldn't give a shit what you prefer. There's a cargo of medical supplies waiting at Kabul that needs to be delivered to Kakulah. That's the village those MCF medics are heading for. There's no point in going out empty, so they're loading a cargo for me right now. You'll need to collect the medical supplies from Kabul, and then make a stop on the way back to Pakistan to unload the cargo they're putting aboard now. It's an easy stop close to the border. They have a temporary airfield, no control tower or landing lights, but it's no sweat for a daylight landing."

"Is there a strip at Kakulah?"

"There's a flat field, it's been used before, and you'll have no trouble getting down."

"And what's this other cargo?"

"It's just my cargo, Hoffman. That's all you need to

know. I want a fast turnaround, so get your wheels up inside of two hours."

I left him then and went to supervise the loading of the cargo. The wooden crates were heavy, very heavy, so I assumed they carried weapons of some sort. Walker's two men, McDonald and Madden, had their things together ready to leave. I went over to them.

"I'd like Luk's satphone back if you don't mind."

Saul Madden looked surprised. Clearly, he hadn't realized it had been stolen. McDonald opened his pack without a word and handed it to me.

"I trust the satphone was useful to you," I remarked.

"Yeah, it worked fine."

"Good. I'd hate for Joe Ashford to be left out of the loop."

He glanced at me in surprise, then shrugged and left. Madden started to follow, but he turned and shook hands.

"I never knew he'd taken that phone. Did it cause you any problems?"

"No. Joe Ashford doesn't need any help to make our lives difficult."

"You're right there." He seemed to stop and think. "Look, are you returning to Kabul?"

"Yes, we are. Why?"

"Could I bum a ride? I've had a gut full of Joe Ashford and the psychos he had on his payroll. I need to look for a new contract, and there's plenty of work going there."

"I imagine there is. You're not planning to ask Ashford for a new job?"

He grinned. "In your dreams. I lost some good friends when Walker led our people into that ambush. It was Ashford who put him in charge, and he knew the guy was inexperienced. I don't need that kind of work."

"I guess not. I'd be glad to take you back to Kabul. We leave in two hours, maybe less, so stick around."

"I appreciate that, Max. How about I wander over to the passenger terminal and rustle up some coffee?"

I nodded. "It'll pay the fare to Kabul."

I handed Luk the satphone, and he nodded his thanks. He stuffed it into his pack and was about to speak when Najela signed something to him.

"She says that she'd like to make a quick visit to her uncle who lives here in Peshawar. He lives close to the airfield, so we'll be back in just over an hour."

"Ok, but don't be late. It's a long walk to Kabul."

They waved and walked over to the terminal where there was a line of waiting taxis. Rachel had been in the cockpit, making the usual shutdown checks and calculating the figures. She jumped down.

"So we're going back to Kabul?"

"That's right."

"I've calculated the fuel, and the tanks are just under half full. It's not a problem, provided we don't fly to any distant destinations with no refueling facilities."

I explained that we had a series of short hops, to Kabul, a stop on the return leg, close to the border, and then back into Pakistan with the medical supplies.

"I'd assume that we'll be come back here, to Peshawar, for the next cargo."

She looked doubtful. "That won't be a problem, but if Ashford wants us to pick up anything else, we could run low on gas."

"I'll tell him to keep it in mind."

We stood in silence for a few moments, watching the activity taking place around us. A military helicopter clattered in for a landing. A few minutes after a commercial jet made its final approach and dropped neatly onto the tarmac. It had the letters PIA stenciled on the fuselage, Pakistan International Airlines. Their safety reputation wasn't the most envied in Asia, and more than once I'd been advised to stay clear of them. Maybe it was true, or maybe it was sour grapes.

"I'm sick of this," Rachel spat out abruptly in a show of passion that surprised me.

"Sick of what? Pakistan, Afghanistan? Or something else?"

"Working for the CIA. When we've finished the immediate contract, I'd like to get out. For both of us to get out and start again."

I thought about that. The airline industry was in dire straits worldwide, and they were going broke in large numbers.

"It won't be easy to get a regular job flying commercial," I pointed out.

"I realize that. But if we can get out of this with a single aircraft intact, say the Twin Otter or something like it, we could make a new start. I don't care where we fly, or what cargoes we carry, except for drugs and guns, of course. But I draw the line at the CIA. I'd almost prefer to fly cargoes for the Taliban."

"Almost," I grinned.

"Yeah, ok. Almost."

"I agree. We'll finish up this current contract, and we're out of here. Even if we don't get out with the aircraft intact, we'll find a way to start again."

"The two of us?"

I pulled her into my arms and kissed her long and hard.

"That's a given. I'm not letting you go, Rachel."

"Do you love me, Max?" she asked, her eyes misty but watching me carefully.

"I love the fact that I don't have to pay you wages."

She pushed me away. "You bastard. Is that it?"

I reached for her again. "No, that's not it. Of course I love you."

"It's not just the slave labor pay rates?"

I chuckled. "That does help."

She punched me on the arm. "Bastard."

But it was an affectionate blow. She was one tough girl,

and if she punched me and meant it, I'd sure know it.

Saul returned with three coffees, not quite Starbucks, but it was fresh and hot. We drank it and began making the preflight checks for the short flight to Kabul. A taxi rolled up, and Luk got out with Najela. They looked unhappy about something as they climbed aboard. I wondered whether to ask them about it but decided it was their business. Rachel started engines, and I radioed the tower for clearance. They were not quite ready for us, and we had to wait while a pair of Pakistan Air Force F16s swooped in for a landing. Rachel watched them in frank admiration.

"Hey, look at those two beauties. I was too late to fly one of those. They're obsolete in the USA, but they're still a great aircraft."

"They're sure nice to look at."

"They call them the Fighting Falcon," she went on. "Look at them, a frameless bubble canopy that give all round visibility. They have a side-mounted control stick to ease control while maneuvering, and a fly-by-wire flight control system that makes them handle like a racing car. They carry an internal M61 Vulcan cannon and eleven hardpoints for mounting weapons and other mission equipment. They kick ass, those babies."

"Rachel, let's concentrate on getting this particular baby airborne first."

"Yeah, boss, I hear you," she grinned. The tower came

on with our clearance now that the Pakistani military aircraft had landed, and we taxied out to the main runway and took off for Kabul.

The flight to Kabul wasn't quite uneventful. Luk had been back in the cargo space with Najela. They came forward and sat on the jump seats. They obviously had something important to say, so I waited. Rachel was flying the plane, grinning from ear to ear. We both expected them to announce an engagement or something like that. They'd got so close in the past few days it was impossible to imagine one without the other.

"Max, Rachel, there's something important Najela has to say," Luk began.

"Hey, don't hide behind her," Rachel shouted good naturedly, "speak up for yourself."

He looked mystified. "But, it's about her uncle, about what he said."

Rachel and I exchanged glances. It wasn't what we expected.

"Ok, Luk, shoot! What did he say?"

"It's a message from her father in Yaluk. He wasn't sure if he was doing the right thing keeping it secret, but he decided he wanted you to know. It's about the man you saw in the stone hut on the outskirts of the village."

I pictured him, the magnetic gaze, and the astonishing sense of overwhelming strength in the feeble body.

"Luk, don't string it out. What has he found, a cure for

cancer? Or is it for AIDS?"

"Neither. He's there for treatment, and he's very ill. His name is Omar."

"Ok, and?"

Then it hit me, like a meteorite in the guts. "You don't mean…?"

"Yes. Mullah Omar. He's there for treatment, and Yaluk was the only place that would treat him."

"Christ, Luk, we were there with a force of infantry and mercenaries. We could have picked him up and walked out with him. And we didn't know!"

He shrugged. Najela looked miserable. "He couldn't make his mind up whether to pass on the information or not. But since we left, he started to get serious about the women, making them cover up, you know what they're like. His men punished a couple of women who defied him. They were whipped, and it was nasty. They thought that the presence of Western soldiers meant that they could relax a bit, but he cracked down hard. Ban said he was sickened by it."

"So what the hell do we do with this information, Luk? Pass it on and see the village saturated with drone launched missiles?"

"That's your choice, Max. You're still the boss."

I nodded. "Thanks."

There were times when I regretted that title. Times when I'd like to walk away, and let someone else take responsibility. And then I thought of my grandfather. He'd earned his spurs in Russia, fighting as an SS officer, and battling the overwhelming Red hordes that fanatically defended their homeland from Hitler's invading armies. Then he'd joined the French Foreign Legion and earned a reputation as a tough and uncompromising warrior. And then he'd started his airline, the one that I was faced with losing. What would he do? But the answer was simple. He'd fight to his last breath. So be it. I'd work this problem through, and all the others as well.

Once more the military held us up. Flocks of helicopters were taking off, followed by a squadron of F18 fighter jets. From a far corner of the airfield, I could see a ground crew getting ready to launch a drone, one of the Predators or even the lethal Reaper, the MQ-9. Finally, we received our clearance, and I took her straight in for a landing. I taxied over to the cargo area where a ground crew was waiting to unload the cargo. Saul came into the cockpit.

"I wanted to thank you for the ride. Is there anything more I can do?"

I was about to say no, but something flashed across my mind. He was a tough, brutal fighter, and no friend of Joe Ashford. I remembered the old proverb, 'the enemy of my enemy is my friend'.

"Saul, we could do with someone to guard the aircraft, at least until we know what's happening around here."

"You think Ashford will try something funny?"

I shrugged. "I've no idea. But we've had enough problems lately, and I'd like to be ready if something did happen. At least until we're out of his hair."

He nodded. "I'd be glad to. I'll stay by the aircraft as long as you wish."

"I can't pay you, Saul. Not yet, anyway."

"If I get a shot at Ashford, it'll be worth it."

I smiled. "I think you've just joined a long queue."

I sat in the cockpit filling in the flight log, chatting idly to Rachel, when a military police Humvee rolled up and a squad of MPs jumped out. They stood outside the cockpit window, and I slid it open.

"What's up?"

"Max Hoffman?"

"That's me."

"We want you to come with us, Sir."

"Where to?"

"To Camp Phoenix."

"And if I don't?" I had a bad feeling about this. What the hell had I done wrong?"

The MP sighed. He looked hard and competent, and probably a veteran of countless Saturday night squabbles between rival groups of soldiers. He wasn't particularly tall, maybe five feet eight inches, but his body was about the same width.

"It'd be better if you didn't force it, Mr. Hoffman."

"Ok, no need for any rough stuff, I'll come."

"I'll come too," Rachel exclaimed.

"There's no need, I'll be fine."

"Yeah, but I've seen these military types. I don't want you railroaded by some desk jockey colonel. I'm coming."

"Luk, stay here with Najela. Keep an eye her, and on the aircraft."

He nodded. "Don't worry, I'll keep everything safe."

The MPs escorted us into the Humvee. It was cramped and hot when they piled in after us. It was only a short drive to Camp Phoenix. It was one of the most depressing places I'd seen. The journey through the impoverished capital was bad enough; ragged civilians, beggars, cripples, women in blue burqas, and men driving donkeys loaded with miscellaneous goods. I doubted it was much different to the way it looked hundreds of years ago. The presence of motor cycles and battered old trucks struck a modern chord, as did the occasional military unit, soldiers with M-16s patrolling the streets, fully kitted for war in camouflage uniform, Kevlar helmets and full body armor. There sure was a long way to go before this war was anywhere near won. Camp Phoenix did nothing to lift my spirits. Concrete and barbed wire were its main features, decorated with sandbags and machine guns at regular intervals. We drove straight through the gate and stopped at a low building.

"We're here," the sergeant said. "If you'd like to step out of the vehicle, we'll see you inside."

I bet you just would, I thought. We walked through the double doors, flanked by the MPs. Inside, stood a group of soldiers. They looked as if they were waiting for us. Then I nearly collapsed with shock. They clapped and cheered. One soldier stepped forward, and his cap had four stars on it.

"I'm General Mann. Congratulations on what you did for my men. You saved a lot of lives. My thanks to you, Sir."

"That's ok, General. They'd have done the same for us."

"Yes. Come on inside my office, Son. I want to hear all about it. Someone bring us a tray of coffee."

We sat down in his office, and I looked around. It was austere and functional, maps pinned to the walls, filing cabinets, and a huge desk. Apart from the folding chairs, there was little more furniture on display. I had to go through the account of our encounter with Lieutenant Rains and the MSF medics, the fight with the insurgents at the foot of the Khyber Pass, and their rescue by Art Schramm's men. Then our subsequent flight through the tunnel and the take-off and flight to Peshawar.

"So that's about it, General. Here we are."

"You did well, Hoffman. Damn well. I gather your grandfather was something of a military hero?"

So I had to explain again about his beginnings in Russia, then the Foreign Legion, and finally his fledgling airline. I got the impression that he took in every single detail. This wasn't a man who'd got where he was by missing any part of a conversation. When I'd finished telling him about Jurgen Hoffman, he had more questions.

"What about the CIA? I gather you're working for them."

I nodded. "No disrespect, General, but I'll be finishing this contract, and then I'm out. It's not my kind of employment."

"Too violent?"

I chuckled. "It's a violent world, Sir. No, it's not the violence that concerns me. It's more a matter of who you trust."

"Yeah, they do have a certain reputation. And then, when you move on?"

"If possible, I'll carry on hauling cargo over South East Asia."

"Right, we always have cargos looking for aircraft to move them. I'll keep you in…"

"General, you're needed urgently on the phone."

"Can't it wait?"

"It's the White House, Sir."

I got up to leave, but he waved me back to stay. "This'll only take a moment. Sit yourself down."

He picked up the phone. "Mr. President. How are you, Sir?"

I only heard one side of the conversation, but it didn't

take a genius to fill in the gaps.

"Things are going well, Sir. Very well. We've blunted their attacks, and we're hitting them back strongly."

He winced as the other party said something that hit hard.

"That's true, Sir, but until our intelligence comes up with any…"

He listened again. His eyes closed as a torrent of words slammed into him from several thousand miles away.

"Yes, Sir, I understand. Yes, they'll keep coming back at us until we cut off the head, but until we find the head…"

He grinned at me, but it was an effort, I could see that.

"You can't be serious! If we pull out prematurely, it'll mean another Vietnam for us. That's unacceptable, Sir…"

"Yes, Sir. How long?"

He looked grave. "I understand, Sir. I'll do my best."

He put the phone down and looked at the silent instrument for a few moments. Then he looked up.

"You got the gist of that?"

"I did, yes. He's not happy."

"Damn it, Hoffman, I'm not a miracle worker. He's saying that we've got to take out the leadership, and that means Mullah Omar. And that's like looking for a needle in a haystack. The Man says that we need to catch up with him, like we did Saddam Hussein, Gaddafi, and Noriega in Panama. It puts an end to things. If we'd taken Giap or Ho Chi Minh in Vietnam, history may have been different. He feels that it's a simple equation. Catch up with the bastard or lose." He looked troubled. Very troubled. "You know what really upsets me, Max? It's the women in this damn country. You remember the Taliban using that football ground for executions, women being beheaded in front of masses of people? And for many of them, a quick death is preferable to what they have to put up with here."

I thought of what Luk had told me, in the village where the women had been severely punished for not covering their hair properly. Whipped, beaten tortured. I thought of Rachel. What if someone did that to her? I came to a decision.

"So you need to locate Mullah Omar."

He stared at me. "In a nutshell, yes. That's what we need, and that's what we can't do."

He slumped, and put his head in his hands. I felt sorry for the guy. There was no doubt he was a successful career soldier in an impossible situation. But more than that, I felt sorry for the women of Afghanistan; the women who would suffer the torments of hell if a Taliban dictatorship returned. That was what prompted me to speak.

"I know where he is."

He nodded absently. Then he looked up and stared at me. "Who?"

"Mullah Omar."

"You're kidding, right? No one knows where that guy is."

"I do."

His gaze intensified. "What's the punch line, or the catch? Maybe the price, there has to be something."

I'd given it a lot of thought; how it could play out if I told the Americans where he could be located. I returned the General's gaze. "He's in a village, close to Jalalabad. There's no price, but there is a problem."

"First off, why haven't you said anything before?"

"I only found out on the flight here back from Peshawar."

"Ok. Go on."

"He's in a small, very peaceful village. I'm concerned that if your troops go in heavy handed, or you send over a swarm of drones to rain down a hail of missiles on the place, the village will suffer badly. They could even be wiped out."

"Yeah, collateral damage. It's regrettable, but it's part of modern warfare."

"I'm sure that's true, General, but I can't allow that to happen here."

"You know these people, these villagers?"

"I've met them, yes."

"Ok, I understand. So what are you proposing, what's the price?"

"Price? I'm not a bounty hunter. I'm just trying to do the right thing."

"I see. Spell it out, Son. I don't understand, what exactly

do you want?"

I'd worked out the idea in the short time since Luk had told us of Mullah Omar's whereabouts. Maybe it was crazy, but no, there was no maybe at all. It was crazy. But I wasn't going to stand by while an innocent community was flattened in an awesome display of military power. I couldn't be a party to that kind of indiscriminate bloodletting.

"I want to lead a small party in to arrest him and bring him back. There's no other way to do it without endangering the lives of the innocent civilians around him."

His jaw dropped open. "You? Do you know about this guy? It won't be easy. He's very slippery and very clever. Do you have military experience?"

"Some. A bit."

I winced inside. My military experience had been gained at the expense of a man's life, at the expense of creating a widow, and fatherless children. It was a load I would have to carry all my life, and one I'd need to put aside for the duration of what had to be done to help bring this war to an end.

"A bit! How could you lead a team in on an operation like this? It's crazy!"

"Crazy or not, that's the deal. Lieutenant Rains didn't ask about my military experience before I helped him out."

He nodded thoughtfully. "Yeah, that's true."

He hadn't asked me the sixty-four dollar question yet. He was too smart to push me that far, and he knew that I wouldn't part with the location until I was satisfied.

"Tell you what, Max. Why don't I call in some of my staff for a meeting, and we'll toss your ideas around, see if we can't come to some agreement? We need to act fast, before this character changes location."

"There is another problem. I have a cargo on board that the CIA chief, Joe Ashford, wants delivered right away."

"Cancel it. I'll square it with Ashford. Any problems, tell him to talk to me. I'll arrange for the cargo to be unloaded and stored in one of our military warehouses inside Kabul International. He can arrange for someone else to collect it when he's ready."

"That sounds fine to me. I'll want my co-pilot, Rachel, to join us for this meeting. She is here with me."

"Good. A bit of glamour never did anyone any harm."

* * *

Master Sergeant Carol Wendelski watched her screen carefully. She'd already had a fruitless day. Her Reaper drone wandering the skies of Afghanistan, loaded with the most advanced weaponry known to man, yet found nothing to aim it at. It's ordnance stores of AGM-114 Hellfire II air-to-ground missiles and the GBU-12 Paveway II laser-guided bomb, were still safe on the hardpoints, awaiting a successful enemy sighting. It was so frustrating, to be master of such a sophisticated weapon, to know that the bad guys were down there, yet she couldn't locate them. Her headset cracked into life.

"Creech, this is ISAF control Kabul, the Reaper pilot operating north of the Khyber Pass. We have a target for you."

Her blood raced, and she felt the adrenaline high as her nervous system began pumping the blood around her body at an increased rate, readying itself for action.

"This is Creech, MQ-9 operator Wendelski, Master Sergeant. What have you got?"

A minute later, she moved the joystick a fraction, and her bird swung onto a new course. In less than a minute, she was over the new target, or at least, she was at the correct coordinates. Where were they? She banked the Reaper and sent it lower, the unmanned aircraft obediently moved onto a long, curving trajectory that would take it closer to the ground.

* * *

Ismael Raqim never knew why he looked up at that moment. He'd heard nothing, seen no movement or even a shadow. They were the advance party, a small band of fighters to secure the route for the larger warband of a hundred men that followed a mile behind. Their mission was to reach Yaluk village and escort their leader to a new safe house over the border in Pakistan. The venerable Mullah was old and frail. He'd be a sitting target without a fit, tough escort that could help him across the high mountains. They'd carry him if necessary. In fact, they'd probably have to. One of his men carried a folded gurney on his back in case it was needed. He held up his hand, and the twenty men behind him stopped instantly. At first he saw nothing, but it must have banked, for he saw a reflection from the wings. At once, he shouted a warning.

"Drone! Get under cover!"

His men scrambled off the narrow track they were on and dived behind the loose rocks at the side. He squinted up at the sky, had he acted quickly enough to prevent their discovery?

* * *

There! The human eye often finds it difficult to detect irregular shapes in a scattered and broken landscape. It was the principle on which camouflage was designed. But movement is something else. She saw the movement several thousand feet away and automatically adjusted her controls to bring the drone closer. It was a Taliban warband, there was no question, and they were scattering for cover in the rocks. 'Too late, you assholes', she muttered to herself. She brought up the weapon selector and chose the

Hellfire. The aiming system aligned itself to the location of the hidden fighters and flashed a 'ready' warning. She checked across the board, it was all green, no ISAF forces in the area. Nope these were bad guys for sure. Not for much longer! She hit the button and watched the missile fly off the rail and roar straight down to the track. It was uncanny watching it impact, the explosion of smoke and flame, chips of rock, bodies, earth and foliage all flew into the air. Yet it was silent. That was so weird. She took the Reaper down even lower and made several passes over the area. She could see at least three of them still moving. That was no problem, and she selected a second Hellfire, checked the aiming point and fired. The drone was almost on top of them now. The missile launched and within a few seconds had impacted. She moved the controls to climb higher, then circled to inspect the impact site. There was no movement. She'd done her work well. If she'd searched an area half a mile to the north, she may have found what she was looking for. Instead, she spent the time making certain of her kill.

"ISAF control Kabul, this is Creech. Your fire mission successful, repeat successful."

"That's good to know, Master Sergeant. Score one for the good guys."

"Yeah. Let me know if anymore business comes my way."

"That's affirmative, Creech. Good work. We'll keep in

touch."

Carol Wendelski continued on patrol. She'd struck a blow against the enemy, and at last she was blooded. And it felt real good; now for the next one.

* * *

The agony was terrible, more than he would have realized was possible. Ismael Raqim lay on his back. He knew he was dying, as were his men, either dead or dying. He turned his head and saw the pool of blood in which he lay, his blood. He'd failed, failed to provide the protection that his leader so sorely needed. He thought of his wife, waiting for him at home. She'd become very bitter of late. They had three daughters, and she always blamed him for not giving her a son. She said that the lot of women in Afghanistan was so terrible it would have been better if they were not born. He'd wanted to talk to Mullah Omar about her strange ideas, he didn't understand it. Women in this country were treated entirely according to the laws that were handed down to them. Surely his wife knew that? It should be sufficient. A hot agonizing spasm ripped through his body. He tried to move his head to look for any survivors, but nothing moved. Nothing would save him now, and he could feel a darkness creeping over his body. Perhaps Western medicine, nothing less than their hospitals and drugs would save his life, and that probably wouldn't be enough. A pity they'd bombed that new hospital in Jalalabad, but there was no choice. His leaders had reported the staff were not obeying the correct Islamic rules, so it had to be destroyed. He closed his eyes for the last time, still not understanding the irony that he had personally destroyed the very institution that may have saved the lives of those men that had survived the Hellfire missiles and lay wounded amongst the rocks. Instead, they would die, like him, as much victims of their own stubborn ignorance as the missiles that exploded amongst them. Now it was up to the men who followed behind.

* * *

Abdul Qadir watched impassively as his advance force was destroyed. It was as well he'd sent them ahead, so that any drone that sighted them could waste their energy wiping them out, and his main force survived. He looked back at his warband; a hundred men crouched in the shadow of a shallow ravine. They would wait for an hour, to give the cowardly drone enough time to vector to a different location, and then they would move off again. He searched for the man he needed.

"Rashid Osman, take ten men. You will form the new advance party. Move off in half an hour, and watch for any movement in the sky."

His man nodded. "You think the enemy drone will be gone by then, Commander?"

"It should be, yes. If it has not, you will be attacked. Better a few men than our entire force. This mission is holy, and it cannot be allowed to fail."

"As the Prophet wills it, we are certain to succeed," Osman replied. It was the correct response to his leader's order. But he looked up and scanned the sky, trying to hide his inner qualms. All of them had seen the explosions, and the debris hurled into the sky. They all knew that some of that debris was all that remained of their friends. Some men had brothers who'd been slaughtered in the drone attack. It was not the way of the fighter for Islam, for their bodies to be ripped apart and tossed in the air like so much rubbish. Yet there was nothing he could do. It was the sensible way to send an advance party. It was just a pity that it hadn't been someone else to lead it.

CHAPTER TWELVE

We are certain that NATO member states will take more effective steps to accelerate the readiness of the Afghan National Army and police. This is the only way that Afghanistan's wish for the soldiers of our friends to return to their countries soon can come true, and for the Afghans themselves to take full responsibility of their security… We hope that the Afghan forces will lead the task of security and stability throughout the country in the coming five years.

Hamid Karzai

"Secure the room, Colonel. I don't want any of this getting out."

The room had cleared after the meeting. Marine General Daniel Westwood waited until his intelligence officer came back and reported that they had total privacy. Only then would he continue. Without Max Hoffman. He glanced at his infantry commander, Lieutenant Colonel Vance Everard.

"What's your state of readiness, Vance?"

"One hundred percent, Sir. We're ready to go out and hit the enemy hard wherever they are. This defensive posture is getting on all our nerves. The men are raring to go. All we need is a target."

"You may have one. It's a biggie."

"How big?"

"As high as they come."

"Jesus Christ, that can only mean Mullah Omar."

"I'm not sure the connection with Jesus is appropriate for that one-eyed murderer, but yes, that's who we're looking at."

He went on to explain the report from Hoffman, and his insistence on leading a small force in to arrest him and bring him back to face trial.

"That kid?" Everard scoffed. "He's not an American, not even military. We don't know where the hell he's from."

"He's one quarter American, actually," General Westwood corrected him. "And the rest French. He's a skilled pilot, the son of a war hero, and he did fine work helping your Lieutenant Rains out of trouble. I wouldn't underestimate him. Besides, he's the only one who knows where this Mullah Omar is holed up."

"Even so, we're talking about the Taliban leader. It's a hell of a gamble, letting him go it alone."

"Not quite alone, Vance. He'll have Rains' men along with him."

"It's not enough. He needs more."

The General nodded. "I don't want to risk too many casualties amongst our own men, Colonel. Rains' platoon is enough for the initial recce. If this goes wrong, I don't want more of our troops at risk."

"What about the Delta Force?" Colonel Brooks suggested. "This kind of mission is right up their street."

"Except we don't know where to send them. But it's a good idea. Contact their CO, have him shadow Hoffman's unit with some of his men. If they use helicopters, they can stay well back and get in quick if the shit hits the fan. You're right. It's their kind of work. Get in fast, do the job and get out fast." The General was quiet for a few moments, thinking hard. "That gives me an idea. Are those mercenaries still in town, Schramm and his men?"

"They are, Sir. They're helping drink the local PX dry, last time I heard. They were due to fly out but their principal cancelled on them, so they're waiting for their next contract."

"Maybe we could offer them one?"

Colonel Everard stared at the General. "Mercenaries?"

The intelligence officer, Lieutenant Colonel Brooks, leaned forward. "Sir, that's against military law. We can't do that. The President would have us hung, drawn and quartered."

General Westwood fixed him with an intense stare. "Vance, do you think I'm that crazy?"

Everard looked down. "No, of course not, Sir."

"No. We are only allowed by our UN charter to employ security personnel. My proposal is that we offer Schramm and his men a temporary security contract. They'll travel with Hoffman and Rains, who incidentally they got on well with, according to my reports. That'll be a tight, compact force to send in."

"Excuse me, General," Colonel Brooks, the intelligence officer interjected. "That's still not much more than platoon strength. Against this man, Omar, it's not enough. Not if we want to be sure."

"You're right, Charlie. That's why I asked Colonel Everard to stay here to listen. My intention is for him to track Hoffman's force at a distance, and be ready to move in at a moment's notice if he runs into trouble."

Both Colonels smiled. "I assume Hoffman knows nothing about this?" Brooks asked.

"No, nothing. And it's to stay that way. Clear?"

They both nodded.

"Good. Let's go over your strength, Vance. How about APCs, you've plenty of Strykers to carry you cross country?"

* * *

We had to wait until the morning before we could meet with Rains. The plan was that we'd meet at five, load his platoon onto their vehicles, and set out on the mission. I had more than a few misgivings. Although the man I'd seen had little obvious security, I doubted that the most senior leader in the Taliban movement would lack for protection. We'd come upon them without warning before, and they were unaware of the existence of a viable tunnel leading to the village. Now that they knew, they would without doubt have called in fighters to protect him. The question was, how many. We'd only get the answer to that when we got there.

Then there was Rachel. She'd gone with Najela and Luk to fix up a hotel for us to stay in overnight. I knew she'd be determined to come along, and I was equally determined that she wouldn't. And Luk had a similar problem with Najela; he'd want her to stay back, and she'd want to come with us. In her case, it was even harder. We were going to her home village, and her local knowledge could be invaluable. There was Joe Ashford, and he wouldn't take too kindly to having his cargo held back. At least I had General Westwood to watch my back now, but that could change at any moment. He was a senior army general, and no man achieved that lofty height of command without being an astute and wily politician. I'd been looking at some of the local maps in the Camp Phoenix operations room, and he'd agreed to give me free rein. I had to look at maps covering a much wider area than I needed. I was well aware there would be plenty of sets of eyes on me, now that I had the prized secret of the whereabouts of Omar. I needed an edge, and something that would offer me a defense against the inevitable problems I knew I'd be facing in the near future. I was thinking of Art Schramm and his gang of cutthroat mercenaries. They'd be the best possible edge any man could ask for. It was right then, when I was thinking about him, that I felt a tap on the shoulder, turned, and stared into his smiling face.

"Art! What are you doing here? I thought you were leaving for another contract."

"Not while there's cheap beer on sale in the PX. Why don't you join me? Some of the boys are already in there."

"I don't mind if I do. What are you going to do now that you're out of work?"

We were walking towards the camp PX. It suddenly occurred to me that I'd met Art in an odd place. Why was he there? Unless…

"They told you where to find me."

He smiled. "Sure, they asked me to look you up. What're we going to do? That's up to you, but the General said that if you'd take us, the contract's ours."

"You mean…"

"To take out the one-eyed monster, Omar the Merciless," he chuckled.

"Is that what they call him?"

"I've heard it said, yes. So what do you say? I gather you're the only one who knows his location."

"That's right. It would be good to have your men with us. You know that Rains will be along? Of course you do. What do you think about him?"

"Same as you. He did well, once he'd ironed out a few wrinkles. His men are ok, especially that sergeant of his. So where exactly are we headed?"

"Sorry, Art. That's classified, until we're almost there. But it's in the general direction of the Khyber Pass."

He nodded. "Fair enough. Come on and meet the boys."

I spent the next two hours talking to his men, listening to the colorful stories they had to tell. It was almost midnight when I walked back to the hotel Rachel had booked us into. I gave the receptionist my name, and he handed me a key. We were on the fifth floor, which was well away from the blast areas if terrorists struck, he assured me. I wasn't assured, but I went up the stairs, there was no elevator, and entered the room. I thought Rachel was asleep, so I undressed quietly. As I got into bed, she spoke.

"You're late."

"Sorry, I bumped into Art Schramm. You know he's bringing his men along?"

"No, I didn't know. But I'm pleased. Max, I don't trust the Americans."

"Me neither."

"How do we know that they won't follow us and carpet-bomb the village as soon as they know the location?"

"I've no doubt they'll try exactly that."

"Max! Those villagers, I can hardly believe it."

"Don't worry, I've got an idea. I'll tell you later. For now, there's something else on my mind."

"Something good, I hope?"

"Oh yes."

In the morning we dressed, and after a short argument, I was overruled.

"Max, I'm your co-pilot and your partner. My place is with you, and if nothing else, to watch your back. Don't try that macho bullshit with me about women staying behind when men go to battle. My job was flying fighter planes before I met you, not knitting cardigans. You need me."

I wondered about the partner bit, but she read my mind, correctly as usual.

"I'm with you for the long haul, buddy. If you think you're going anywhere without me, you've got another think coming. And besides, I reckon when this mission is over, we'll be looking to restart the airline. We still have one aircraft, and General Westwood is sure to look favorably on handing us enough contracts to borrow the money for another."

"I would remind you that we're still in debt to Joe Ashford's outfit for our aircraft."

She snorted. "I couldn't give a rat's ass about that

asshole. If he wants to come after us for the money, I'll tell him to collect it from the DEA."

The Drug Enforcement Administration was a federal law enforcement agency, tasked with combating drug smuggling and use within the United States. They had the sole responsibility for coordinating and pursuing US drug investigations abroad. But Ashford was CIA.

"I wouldn't threaten him, Rachel. He's too powerful for that."

"Not if he's locked up in a Federal Penitentiary."

"I wouldn't bet on it. Leave him alone. I'll deal with Ashford when the time comes."

"I'd like to put a bullet through his fat head," she snarled.

"I know, but forget him, I'll find a way out."

We joined Luk and Najela in the lobby and walked together back to Camp Phoenix. Lieutenant Rains had a small armored column prepared, four Strykers, enough capacity to carry all of our supplies and us on the mission. And bring back one prisoner. Art Schramm's men lounged around in the morning sunlight, and like Rains' men they were dressed in modern Uniform Camouflage Pattern combat clothing. The only way to tell them apart from the infantry was weapons, an exotic array of pistols, rifles and submachine guns. Unlike Rains' men, they wore little in the way of body armor. I'd asked Schramm about it before.

"It's like this, Max. We operate as a small, tightly controlled group. Our specialty is getting in fast and hitting them hard before they realize we're even there. If we're slow getting in, and they get wind of our coming, we've lost before we begin. Body armor isn't going to help us then."

Rains stepped out of the General's HQ building. "It's time to mount up. Let's lock and load!"

His men scrambled for their vehicles and tumbled aboard. I climbed into the lead vehicle with Rachel, Luk and Najela. We shared the space with ten of Art Schramm's men. The only infantry we had with us were the driver and the weapons technician, who sat in front of the tactical screen that monitored the turret-mounted weapons systems. Rains' man handed me a headset, and I put it on.

"This is Rains. We're ready to go. It's up to you to lead the way, Hoffman."

"Understood. Our direction is Jalalabad. Driver, take the main A1 road, let's go."

We lurched forward out of the gates of Camp Phoenix, leaving behind the reinforced concrete blockhouses, the rolls of razor wire and alert guards manning heavy machine guns. Before we got out on the open road, we had to pass through an Afghan national Army checkpoint, manned by nervous looking dark-skinned Pashtuns. Theirs was not a secure occupation and were distrusted by both their ISAF allies and their Taliban opponents. They were constantly aware that when ISAF pulled out, they were threatened with being totally overrun by the Taliban, just like the North Vietnamese steamrollered the ARVN after the American withdrawal.

"I wouldn't be in their position if I could help it."

I looked around. Art Schramm was next to me, staring out of the viewing port.

"What would you do, it you were an Afghan soldier?"

He grinned. "In this hellhole? I'd emigrate. But a lot of their problems they bring on themselves. Their loyalties are more tribal than to their commanders and the government. It makes them ideal candidates for suicide missions. If they tidied up their act, and started fighting the enemy instead of squabbling amongst themselves, they'd be a lot better off. Instead, they're always looking for a kickback, and they're not above selling their kit to the highest bidder."

"Just like the ARVN in South Vietnam."

"Yep. It's not their fault. It's the crap system they live under. The men at the top could change it, but why should they when they're getting rich out of billions of dollars of aid from overseas."

"So there's no answer to it? The people have just got to keep on suffering?"

"That's about the size of it, yeah."

I shook my head. It seemed the only solution for most

of them, was to get out. But get out to where? The poverty in Pakistan, just over the border, was as bad if not worse in some cases. And Pakistan was the limit of where these people could travel. They had no papers, no money, and no possessions. Nothing.

I opened the hatch and looked out. Close to me was the formidable remote turret, controlled by the weapons technician inside the vehicle. Either side of me was the rugged wastes that bordered the Kabul-Jalalabad Highway, the A1. The remote turret moved suddenly, and I realized the operator was panning it around, constantly seeking out any possible enemy threat. The other vehicles' turrets were doing the same, so that all four turrets were moving around in a balletic, high-tech dance. In the distance, the mountainous countryside loomed above us, almost threatening in its overpowering desolation. Closer to the road, the ground was a mix of shale, sparse grass covered meadows and more expanses of broken rock. There were no people, no buildings, just a vast expanse of harsh landscape. I climbed back inside and closed the hatch; we were nearing Jalalabad, and the chances of ambush were greater. I'd had a conversation before we left with Rachel about a possible ambush, but from our own side.

"How will you hide the direction we're heading in?" she'd asked me. "Once we get near Yaluk, they'll know where we're going."

"Remember that first abandoned village, where we left

the aircraft?"

She nodded. "Of course."

"That's where I'm leading them. With any luck, I'll be able to convince Rains that Mullah Omar is hiding close to the village. Somehow, I need to get us all into the tunnel that leads through to Yaluk. If General Westwood's people are focusing on that empty village, we can go through the tunnel to Yaluk, sweep in and grab Omar."

"But surely, once we're in the tunnel, Rains will know where we're headed and radio Kabul."

I smiled. "If he has a radio that works underground, he will. Otherwise, he'll be out of radio contact."

She still looked doubtful. "I hope you're right, Max. If they attack Yaluk, a lot of people are going to be killed. Don't forget, Najela's family are from that village."

"I haven't forgotten."

We reached Jalalabad, skirted the city and stopped for a break. We parked the vehicles in a small circle, like the wagon trains of the Old West, and sat inside their protective cover. Rains came over to where I sat with Luk, Rachel and Najela.

"This road only leads one way, Max, over the Khyber Pass into Pakistan. As I recall, there are not many villages along the way. There's Basawul, just before the pass, and that abandoned village just before the Torkham Border Crossing Station. So which is it?"

"He's hiding close to that abandoned village, just

outside, in fact. Do me a favor. Don't pass if back to Kabul. We'll have a B-52 raid inbound if they think he's hiding there."

He chuckled. "I don't think they use that kind of tactic these days."

"No? Would you bet your shirt on it?"

"Ok, no, but I won't say anything, it's your show. We'll be there in an hour, so how do you want to play this?"

"We'll use Art's tactics, and go in hard and fast. My vehicle will go in first. Deploy the others in a covering formation. As soon as we know it's not heavily defended, we'll go in on foot and grab him. He'll have a few guards with him, so we need to be careful and take them out before they even realize we've arrived. Art's men can do that. As soon as we have him located, I'll call you in with your men to make the arrest."

"Really?"

"Sure. It makes no difference to us, Dwight. But you'll go down in the history books. It'll be Captain Rains by the end of the day."

His eyes shone, and I could see he was hooked.

"That'll be something to tell my folks."

"Yep. But don't screw up, Lieutenant. Let us go in first, and you provide the cover."

"I've got it, don't worry."

We got moving again and covered the remaining distance to the village. It was just as I'd remembered it;

a few mean, miserable stone huts, most of them with their roofs tumbled in. There was no sign of life, and not even a bird sang. I ordered our driver to go straight into the center of the squalid ruins, and Rains deployed his three Strykers just outside with their guns trained on the buildings. One of Art Schramm's men opened the door to exit the vehicle, but I pulled Art to one side.

"He's not here."

He stared at me. "I wondered about that. It didn't seem a likely place for the Taliban's chief mullah to be holed up. So where are we headed?"

"To Yaluk. I saw him while we were there."

"Christ, he'll be long gone."

"No. He didn't know that I'd seen him, or recognized him anyway. The message from Najela's father suggested that he was very ill and needed treatment. He'll be there. But you know what'll happen when General Westwood finds his location?"

"An airstrike."

"Yes, exactly. Probably a drone strike, followed by a huge influx of troops who'll be shooting at anything that moves. I'm trying to save those villagers who protected us from being caught in the crossfire."

"Understood. But you know Rains will already have called them."

"Yeah. Let them come and saturate bomb an abandoned village. We'll be halfway to Yaluk, underneath the mountain in the tunnel."

He smiled then. "Yes, I like it. I'd suggest we pull the vehicles back from the expected attack site. Five hundred yards back from the village should do it."

I could hardly believe what he was saying. "They surely wouldn't target their own vehicles. There could be soldiers inside!"

"Are you prepared to bet on that?" He looked grim and hard. "It happened to me once before. So-called friendly army saturation bombed our position, and I lost half my men. Never again."

"Were they American?"

"No. French." His face relaxed. "But they could have been any nationality. Soldiers are the same the world over. They have fixed objectives, and they'll usually use whatever force they have at their disposal to reach their objectives."

I thanked him and called up Rains on the radio.

"We should laager our vehicles five hundred yards outside the village."

"Yeah, I've already given the order, Max. We're about to move out now. Is this guy in the village itself?"

"No, we'll need to go in on foot. He's outside the village."

"Got it. We're moving out now."

I watched the puff of smoke as his driver gunned the engine and drove back out of the village to the road. Our driver followed and they parked their vehicles in laager, just as we had outside of Jalalabad. Rains detailed one man to remain with each vehicle then assembled his men ready to move out. I noticed him look up at the sky and smiled. "We're ready to move, Hoffman. Do you want to take the point? It's your show."

"I'll do that, Art, would you and your men travel right behind us. Dwight, you can take the rear. Is that ok?"

He nodded. I could see he wasn't too happy to be in the position that would put him closest to whatever action the General had planned, but he nodded his agreement and gave the orders to his sergeant. Vince Mason issued the orders and got his men into formation, ready to move. The tough sergeant was no fool, and his men were spread out in a loose spearhead formation, far enough away from each other not to present an easy target to an enemy, but close enough to give each other supporting fire. Mason himself took the position at the rear. I wondered if he knew what Kabul had planned, maybe not. Probably only Rains was privy to that information.

"Max, up there!"

I followed the direction of Art's gaze. A drone banked lazily in the sky. It was perhaps five miles away and about three thousand feet high.

"I see it. I hope I'm wrong, and it's just an unarmed Predator on a routine reconnaissance."

"Yeah, and my mother was the Queen of England," he returned grimly. "I'd bet my pension it's a Reaper, and carrying a full weapon load."

I looked at him. "I wasn't aware that mercenaries had pension plans?"

He shrugged. "Well no, we don't. But I've never liked to gamble."

Rachel heard his sardonic comment, and we both laughed. If it was a Reaper, it was early. I just prayed that whoever flew it was patient enough to wait until we'd cleared the area.

* * *

Master-Sergeant Carol Wendelski touched the joystick and brought the MQ-9 back to the straight and level. She had the village in sight, and now all she needed was a target. Her orders were clear. She was to use the Hellfires, of which she carried a full load on the drone's hardpoints, and not to use her ace-in-the-hole, the laser guided bomb, until she had cleared the order with local control, Kabul. She could see the Strykers, which meant ISAF, so she had to be very careful. Where was the enemy? Corporal Vernon Munch stood at her shoulder, watching. He was due off shift, and he'd been flying a Predator for the past four hours, patrolling the skies between Kabul and Helmand. He should have gone home, but the buzz in the Ground Control Station was too much, and he'd stayed to watch.

"I have to see this, Sarge. I've never seen one of those

laser guided babies fired in anger. Not yet, anyway."

His Sergeant kept her eyes glued to the screen. "I've only done it in practice, Vernon, on the simulator. I don't even know if I'll get clearance to use it yet. It's Hellfires only on my command, and they'll let me know when I can toss the big one. Hold up, there's something coming in from Kabul."

She listened intently, and her eyebrows narrowed in puzzlement. "Could you repeat that, Sir. You want me to launch the laser guided bomb on your command, even if it endangers our own people?"

She waited for the reply. Then, "I understand, Sir. But it could mean inviting a friendly fire incident. Are you certain about that order?"

The reply left her in no doubt as to their intentions.

"Yes, Sir, I understand, crystal. I shall fire immediately on your order. Creech out."

Ok, it was obvious what they wanted. And what they intended. But it wasn't obvious to her how to play this one. She had a sneaking suspicion that she was about to receive an illegal order. One that she could obey, and be hung out to dry in the subsequent furor. Or disobey, and be put through the ringer, all the way to court martial. Or was there a third way?"

* * *

I led the way through the village, towards the tunnel. When I turned around, I could see Dwight Rains looking around with an uneasy expression on his face. A few yards from the entrance to the tunnel, I slowed and waited for his men to catch up. He came up with his Sergeant, wearing a puzzled expression.

"What's the deal, Hoffman? Where are we headed? There's no one here."

"Lieutenant, would you follow me into the tunnel. Art, you take the rear, we're going underground."

"Sure, we'll be here," he acknowledged and winked at me, enjoying the conspiracy.

We entered the tunnel, Rachel, Luk and Najela in the front with me, and Rains following with his men. About five hundred yards in, there was an open space where the tunnel widened into a natural cavern. I called a halt and told Rains I needed to talk.

"I'm sorry, Lieutenant, but I deceived you. Mullah Omar isn't anywhere near the village."

"The hell you say! You mean you've led us all this way for nothing?"

"No, not for nothing. He's not far away, but not where I said."

I explained my belief that General Westwood would launch a bombing raid as soon as he knew the target.

"You can't think he'd drop bombs on top of us, Hoffman? The man's a tough soldier, but he's not a homicidal warlord."

"Perhaps you're right. What message did you send him?"

His eyes darted away then came back to me. "I don't know what you're talking about."

"Come on, Rains. You know as well as I do that he wouldn't allow you on this mission without making sure you kept in contact. What did you say?"

His hesitation was brief. "I sent the coordinates of that ruined village, which was all. If you're right, it's about to be flattened, but I don't hear any bombs dropping."

He was right. There was only silence in the tunnel, no loud explosions, and no shuddering vibrations as the earth shook to the detonation of high explosives. I wondered for a few moments if I was wrong, but only for a few moments.

* * *

She'd lost sight of the soldiers. One moment they were visible in the village, moving through the buildings, checking for enemy activity or IEDs, she presumed. The last she saw of them was when they were close to a heap of rocks at the foot of a nearby hill that formed the southernmost border of the village. When she'd brought the Reaper around again they'd gone, but she'd no idea where. Back to the village, or somewhere else, but where?

Her headphones crackled, and she listened intently.

"Creech, this is Kabul. Are you over the target?"

So it was a target now, not a village. Of course, in the post operation report, it would sound much better, colder, more military; a target, and something to be hit, to be destroyed.

"That's affirmative, Sir."

"Confirm the location of our troops. Are they in sight?"

"No, Sir, I cannot see them."

"Roger that. You have permission to fire, do you understand, permission to launch a single GBU-12 Paveway laser guided bomb on that village? Flatten it for us, Master Sergeant."

"But, Sir, I can't confirm that our troops are clear of the area."

"You have a fire order, Master Sergeant. Do it, now!"

She sighed. She'd seen the soldiers disappear to the south of the ruins, and she could give them a chance. She sighted the laser target designator to the north of the buildings and pressed the fire button. There was brief spurt of smoke and flames as the rocket motor fire, propelling the bomb towards its target. Seconds later, it impacted in a huge explosion as debris was thrown skywards; rocks, earth, lumps of wood and rusty old iron used to patch the roofs of the decaying buildings, but as far as she could tell, no bodies, no torn scraps of uniforms or equipment. Thank Christ for that. Except that she knew it was a wasted shot, there was nothing down there. Whichever Taliban warband they were attempting to take out, they were nowhere near. But neither was her side. They'd be pissed that she'd skewed the shot, but that was tough. She had one GBU-12 Paveway laser guided bomb left on the rails, now how could she use it to inflict the maximum damage on the enemy?

* * *

The blast brought down a shower of rocks and stones near the entrance to the tunnel, and a mass of small pieces of rock nearer to where we waited. A huge cloud of dust swirled around us, blotting out our vision, so that it was as if we were in one of the fabled London peasoupers; the fogs that blanketed the city during Victorian times. Several of the men started to edge further away from the tunnel entrance where the explosion had occurred. Rachel held my hand tightly, more a woman and less a tough fighter pilot now that we were inside a dark cavern, waiting for the roof to collapse and bury us alive. The dust eventually settled, and we were able to see again in the beams of the flashlights the soldiers carried. Rains was frozen, unmoving. I borrowed a flashlight and looked at him closely, shining the beam into his eyes. They were wide, dilated in the abrupt shock caused by the explosion, and the knowledge that everything he'd believed about his army, about the honor and principles that were its guiding light, had just been shattered. At last, he'd left West Point behind for good and planted his feet firmly in the soil of Afghanistan. I pitied him the terrible culture shock, but there was not time for pity. War was a pitiless occupation, and we were stuck in the middle of it. I looked at his sergeant.

"Are any of your men injured?"

He shook his head. "I don't think so. It was just the, er, surprise, I guess you'd call it."

"You'll need a couple of men to look after the Lieutenant. I think he's out of it for now."

"Yeah, you're right. Johnson, Venner, come and look after the LT."

Two PFCs came forward. "Is he injured, Sarge?" one of them asked, a pale, pimply youth of no more than nineteen years of age. He looked half starved, his helmet oversized on his thin face. Too young and frail to fight, except for his eyes. They were eyes that had seen combat, eyes that measure, assessed and then acted in a split second. I'd noticed those eyes many times in the past few days.

"Nah, he's just a bit shaken. Keep him at the back of the column."

" I assume we're going forward, Sir?"

"We are, yes. There's no going back."

"Why's that, Sarge?"

Vince Mason nodded towards the direction we'd come

from. The roof was down and the entrance blocked.

"We're trapped, oh Christ, we'll never get out of here!" the other trooper shouted. His companion sniggered. "You crazy fool, Johnson, we just go out the other end, like we did before."

I interrupted them. "We need to get moving. Make sure Rains stay in the rear. Art, when we get near the tunnel entrance, your men need to be ready for anything. That bomb will have alerted them that something's going down."

"I hear you, Max. We'll be ready."

We started again moving along the tunnel, crawling where the roof got lower and lower and then we were back on our feet, and I quickened the pace to the end. When we saw the daylight, Art and three of his men overtook us and went ahead. As we came to the end, he turned to me.

"It's all clear. How do you want to play this?"

"You're not going to like this, but we need to split our forces. I want about half the men to go to the north and half to the south. We'll leave four soldiers here with Rains. They can stay out of sight inside the tunnel entrance.

"It's going to be a long walk back now that they've brought the roof in. I'd guess about fifty miles, and we won't make that in less than two days in this terrain."

"No, that's why I'm going to radio the Strykers to start heading this way. They'll get here in two or three hours. That's time enough for us to do what we have to do and move out."

He looked chagrined. "Christ, I'd forgotten the Strykers. I must be getting old."

I laughed. "Not old, Art. You're just not used to that kind of luxury."

I called up the infantryman who carried the radio and used it to contact the Strykers. The corporal in charge was dubious at first about taking orders from me, so I called Sergeant Mason to come over. He put on the headset.

"Who's this? Corporal O'Shea? Right, Mr. Hoffman is in charge, you know that. So get your ass into the APC and get its wheels turning."

"Hold on, Sergeant. Tell him to stop five miles short of Yaluk. We'll call them in when we're ready."

He passed on the order, ended the call and looked at me. "Anything else?"

"Yes, get your men up and ready to move off. We're going in. Take your squad south, we're going north to encircle the village and then move in."

"You've got it, Sir."

CHAPTER THIRTEEN

This is a government based on nothing because of the continuing presence of foreign troops in Afghanistan. Karzai's call to the Taliban to come to the government has no meaning. He became president through fraud and lies.
Taliban spokesman Zabiullah Mujahid

"What's the story so far, Charlie?"

General Westwood put the question to his intelligence officer without looking way from his wall map.

"We're not making much progress, General. One Paveway hit on that village, but by the looks of it there was nothing there. Hoffman's team has disappeared."

"What are they up to? Soldiers don't disappear."

"I've no idea, Sir."

"Damn. That Mullah Omar is almost within my hands.

I can smell him. Are the backup forces on standby?"

"Everything's ready. We've a squadron of Deltas. You may have met them. They're the Night Stalkers. The guys are waiting on the tarmac, waiting to get their choppers airborne."

"What are they flying?"

"Little Birds, General. There are ten of them, forty Deltas in all."

"What about ground forces?"

"Vance Everard is already on his way to Jalalabad, and they've been shadowing Hoffman's' mission at long range since they started. There are twenty Strykers, about three hundred aboard."

Westwood grunted. Where the hell was Hoffman, where was he headed? He pored over the map, checking, rechecking, and making calculations. Then it hit him.

"Charlie, that village where they pulled back to after that attack when Rains was hit, what's it called?"

"Yaluk, General."

"Yeah, Yaluk, that's right. Hoffman was playing us for suckers. I don't know what his game is, but they're headed to Yaluk."

"But General, that's another fifty miles and they're on foot."

"It didn't take them that long to get there last time. There must be a tunnel under the mountain. That's where they've gone. Through a tunnel to Yaluk."

"Are you sure, Sir?"

"Damn right. Get onto them, and get the Deltas airborne. Tell Vance Everard to put his foot on the gas. Send his company in. They're headed to Yaluk, and you can get onto Creech. I want that Reaper overhead with a feed to this headquarters. This time we'll nail that bastard Omar once and for all."

* * *

I led the group to the north of the village. Luk and Najela were with me. We needed her knowledge of the local terrain and Luk to interpret her sign language. Rachel was there too, despite me trying to get her to travel with Art Schramm. I tried to persuade her to stay in the center of the group of mercenaries, but she'd refused.

"I'm coming with you."

I didn't argue further. She was a woman, but she was also ex-military and knew how to handle herself and her weapons in a scrap. I could see Sergeant Mason leading the infantry towards the south of the village, and so far we'd hadn't encountered any of the enemy. Three hundred yards ahead of us lay the village itself, and two hundred yards further the stone hut where I knew that Omar stayed.

"What do you think?" I asked Art.

He stood next to me. I'd called him forward to decide on how to move in. His usual tactic of hurtling in, all guns blazing, was not what I wanted for these villagers who had done so much to help us.

"You mean other than an all out assault?"

"That's not going to happen, Art. They were good to us when we needed them."

He nodded. "That's right. But Omar is certain to have sentries out, and they could start shooting at us anytime."

I saw Najela signing to Luk, and her hands were moving frantically, like semaphores. Luk turned to me.

"She says she will go into the village and see if there are any enemy soldiers lying in wait."

I didn't like it, but it was her village.

"Ok, Luk, but you go with her and protect her."

"I was going anyway," he smiled.

They walked quickly towards the silent mass of stone huts and disappeared around a corner. At first I thought the place was empty, and I had a feeling of dread that I'd led them here for nothing. Then two children appeared, playing with an old motor tire. It was slightly incongruous. We were watching with a force that could bring down overwhelming military might on their tiny community, and yet here they were, playing as if there never had been any threat to their peace and security. So the village was still occupied. I turned to Art.

"Remember, no massive shows of force. We don't want those children hurt."

He shook his head. "No, of course not. We'll be careful.

When do we go in?"

That was the next question, whether our main target was still in residence, and if so, how to tackle the task of taking him alive.

"Let's wait a little longer, and see if anyone appears."

A few minutes later, we were rewarded with the sight of a bearded tribesman carrying a water container to the village well. That was unusual. It was the norm here for such work to be done by women. But what was significant was that this man didn't just carry a water container. He also had a Kalashnikov assault rifle slung over his shoulder, the iconic AK-47, together with crossed belts over his shoulders bearing pouches for spare clips. He also wore a black turban. Everything about him screamed Taliban insurgent, so they were keeping a guard post in the village. I whispered to Art.

"I think we're in business. The stone hut I saw Mullah Omar in is over there, a couple of hundred yards from the center of the village."

I pointed it out to him. "I suggest we circle around behind and rush it when we're a few yards away."

He nodded. "We're ready."

At that point everything started to go wrong. My intention was to make a clean, incisive attack on the area where Omar's house stood, so we'd stay away from the main village and avoid any threat to the inhabitants. Sergeant Mason was waiting for the order to go, but I saw a figure running towards them, several hundred yards away. Even at that distance, I could see it was Rains.

He was shouting, "Attack, attack, go in and get him before he escapes!"

The fighter with the water container looked up in alarm and dropped it. He unslung his AK-47 and cocked the action. Then he released a burst that threw up chips of stone near to where the infantry were milling, uncertain whether to obey their sergeant's order to wait or their lieutenant to move in. The military has a hierarchy, officer's trump sergeants, and they came to that decision automatically, as they were trained to do. They charged.

Mason was running alongside, them, shouting, "Get back, and get under cover."

But they ignored him. They were committed. Their blood was up, and they were following a legitimate order. I cursed the men at the tunnel for letting him go, but it was no time for recriminations.

"Max, look!"

I followed Rachel's gaze. Four black turbaned fighters had materialized, but these were armed with RPG-7s, the shoulder launched missiles that were the preferred weapon of Islamic terrorists worldwide. Two of them launched; one missile went wide, and the other detonated close to Rains' men. I saw them diving for cover.

"Hoffman, we have to go," Art shouted.

"You're right. Lead your men in to help Rains' people.

I'll go into the village and try to locate Luk and Najela."

He led his men off without a word, charging in the direction of the fighters with the missile launchers.

I shouted at Rachel. "Let's go, we need to find Luk and Najela."

She followed me on a curving run that took us into the village, keeping us out of sight for most of the way from the missileers. I heard the sound of automatic gunfire. First there were only two assault rifles, and then they were joined by many others."

"I wish I knew who was firing," I shouted at Rachel. "We don't know yet how many enemies there are."

"They taught us to hear the difference," she panted as we ran. The slower rate of fire, it's a deeper sound as they shoot, are the AK-47s."

"There seems to be more of those," I replied.

"Yeah, one hell of a lot more."

We rounded a corner and ran into Luk and Najela. Luk had his sniper rifle ready to use. He stared at me as we rushed up.

"What's going on? It sounds like a war has broken out."

"That's about right, yeah. They saw us coming, so we'll need to fight it out with them."

"Do you have any idea of their numbers?"

"No, none."

Najela signed rapidly. Luke turned to me to interpret.

"She says there are more than a hundred fighters. Most

of them were staying in a cave on the hillside just above the village, so as not to attract attention from enemy drones. But they will be on their way here."

The firing was increasing by the second, and a full-scale firefight was developing.

"I think we can work that one out for ourselves, Luk." I turned to Rachel. "You need to get her somewhere safe. She's too important to risk out in the open." I saw her open her mouth to argue, but I overruled her. "Just do as I say, and try to keep the villagers safe if you can."

"Where are you going?" she asked, not moving.

"We've got a battle to fight, Rachel. Now get her under cover."

I left them and Luk, and I headed for the firing. We reached the edge of the main village square and joined Art's men who were pinned down by heavy incoming machine gun fire.

"They tell me there are more than a hundred enemy fighters," I shouted to him. "Do you know what Rains' men are doing?"

He pointed to a larger building down a side street. "Last I saw they were pinned down behind that place. I only hope to Christ..."

Before he could speak, two rockets hit the building in quick succession, and when the smoke cleared it was almost flattened. We could hear the cry of at least one soldier who'd been hit, but there was no time to go and attend to the casualties.

"Art, those men, we have to draw the enemy off them, and give them a chance to regroup."

"That bastard Rains! They're good troops, and he led them straight into trouble."

"Forget Rains. There's only one way to do this."

"What's that?"

"Your way. Straight in and hit them hard."

He gave me a broad smile. "That's my way of thinking." He turned to his men. "We're going in fast, are you all ready?"

A chorus of shouts announced their enthusiasm. These men did this for a living. The money was good, but what drove them were situations like this, and I guessed that some were as addicted to the adrenalin rush of battle as a junkie to his crack pipe. Then Art leapt up, and they followed, running at breakneck speed straight for the enemy, but not all of them. Art had deployed four of his men with light machine guns to give covering fire. Luk joined them, shoulder to shoulder, aimed and firing his sniper rifle at high speed. It could have been another Charge of the Light Brigade, magnificent but foolhardy. But if there was a massacre, it was the enemy who fell, not the mercenaries. I ran behind them and got caught up in the adrenaline-fueled chase. One man next to me went down. I bent to him, but his companion shouted, "Leave him, he's ok. We need to kill these bastards first.

We'll worry about the wounded afterwards."

I nodded and ran on.

We were still a hundred yards from the stone hut that was temporary home to Mullah Omar, and the Taliban were dug in fifty yards back from that. We threw ourselves through the gaping holes in the stone building that stood directly opposite. Art was already deploying his men to bring their fire to bear on the enemy. I ran over to him.

"Why have we stopped, Art? We're nowhere near the hut."

"Look!"

He gestured to the ground that lay in front of us. It was open ground, and the Taliban had been crossing it to intercept our force. Art's shooters had killed a score of them, and their bodies lay strewn over the ground.

"The reason we killed them so easily was because of the flat, open nature of the ground. If we try and cross it, they'll do the same to us."

"You're right. They still outnumber us by more than two to one, and we don't know yet about Rains' casualties. I need to send someone back to bring his men forward."

"Max, they're coming!"

It was Luk who'd shouted. I searched the ground ahead of us.

"No, behind us. Sergeant Mason, he's bringing the men forward to join us."

I looked, and there they were, Rains' platoon of

infantry, dashing forward to join us. Mason slid in next to me and grinned.

"I thought it was time we did some good."

"What about Rains?"

He shook his head. "The Lieutenant's dead. He was the only fatality. A couple of the men took minor flesh wounds but nothing to stop them fighting. At least Rains is out of our hair."

"Forget Rains. We'll record he was hit when leading his men into action."

He gave me a scornful look.

"It's too late for him," I continued. "But at least his family won't suffer."

He stared at me silently for a few moments then nodded. "I copy that. I guess the poor bastard just wasn't ready for all the flak that was thrown at him over here. What's the next move?"

I was about to reply when there was a burst of firing and bullets zipped around our position. They weren't coming from directly in front of us, to the east, but this time from the north. Reinforcements!

"Luk, I'm worried about those missiles. Cover our front with your sniper rifle. Sergeant Mason, could you deploy your men to cover the north. We need to find out how many of them we're dealing with. What's the situation with machine guns?"

"We have two, M249 light machine guns. They'll keep

their heads down."

"Good, get them firing as fast as possible. We don't want them overrunning our position."

He gave orders to his men, and they moved their positions to cover the north side. Almost immediately, they began to fire, blunting the new attack that had materialized from the north of the village. I turned to Art Schramm.

"Art, we've got to face the obvious. We can't defend this position. They can pin us down here with machine gun and rocket fire, and we've nowhere to go. It seems to me we either break out or stay here and die. The only other alternative is a miracle."

"You're right. A frontal attack will result in casualties, and a lot of the men are going to get hit."

I checked my watch. We had several hours to go until darkness. It was going to be a difficult choice to make. There was a renewed burst of heavy gunfire. I strained to make out the direction it had come from, but everything was covered in a thick cloud of smoke that had swirled down around us as if by magic.

"Well if that don't beat all," Art exclaimed.

"What?" I still couldn't see anything.

"It's the damned cavalry, and in the nick of time, as always. It's a flock of Little Birds, coming down on us."

"Little Birds?"

Then I saw them, small, agile, attack helicopters. They swooped in, peeling off one by one in formation to fire a salvo of rockets into the enemy position. They carried on down, firing the twin thirty millimeter chain guns mounted on a stubby wing either side of the fuselage. I could see the troopers clinging to the cockpit, two to each side, heavily armed and heavily armored. They were waiting to land and deploy, and we all knew that hell would break loose the second their boots touched the ground. From below, they seemed like mythical lords of war, watching the results of their savage gunfire on the enemy below. It was cold, clinical, dispassionate killing. It was magnificent. The Taliban were jumping to their feet, attempting to fire on the helicopter borne troops. It was no time to sit and do nothing. I jumped up, shouting at the men.

"Luk, keep pouring it onto those bastards. The rest of you, we're attacking. Sergeant Mason, take out those enemy to the north. Machine gunners, cease fire as soon as we move off unless you have a clear field of fire. We'll take down those bastards in front of us. Let's go!"

I ran out, uncaring about who would follow me. I knew they'd be there, right behind. We flung ourselves down in a narrow ditch that crossed the open ground. We were less than fifty yards from the enemy, and now they'd seen us some had started to fire in our direction. I waited for an opportunity for us to start forward again, scanning the enemy position, watching them try desperately to fight off the assault from both sides. The tide had turned. They'd been part of a two-sided assault on us, but now they were on the receiving end, and already the panic had begun. It was time to finish it.

"Max, behind you!"

I whirled. We'd climbed the rocky ledge the enemy were using as a barricade and jumped down amongst them. I fired again and again. It was as if time had slowed, and there was no universe except for this tiny place, where expectations became a brutal binary reality of life or death. A fighter had just tossed down his assault rifle, out of ammunition, and he was jumping at me with a huge blade in his hand, a richly ornamented Afghan fighting knife.

I knew that in societies like this these blades were handed down from father to son, as a sign of adulthood. Some were not functional, and purely used for symbolic, ritual purposes. Others were savage killing blades. I realized at once that this was the kind of weapon I faced. I dodged to the side and missed the first killing stroke. He back swung the knife, and I pulled the trigger, but my gun had jammed. I used the rifle to ward off the blow, but his blade slid down the barrel and the stock, slashing into my hand. It felt unreal. In the midst of the high tech action, where men fought with machine guns, assault rifles and missiles, I was in a fight with a man using a weapon that could have been made two thousand years ago. I felt the pain as the blade cut in. The man smiled and lifted the knife again for the killing stroke. He swung down, and I kicked him hard in the groin. His breath left his body in a searing scream of pain, and he hesitated for that one moment; it was enough. I still had my Colt .45 in the holster, and in one fast, smooth action, I ripped it out, levered off the safety, then for a second, a whirlwind of images flooded my mind, and I saw the face of that Vietnamese. Then I cocked the pistol and fired. The heavy bullet caused him to stagger, but he still made another lunge, and I fired again, two more shots. This time there was no more resistance. He doubled over in agony and fell to the ground, blood pouring from his wounds. In that moment, I knew I'd thrown off some of the chains that shackled me to that image of long ago, on the Vietnamese border. It had been a question of life or death, and I'd chosen life. I was also certain that the decision I'd made all those years ago was based on the same, fundamental premise. He'd meant to kill me, and I'd chosen to live.

It was time to get back into the fight. I looked down. My hand was bleeding badly, but not enough to stop me fighting. I picked up a dropped rifle, a Soviet AK-47, distinctive with its banana magazine. I'd no idea if it was loaded, but when I pointed it at a pair of insurgents hacking towards me, a stream of bullets came out of the barrel, and they fell dead. There was the sound of screaming and shouting. I looked up, and my blood chilled. We'd hacked clean through the line of Taliban, but a second wave was coming in.

"Take cover," I shouted. "Get behind the rocks, and

pick them off as they come."

The men jumped behind cover as the new assault came at us. One of the men shouted, "Holy shit! Look at them go."

I looked around. For a moment I thought even more enemy had appeared to join the battle. But this time the Gods of War were smiling on us. The Delta Force, they'd deployed from the helicopters and begun their fearsome killing work. They came in on the run, fast, expert, sliding from cover to cover, each man protecting his partner, laying down a lethal curtain of fire as they attacked. Pure poetry, at least, of the efficient, killing kind. The enemy had formed a defensive curtain around the area where Mullah Omar's hut stood. I still hadn't seen him, but he was here. These Taliban were fighting ferociously for one reason only, to protect their leader. The Deltas forced them back, and they retreated over a carpet of their dead and wounded. The assault never let up. The Little Birds poured down fire from their miniguns, decimating the robed ranks, whilst the Deltas pressed forward, pushing them further and further back. We came in behind them, although there was little we could do, except make certain that there were no survivors waiting to hit the Deltas from behind when they'd gone past. Slowly the battle wound down as the fight ascended the rocky slope above the village. Then it was as if we'd hit a brick wall. The enemy staged a last stand, manning a defensive pile of loose boulders and shale that stretched across the narrow pathway leading into a cleft between the rocks. Bullets and rockets hammered towards us, and we dived for cover. I knew instinctively what was happening. These were the sacrificial rearguard, making a suicidal last stand while their leader escaped. And there was nothing we could do about it. The gunships zipped around like angry bees, unable to locate a target. And we still had a formidable blocking force to fight before we could even begin to give chase. In that moment, I knew that we'd won, and yet we'd lost. And then something happened. Something strange. The question in all of our minds was Mullah Omar. Was he ever here, or was it all for nothing?

"Max!" I looked around. Luk had been using his sniper scope to spot for the enemy. "He's there, look!"

I gazed in the direction he was pointing and focused my binoculars. Just where the rocks parted to give way for the dark cleft that led into them, a group of men stood; insurgents, Taliban. They were staring down at us, and almost daring us to take a shot at them. In the center of them stood a man dressed entirely in black. A patch covered one of his eyes. Mullah Omar. The rest of our force stopped to look, and we all looked up at our main foe. It was like a frozen tableau that lasted for a couple of minutes, a frozen moment in time. No one fired, as if it was some ancient battlefield courtesy, facing the enemy after a hard battle. Then there was a flurry of movement, and they were gone.

"Sergeant Mason, over here!"

Two of the infantry searching the area where Omar's stone hut lay had emerged with two men. They were so ragged I thought at first they had caught two more prisoners, but when I focused my binoculars I saw they were American. I walked towards them with Mason and Art Schramm, and as we drew near, it became clear they were an officer and an NCO. The officer held out his hand to us.

"Major Roberts, and this is Corporal Blakeney. My thanks to you gentlemen, I thought we were going to be here a lot longer than this. Maybe forever."

We shook hands. "How long have you been a prisoner, Major?" I asked him.

He shook his head. "I wish I knew. We lost track of time. A year, I guess. We were captured in the winter of 2009."

"It's 2012 now, Major. I'd guess you've been there for three years."

Their faces fell. Three lost years! "We were hooded for most of the time," the corporal explained. "It was disorientating."

I nodded. I'd bet it was all of that, and more.

* * *

"Mr. Ashford, my employer has been very fair with you. Yet now you tell me that the shipment has not arrived, and you do not have the money to repay what you owe. I'm afraid that his patience is finally at an end. Do you have his money?"

Ashford stared at the phone. He wanted to recruit a team, send it in to those spic drug dealers, and blast them all to hell. Except that they were too strong, too heavily armed, too numerous.

"Listen to me. It's all lined up. The guns are stuck in a warehouse in Kabul. As soon as I can get them moved to my contacts, I'll have the drugs, and I can swap them for the money. Just a few days, that's all."

"But Senor! That is exactly what you said last time we spoke. My Jefe has given me explicit instructions, no more extensions. Either you pay, or we shall have to proceed with the alternative."

He pictured his life, as it would become; a fugitive, running from the South American hit squad. The Agency wouldn't support him, and if they found out what he'd been doing, he'd be facing a lifetime in a Federal prison. He had to get more time, had to!

"I'll give you more money."

There was a slight hesitation the other end, and then a sigh. "But you have no money."

"As soon as the deal's done, I'll up the ante. Twenty-five percent on top."

Another hesitation. This time it was briefer. "Five days, no more. After that, there will be no more calls. You would be advised to make your peace with God if you fail to keep your side of the bargain, Senor Ashford."

"Don't worry, you'll get your money."

"It is not I who should be worried, Senor Ashford."

The line went dead, and he hung up. The damn spic had gone. Ashford started working out how he could play this. The first task would be to get the crates loaded back onto the Twin Otter, and he'd need to arrange to divert some extra ordnance to make up the amount he'd promised the Taliban. That was easy. He knew who would issue the necessary orders, and they'd have no choice but to carry them out. As soon as that little shit Hoffman got back to Kabul, he could fly out to the field and do the swap for the drugs. The intelligence officer had told him they should be back by the following day. He'd have to move fast. He climbed into his SUV and started to drive to Kabul International. Now what would make Hoffman do as he was told? Hadn't Ed Walker said that he was sweet on that co-pilot of his? That should do it. Perfect!

CHAPTER FOURTEEN

After our victory in Afghanistan and the defeat of the Soviet oppressors who had killed millions of Muslims, the legend about the invincibility of the superpowers vanished. Our boys no longer viewed America as a superpower. So, when they left Afghanistan, they went to Somalia and prepared themselves carefully for a long war. They had thought that the Americans were like the Russians, so they trained and prepared. As I said, our boys were shocked by the low morale of the American soldier and they realized that the American soldier was just a paper tiger.

Osama bin Laden

President Barzai looked tired and irritable. He glared at the two senior men. The man in uniform was his Army Chief of Staff. The other was a constant thorn in his side.

"What is it, Defense Minister Wardak? You have called

me away from vital work to attend this meeting. Tell me why?"

Abdul Rahim Wardak spat out one word. "Drones." He looked at the President and the Army Chief of Staff. "These hideous aircraft fill our skies, killing our people and destroying our mosques. Shall I tell you who they're fighting for, Mr. President? The Taliban. Every time one of their missiles attacks our innocent people, they cry out for revenge, for the blood of the Americans."

"Yes, yes, you have said this before, Abdul. But remember, the drones are doing a fine job, destroying the Taliban leaders wherever they gather."

"A fine job you call it? When every missile recruits more fighters for the enemy cause."

"And how would you deal with the Taliban leaders, Abdul," General Kadim asked gently.

"By negotiation. It is time we talked, instead of driving more fighters to fill their ranks."

Barzai stood up and leaned on the table. "Talk to them! Are you serious? Do you know how many times I have tried to talk to these people? Every time it is impossible. Do you know they don't even have an address, and somewhere I could contact them? How can you talk with non-existent ghosts, Defense Minister?"

It was true. Wardak knew that. The Taliban were virtually unreachable. They made contact only when they had something to say, and then the conduit would quickly be broken off. He stayed silent.

"Yes, you know the truth of it, don't you? Talk to them, you say, but I say, talk to who? Stop the use of drones, that's what you suggest. But how then do we take the war to the enemy? When we talked about the American mission to target the Taliban leaders with mercenaries, you protested. I'm beginning to think you don't want to win this war, Abdul," The President ended scornfully.

Wardak flushed. He knew he was on dangerous ground, and Barzai had a harsh way of dealing with his ministers who failed him. Yet when everything they suggested was tantamount to a recruiting drive for the enemy, what should he say?

"My information is that the American mercenary operation General Kadim was so enthusiastic about ended badly. Our intelligence sources say their people were badly mauled and only achieved limited ends. We have to stop this nonsense now. Even the tribes that formed the Northern Alliance against the Taliban, they're turning against us. Many of them are swearing revenge for the failed American drone attacks. Some have even allied themselves with the Taliban. We're losing this war, Mr. President."

Both men stared at the Defense Minister. Had he lost his mind? His words were tantamount to treason. But Barzai merely nodded.

"We will discuss these things, Abdul. Perhaps there is

merit in what you have to say. This meeting is at an end. General, would you stay a moment? I need to talk to you about an approach to the American military."

Both men were silent as the Defense Minister left the room, and when the door was closed, Barzai picked up his telephone to call his private secretary.

"Bring us a tray of tea, and then we are not to be disturbed. Not by anyone."

He put the phone down. "Now, General, you know what has to be done? I will not have such treasonous defeatism in my cabinet."

"It will not be easy," Kadim replied. He is Pashtun, of course, like us. But his tribe, the Khattak, will swear revenge if anything happens to him. It could even start a civil war."

"We already have a civil war, General. But I take your point. I would suggest an accident. No, I have a better idea. If he were killed in a Taliban suicide bombing, it would strengthen the determination of his tribe to fight our enemies. Can you arrange it? You know how they operate. Perhaps one of your prisoners could be killed and placed in a vehicle on the route that the Defense Minister uses each day."

The General nodded. "It could be arranged, yes. There may be many civilian casualties. It would need a large bomb to be certain of killing him."

Barzai spread his hands wide. "So much the better. We

need to stir hatred against the Taliban. Now listen, there is a nephew of my wife, he is a colonel in the army. I feel he would make an excellent Defense Minister, especially if I instructed him to obey your wishes for the military."

Kadim kept a straight face. He already had a cousin he'd hoped to put forward as a replacement for Wardak, but he'd have to bide his time. Barzai couldn't survive forever. Afghanistan was such a dangerous place. He'd survived several attempts on his life already, and maybe he wouldn't be so lucky next time. He'd even suggested the way to dispose of unwanted politicians that would deflect public opinion against the enemy.

"Excellent, Sir. I will arrange it."

The President nodded. "Good. Anything else?"

"Sir, I've had a request from the American CIA Station Chief here in Kabul, Mr. Ashford. There is a shipment of arms destined for our loyal tribes who are fighting the enemy in the northern provinces. Apparently, there's some kind of bureaucratic foul-up, and it would help immensely if you would issue an order to release the shipment without further delay."

Barzai waited. They both knew that this kind of affair was never quite that simple.

"Of course," the General continued, "Mr. Ashford will be more than happy to make a sizeable donation to your fund for the education of the poor."

"See my secretary and have him draw up the paperwork,"

the President nodded carelessly. "The shipment must be made available without delay." The door opened, and a tray of tea was brought in. Both men sat drinking tea, making small talk. Each one wondered when the other would make an attempt on his life to ease a relative into a promotion, or satisfy some ancient vendetta, or both.

"I'm so glad we had this meeting," the General said to his President. "I feel it will go a long way towards making the kinds of changes and improvements we need to govern this country."

"I agree. It is good to be able to speak frankly with men you trust."

* * *

We sat on the rocks exhausted. All around us the debris of the battle lay strewn on the ground. Bodies, ripped clothing, abandoned weapons and equipment. The Delta Force men were in a tight group on their own, and each was busy checking and reloading their weapons. Their helicopters had landed further down the mountainside, close to the village. There was no sense in their burning up fuel when their main target had disappeared into the deep clefts and caverns of the mountain.

"I've had my men check the bodies. There doesn't seem to be any survivors."

I looked at Mason. He'd done well, taking charge of the

platoon when his officer blundered in and nearly got us all killed. But we were still bitter with the sense of failure. I nodded an acknowledgment and looked up as one of Art Schramm's men cried out.

"He's alive, this guy. One of the insurgents, he must have banged his head when the bullet grazed his skull. He's starting to come round."

I walked over to take a look. Art was already there, bending over him to examine his wounds. He straightened up. "He's right, the guy's ok. I think he's one of their senior officers."

I gazed down at him, but he looked like the usual collection of ragged clothes, bandoliers of ammunition and a black turban. His long beard covered most of his face, but his eyes were open, staring at me.

"What makes you think he's an officer?" I asked Art.

By way of a reply, he reached down and pulled the Afghan's sleeve up his arm. He wore a watch, but not an ordinary watch.

"It's a Swiss Gallet. This model is a Flight Officer time zone chronograph, very, very expensive. There's also this," he picked a canvas folder off the ground. "It's a map case. There are a few documents that we'll have to hand over to the intelligence guys, and a map of this area. A military map."

"American?"

"Pakistani. They actively support the Taliban and supply

them with a lot of intelligence data, especially maps like this. So this guy can read a map and tell the time with a watch that would cost an average Afghan ten years' pay. And that's just the down payment. He's a senior officer, no question."

For some reason the watch disturbed me. I'd seen it before, or one very much like it. I put it to the back of my mind; it would come to me later. I just knew it was important. But how many ten thousand dollar Swiss watches were floating around Afghanistan? I suspected I could count the number on the fingers of one hand and have four fingers left. The major we'd released came over.

"He's an officer alright. That bastard used to enjoy beating us on the back with canes. We had little enough to eat, and he made his men tip it out onto the ground so that we had to eat it like animals. I'd like some time with that gentleman."

I smiled. "I'm sure you would, Major, but we're not like them. Or not supposed to be, anyway."

I looked around as we all heard the sound of engines in the distance. It was the Strykers. They had arrived.

We boarded the APCs and made our way back to Kabul, the long way around. The Deltas climbed aboard their helicopters and took off for a quicker, more comfortable ride. There were no handshakes, no goodbyes. They were soldiers who arrived without fanfare, conducted their deadly business, and left in the same way. Once again we had to endure the bone-jarring ride along the Afghan roads; the ride cross country, following dried up riverbeds and open plains was comfortable by comparison. I had a lot to think about. I knew that the military people at Camp Phoenix would not be impressed by the failure of our mission. Rachel tried to cheer me up.

"It wasn't all bad," she smiled. "We'll get back in one piece. We only lost one man."

"Yes, Lieutenant Rains. A pity about him."

"A pity he fucked up, you mean. Stupid bastard, he screwed the whole plan."

"Maybe." I felt tired and depressed. Then our vehicle stopped, and I popped open the hatch. We were facing a horde of Strykers, the same as ours, but many more of them. Their remote turret guns all pointed in our direction. It turned out to be a company of American infantry. I got down to face a hard-looking officer who'd climbed out to stand on the track, hands on hips. It occurred to me that he'd seen too many American cowboy films. It was like watching a scene from High Noon, and we were cast as the bad guys.

"I'm Lieutenant Colonel Vance Everard. Are you Hoffman?"

"That's right."

"We heard on the radio that your mission was a fuck up, Hoffman. We came in to see if you needed any help."

He was abrasive, to the point of downright insulting.

Clearly, he had no time for me, as a non-military person. I was about to reply, but Art Schramm came up beside me with Vince Mason. The Sergeant saluted, but Everard ignored him. He was about to continue when Art stepped forward to stand six inches from his face.

"What's this about a fuck up? Were you there, Colonel?"

"No, and it's a pity I wasn't. Maybe it would have been different."

"Maybe it would have been worse. Ask your Sergeant here for a mission debrief, and you'll find it was an American officer who fucked up, not Max Hoffman."

Everard gave him an icy stare and turned to Mason. "Is that true, Sergeant?"

Mason hesitated only for a few moments. "I'm afraid Lieutenant Rains was ill, Sir. He went off half-cocked and gave away the element of surprise. But it wasn't his fault, he'd suffered a blow on the head from an explosion."

Everard sighed. "I'll have to talk to the men when we get back. But not a word of this is to get out, you hear me, Sergeant? I don't want Lieutenant Rains to be known as anything other than a hero. That's the story his folks in the US are going to hear."

"He was a hero, Colonel. He was doing a good job, up until he ran into that blast. All of these men are heroes. If you're in any doubt, ask the two American soldiers we rescued."

"From the Taliban?"

I nodded. "That's right. We also brought back a prisoner. A high-ranking Taliban officer."

He finally relaxed. "Maybe it wasn't so bad after all. You need to tell it to General Westwood. He's waiting at Camp Phoenix for the debrief. Let's get the show on the road before it gets dark." He shouted to his troops. "Turn them around. We're heading back."

I heard a ragged cheer. Evidently, his men did not share the Colonel's enthusiasm for roaming the Afghan countryside.

We followed Everard's APCs back to Camp Phoenix. Our driver parked the Stryker near to all the others, a neat, military line of formidable steel and state of the art weaponry. But I thought about Mullah Omar's escape route. These vehicles could not travel where the hardy Afghan insurgents could run and move around at will. Rachel and I climbed down to stretch our aching, tired muscles. Luk followed with Najela.

"What's the next move, Max? Najela and I want to find somewhere quiet for her to clean up and change. She needs to shop for some new stuff too."

"You may as well take her," I replied. "We'll give the General everything he needs to know. I suggest we meet at the hangar in Kabul International, and we can check out the Twin Otter. I expect Joe Ashford will be chasing us for the next load."

"We didn't deliver the last load," Rachel reminded me.

"That's true, but it wasn't our choice. He'll need to talk to General Westwood about that one."

She grimaced. "I don't think Ashford will take it lying down. He's sure to blame us."

"To hell with Ashford," I muttered. "Let's get this debrief over with, and we'll ask Westwood to explain it to him."

She raised her eyebrows. "Yeah, right."

I grinned, "Don't worry, it'll be fine."

Art Schramm and his men had dismounted from the APC that had transported them, and I went to speak to them.

"Art, thanks for everything. I hope they pay you well for what you did."

He grinned. "Don't worry about that, the military squares the bills for our services pretty quick. They don't want disgruntled mercenaries running around in their rear."

"No, I guess not. Where are you headed now?"

"Into town for a meal and a few beers."

"I'd like to fix up to meet, maybe this evening?"

"Make it tomorrow," he replied. "I've got some business to attend to tonight, and she won't wait any longer."

"Tomorrow it is. Lunch at Abe Woltz's place?"

"It's a date."

We shook hands and he left.

"Mr. Hoffman? Max Hoffman?"

I looked around, an American Military Policeman, a sergeant, had walked up quietly behind us.

"I'm Hoffman."

"Yes, Sir, I'm Sergeant Mostyn, a message from the manager of Kabul International. There's a problem with your aircraft, and it needs resolving right now."

I sighed. "Sergeant, I've just got in, and we're about to attend a debrief with General Westwood. You know who he is?"

"I know General Westwood, yes, Sir. But this is an emergency. If the plane isn't cleared, they're going to destroy it."

"What! Cleared for what?"

"I dunno, Sir. That's the message. Either come now and sort it out, or they use a controlled detonation to destroy the aircraft."

I nodded. "I'll come now. Rachel, you go on to the debriefing."

"No way, I'm coming too. The debrief can wait."

"I've got a vehicle outside the gate. I'll give you a lift," the MP said. "But we need to get there fast, before they decide to go ahead with the controlled detonation."

"Ok, we're coming."

We followed him outside the gates of Camp Phoenix and there stood a military Humvee. It was unmarked, which seemed strange, but so did everything else that the ISAF forced did in Afghanistan. We piled in the back, and

Sergeant Mostyn drove us away towards the airport. It didn't seem quite right, any of this. The message about the aircraft, the unmarked Humvee, but when we turned into the airport and drove to the hangar, I relaxed. We both still had our pistols, the Colt .45s that Abe Woltz had given us, so I felt able to defend ourselves if there was any funny business. The Twin Otter was outside the hangar, and Roy Waverley stood by it with a clipboard. We climbed down from the Humvee and joined him.

"What's up, Roy. What's going on?"

He looked up. "Hi, Max, Rachel. The crates are all loaded ready to be shipped out, and the bird's fueled up, so you can get her in the air straight away."

"I don't understand. What's this about a controlled detonation, some kind of security scare?"

"It's news to me." He looked mystified. "Ask Joe, he's inside."

"Joe Ashford? He's here?"

Sure, he sent for you, said you were flying out as soon as you got here."

I felt my anger surge. "We'll have a word with him. I think he needs to understand who's running the war in Afghanistan, and it isn't him."

I stormed into the hangar, and Rachel came with me. Ashford was stood inside, and at first we didn't see him, the interior was too dark. Then I recognized his huge bulk and walked up to him.

"Ashford, what the hell's going on here? We're supposed to be with the General."

"The guy you think is running the war here, isn't that what I heard you say?"

He grinned and held out his hand. Automatically, I shook it. Then I remembered where I'd seen the watch on the Taliban commander. On Joe Ashford's wrist, where there was just a white line marking where he'd worn it until recently. Everything started to click into place, but I kept it to myself. I realized we were in trouble, with the phony MP to collect us from Camp Phoenix. When he released my hand, I repeated my question, "Tell me, what's going on?"

"Yeah, I will. Soon. First, take off those guns, real slow."

"Fuck you!" Rachel exclaimed. "You want our guns, you'd better try and take them."

"I'd be happy to take them off your dead bodies, if you prefer."

We both whirled around at this new threat. Kyle McDonald, Ed Walker's henchman. That reminded me, where was his former buddy, Saul Madden, who we'd left guarding the aircraft? McDonald read my expression correctly. "You're wondering about your friend, that traitor Saul Madden? Don't worry, he won't be coming to help you out, he made a big mistake."

"What was that?"

"He got in my way, so I had to deal with him.

Permanently. But he sure screamed a pretty tune while I carved him up. I dumped his remains outside the airfield where the dogs could have themselves a feast." He belly laughed, a vicious psychopath who'd stop at nothing to inflict pain and injury, and purely for his own personal pleasure. Ashford interrupted him.

"That's enough, McDonald. You want to know what's up? Here's the deal. You're gonna fly this aircraft out with the shipment already loaded, pick up a return load, and deliver it to Peshawar. You'll be leaving in less than thirty minutes, so you can say your goodbyes."

"To whom?"

"To the pretty lady. She's staying here with me. Kyle will go with you, and if there's any funny business, the girl will go the same way as Saul Madden. Savvy?"

I nodded.

"Now take off those guns, it's the last warning."

We unbuckled the canvas holsters and dropped them on the floor.

"Good. Now get into the fucking plane and get it into the air. Kyle will give you the landing coordinates when you're airborne."

I looked at Rachel. "I'm sorry, I don't think I have any choice."

She nodded. "Go and deal with his cargo. I'll be waiting for you when you get back."

"Yeah, very touching." McDonald sneered. "Now do

what the boss says, and fly that plane."

Ashford took hold of Rachel's arm and led her away. "She'll be safe here," he shouted over his shoulder. "Very safe, believe me. Just get up in the air and get that cargo delivered."

"I'll be back," I shouted to Rachel.

McDonald sneered. "This isn't a movie, Hoffman. Now move!"

Roy Waverley was still writing on his clipboard as we came out. He looked at us curiously but said nothing as we climbed aboard the Twin Otter. When I looked out of the window, he was still staring, looking straight up at me. McDonald sat in the co-pilot's seat with his pistol drawn to cover me. He watched as I went through the pre-flight checks and called the tower for clearance. Once more, the CIA chief had smoothed the way, and we were given the go right away. Minutes later, we were in the air.

"I need a heading, McDonald."

"North west."

"Is this going to be the same field as before?"

"Maybe. Just fly the plane."

I didn't ask again, but the coordinates were already in the navigation computer, so I punched in the memory recall and sat back while the autopilot took over. After an hour, McDonald checked his watch and decided it was the moment to hand me the coordinates. The watch, that reminded me of Joe Ashford, and the link with the Taliban commander. First, I needed to get us out of this situation, next, to make a decision on what to do about Ashford. I smiled inwardly; taking down Ashford would end the financial arrangement that bailed out the airline. But that was the way it would have to be, conducting business with traitors, drug runners, thieves and murderers was not my style. We arrived over the field, and I made a preliminary pass to check that nothing had changed, but it looked clear enough. I landed, turned the aircraft around, and taxied to where a group of SUVs waited. McDonald gestured with the gun.

"Outside, Hoffman. I'm not leaving you on your own in the cockpit."

I shrugged. "Suit yourself."

I felt disappointed. I'd hoped to be able to use the radio. A group of Afghan men made haste to unload the cargo. They wore black turbans, and although I couldn't be certain, I felt sure they were the enemy. Not all Taliban wore black turbans. Some rival tribes who weren't Taliban wore them, but their arms and equipment screamed insurgents. This was no ordinary Afghan warband or drug dealer's bodyguard. They started to load the crates that had been stacked on the ground, and the aircraft filled with the pungent smell of opium. So that was it; a straight swap, guns for the Taliban, and drugs for Joe Ashford to sell on. McDonald saw my expression and sneered.

"Yeah, it's opium, Hoffman. You're now part of one of

the biggest business operations in the world."

"So why doesn't it feel good to be involved with something that causes so much death and misery?"

"That's tough," he chuckled. "If you want to feel good, just be happy that you're still alive. For now."

I didn't reply. The loading ended, and I went into the hold to make sure the cargo was secure, and I found that they'd tossed it in an untidy heap. If it shifted in mid-flight, we'd probably lose control and plunge into the ground. I estimated at least two tons of cargo, and a lot of weight to suddenly slide loose in the air.

"This needs to be lashed down," I said to McDonald.

"So?"

"So it's a two-man job. I'll need a hand."

He grimaced. "I reckon you should be able to handle it yourself, but if you really need me, I'll do it."

I didn't need him, and it wasn't a two-man job. But I'd hoped to get him close enough to tackle him without fear of him getting a shot at me. It was not to be. He kept the other side of the cargo from me and gave me an evil grin when I asked him to come around and help me. When it was done, I fastened the door shut and went forward again to the cockpit. My shadow slipped into the co-pilot's seat beside me. I started the engines, and with the brakes on, gunned them up until they were screaming. McDonald started to look nervous.

"What the fuck are you doing, Hoffman?"

"I need the aircraft to accelerate fast when I take the brakes off. This field is too short for a normal take-off. Does it worry you?"

"Fuck off," he snarled.

It was a small victory. I released the brake, and we shot forward for the difficult take-off. When we were in the air, I turned to my guard.

"I assume we're still heading for Peshawar?"

He nodded. "You've got it. He was planning to hop a military flight and wait for us there. So get a move on, Mr. Ashford will be waiting."

"Ashford? I thought he was in Kabul with Rachel. What's happened to her?"

"Don't worry, it's all organized. Your woman will be waiting for you in Kabul when you get back."

If I get back, I reflected. The only consolation was that he needed me to fly his illegal cargoes; at least until he found someone else to do it.

"Who is with Rachel? Who's looking after her?"

"No one." He looked over at me with a broad smile, enjoying my discomfort. "The little lady is safely locked up in a storage locker inside the hangar. You'll get all the details to release her when the job's finished."

But there was something in his eyes. Whatever they planned, it wasn't to tamely let us go. Either they'd kill us both to stop details of their scheme reaching the military, or they'd keep her prisoner to ensure my cooperation.

I had no choice but to follow their instructions, and to find a way out of the mess the second I had the slightest opportunity. I went through scores of different ideas to turn the tables on them, but not one of them would ensure Rachel's safety. I was surprised when I realized we were on the approach to Peshawar. The voice came through my headphones, jarring me out of my thoughts.

"Unidentified twin-engine aircraft heading out of Afghanistan for Peshawar, identify."

I came awake. "Peshawar, this is Helene Air flight to Peshawar requesting clearance to land."

"What was your departure airport, Helene Air?"

I hesitated, but there was only one reply I could give them. "Kabul International."

"One moment. Keep on your course."

They knew very well that I hadn't come from Kabul. We'd crossed the mountains on a heading from the south west of Jalalabad. Would this be the opening I needed? The voice came back.

"Thank you, Helene Air. You are already cleared to land. Come straight in to the main runway and taxi to the Double Eagle hangar. The cargo handlers are waiting for you."

Ashford. Of course, he'd arranged it all, and maybe he had the cooperation of the Pakistani Security Service, the ISI. But however he'd done it, it meant that one of my plans to turn the tables, by making the landing at Peshawar so suspicious that the authorities boarded the aircraft to check it out, had been trumped. I dropped down onto the runway and slowed at the end, following my instructions to taxi to the hangar. I saw Ashford straight away. There was a group of locals dressed in the usual rags, and in the center of them Ashford, taller, bigger, and much more imposing. I stopped next to them, shut down, and went aft to unfasten the door. Ashford's face greeted me with a grin.

"You're on time, Hoffman. Well done. Now get down off that aircraft, and my men will unload the cargo. It's very valuable, believe me." He laughed then. "Oh yeah, it's valuable alright." He looked at McDonald as the mercenary appeared beside me. "Stay with him, Kyle. Don't let him out of your sight."

"No worries, boss. If he even breathes, it'll be his last."

"Yeah, good idea," Ashford nodded absently. "Go around the side of the hangar. I don't want anyone seeing what goes down."

McDonald gestured with his pistol, and we both climbed down. He came behind me so that there was no way I could tackle him. So this would be it. There was no question that the man was going to kill me, and no doubt they had arranged for another aircraft and pilot. I was no longer useful to them. I had to take the chance soon, or it would be all over. We turned the corner, out of the beam of the overhead cargo unloading lights that lit up the front of the hangar, and I made my move. I slowed a little, just enough to let him catch up, then swiveled around and lashed out with my leg to bring him down. But he'd been waiting for me. He stepped back, and my leg only hit fresh air.

"You fucking amateur, Hoffman. You thought I'd fall for that? You must be crazy."

He held up his pistol, and I saw his finger tighten on the trigger. It all happened in slow motion. His teeth gleamed in the darkness, and I noticed for the first time that two of them were missing. He hadn't shaved for days, and his stubble showed coarse on his sallow face. His eyes were dilated and the pupils huge. He was getting a rush form what he was about to do. I tensed my muscles for one last, despairing leap for the gun. It was all I had left. Then there was a soft 'plop', and a dark hole appeared on his chest. Blood flowed down his front to stain his shirt. His eyes widened as his face took on a puzzled expression. His fingers opened, the gun fell to the ground, and he toppled with a crash. I was stunned. What the hell had happened? I stood for what seemed like an eternity, shaking with the tension as adrenalin poured into my body, and my mind went into overload.

"Max, are you ok?" a voice whispered through the darkness.

I turned to see Luk walking towards me, carrying his sniper rifle with a huge silencer attached.

"Luk!"

"Schh, Ashford is still around there. Are you hurt in any way?"

"No," I whispered. "What about Rachel?"

"You wouldn't keep me away from this for a million dollars," a familiar voice rang out in the darkness. Then she limped towards me out of the gloom, and we ran to each other. I held her tight.

"How…?"

"It's ok, Max, we're ok. Let's get ourselves out of here."

"But who…?"

"Waverley, Ashford's manager in Kabul. He was suspicious and came looking around the hangar after Ashford had gone and found me. I got your destination from him and went to find Luk."

"But, how did you get to Peshawar?"

"I hired a Cessna Air Taxi on short notice and flew it in."

"It must have cost a fortune! We haven't got any money."

"Hey, your fiancée ain't exactly broke, you know. I have got some cash from my pension."

"I don't know what to say," I muttered.

"That's ok, don't say anything. We need to deal with Ashford. Don't worry, Luk and I have a plan."

"You're not going to kill him!"

"No, he's too powerful. We just need to make a deal.

He lets us go, and we shut up about what he's up to. At least for the time being."

I hated the thought of him getting away, but she was right, he was much too powerful and well connected for us to touch him.

"One second, there's something I need."

I stooped down and picked up McDonald's pistol that he'd dropped. Rachel carried a pistol in her belt, and Luk had his rifle. It was enough. We walked around the end of the hangar and into the light. Ashford looked up, saw the three of us armed, and smiled. I gave him credit for a quick recovery. He showed no sign of any concern.

"Well, well. So your little friend showed up." He grinned at Rachel. "I trust you were comfortable during your stay in your new quarters at Kabul International?"

"Fuck you, Ashford," Rachel intoned, but there was little expression in her voice, other than a trace of contempt.

"Oh dear, that bad, was it?" he laughed. Then his smile faded, and he turned to me. "What happens now, Hoffman? Or is this some kind of a Mexican standoff?"

"We fly out and leave you here."

"And Kyle McDonald? I assume your friends killed him?"

"After he tried to kill me, yes."

He nodded, and I could see the wheels turning in his brain. Another loose end taken care of, that's all it meant to him. "And what happens when you get back to Kabul?

I guess you'll spill your guts to ISAF?"

But I'd already worked out how to keep him at arm's length if we ever got away. "No. I want full and clear title to my aircraft and airline, all debts paid. You stay out of our hair, that's all."

"All?" he sneered. "I don't believe you."

"There is one more thing, Ashford. You come near us, or any of our people or property, and I'll kill you." He started to laugh, but my next words stopped him. "You know Art Schramm and his boys?"

He nodded. "The mercs, yeah."

"Art is a friend of my family. When we get in the air, I'm going to call him up and spell it all out to him. Don't worry. It'll be on a satphone, and not over the radio for everyone to hear. He'll know what you've done, and if anything does happen to us, he'll come looking for you with his men. You wouldn't like that, Ashford. There's no way out of that. Not even you could deal with Schramm and his mercenaries."

His smile had gone, and he looked grim. "I hear you. You've got a deal."

"What about the aircraft title and my mortgage deeds? Where are they?"

"You'll have them within forty-eight hours. Don't worry," he scowled. "I know what's at stake."

"You'd better."

We left without another word and climbed aboard the

Twin Otter. When we were airborne, I turned to Luk and Rachel. "You know I'll never be able to thank you enough for this."

Luk blushed, but Rachel was all business. "There is something you can do, Max."

I nodded. "Anything, all you have to do is name it."

"I'm the only fiancée in the world without a ring. You can put that right."

I looked her in the eyes. "Is that what you want? Really?"

"You'd better believe it."

"It'll be my number one priority. Anything else? Luk what about you?"

"I'll talk to Najela," he grinned. "Then I'll let you know."

It was all surreal; in the midst of so much death, poverty and misery, they were talking about, well, life."

* * *

They could see he was faltering with the hard, fast pace they had to maintain to cross the mountains without being seen by any wandering drones. But he was weakening. Abruptly, he stumbled. There wasn't room for them to help him along the narrow, rocky path. He walked alone, and he fell to the sharp stony ground. They were horrified.

"Mullah, are you well? Is there a problem, do you feel ill?"

He looked up and surveyed them with his one eye. "The

air is thin and the going hard. I just need a little rest. Do not worry about me. It was just a stumble, no more. Give me a few minutes, and then I will be refreshed enough to continue."

"But, Mullah, it is not safe. The American drones are everywhere. We need to…"

"If the drones find us, it is God's will. If God wishes to protect us, so be it. But I cannot go on. I must have a few minutes rest."

Rashid Osman knew they shouldn't have come this way, but there was no choice. That damned American attack had forced their hand, and it was the only way out. Even so, they'd lost a lot of men, too many men. There would be a great many grieving widows when they returned to the village they used as a base. And even more, if they stayed out here in the open, high in the mountains that bordered the Khyber Pass.

"Sir," he tried once more. "Can you not make a few hundred yards to the group of rocks you can see in the distance. It will give us some cover."

Omar stared at him. "I have spoken, Rashid. We wait here."

"Yes, Sir."

He positioned sentries at all corners of their makeshift camp. But what could they do if a drone appeared? Nothing, except maybe shoot it down. He called over four men who carried RPG missile launchers.

"You know of the danger we face from drones?"

The oldest of the four men replied. "Of course. We are not children that have never learned how to fight."

"Post your men so that they have a clear shot at anything that appears in the sky. Tell them to be ready."

The man looked scornful. "For drones? You know how high they fly, and the range of our missiles."

"I know, but it is all we have. Make sure you are ready, and if God is with us this day, they will have no need to fire their weapons."

"You mean if the Americans do not choose to overfly this area, Rashid."

"That too. Now hurry, do your best."

He'd done what he could. His men were carrying a light machine gun, an old Soviet Degtyarev DP, nicknamed the 'record player' because of its pancake shaped magazines. He considered deploying that but decided against it. Its accuracy was not ideal even for ground operations. No, as an anti-aircraft gun, it was worse than useless. He sat near to Mullah Omar and checked his watch. Five minutes, no more. Then they'd have to move on, even if they had to carry him.

* * *

She was tired and almost at the end of her shift. Master Sergeant Carol Wendelski wasn't looking forward to the long drive home across the Nevada desert, but it was better than living on Creech Air Force base. She was piloting the MQ-9 Reaper. So far she'd fired off all of her Hellfire missiles, and she knew that when they checked the mission camera, they'd find she'd hit precious little. All she had left was a single GBU-12 Paveway II laser-guided bomb, and her eyes, of course. If she saw anything, she could call in an air strike. But she was Air Force, and maybe not a fighter jock, but the next best thing. She wanted, no, she craved a kill. And then she saw it, movement high up on the mountainside. She kept the drone straight and level so that the men on the ground didn't catch any sudden movements and scatter. Then she increased magnification and directed her camera to inspect the target. Yeah, insurgents, had to be. They were too heavily armed, and their direction of travel was too off the beaten track for them to be anything else. She flashed through a mental checklist of her rules of engagement and made a split second decision. She was still operating under the modified RoEs, so she was allowed to go for it. That was good enough for her. She locked the laser targeting system on the party of Afghans, and only then swung the drone over in a hard banking turn that would take it down and directly over their position. As she drew nearer, she armed the Paveway guided bomb at the same moment as she saw the men running around in obvious panic. Two missiles soared into the sky towards her Reaper, and she chuckled.

Who the hell were they kidding? Her finger was over the button, the moment came and she hit it. At the last second, she swore she could see a guy looking up. He was in the center of the group, and he had a black patch over one eye. Surely not? After all this time, it couldn't be that easy, could it? But she'd report what she'd seen. They could make up their own minds; they'd rerun the video and see exactly what she'd seen. The picture disappeared into a blur of smoke and debris. She circled for a few minutes and took another look. There were a few bodies and no movement. That was good enough for her, time to fly the bird back to Kabul and punch out for home.

* * *

We landed at Kabul International. I was sick of seeing the place, but we had to clear up some loose ends; not least was the debriefing that I'd been sidetracked from attending. When we landed, Luk hurried of to check on Najela, conscious of the long arm of Joe Ashford. Rachel and I managed to get a lift on a Humvee driving to Camp Phoenix.

CHAPTER FIFTEEN

We will never allow you to dictate to us how to run our country and whom to employ in Afghanistan. How and where we employ the foreign experts will remain the exclusive prerogative of the Afghan state. Afghanistan shall remain poor, if necessary, but free in its acts and decisions.

Daoud Khan, former Afghan President

"Mr. President, Sir. A message from Kabul."

President Barrani looked up at the aide. His immediate feeling was one of relief. The meeting to discuss agricultural grants for organic fertilizers was one he would gratefully have avoided, but the delegation was from a marginal district, and the congressman had begged for his support. He put on his most regretful look.

"I'm sorry, this shouldn't take long. Keep the meeting

going. I'll be right back."

They all nodded gravely. Affairs of state took precedence. They knew that. When he was outside, he took the aide to one side and grinned.

"Was this a genuine emergency, or were you just saving my ass?"

The aide didn't return the smile. "It's genuine, Sir. They're asking for you in the situation room."

He nodded. "Ok, let's go see if World War III has broken out."

Inside the situation room, he could see smiling faces. So it wasn't war, thank God.

"What's going on?" he asked General Mathew Mann.

"It's good news, Mr. President. At least, we think it is. It's Mullah Omar."

"You think? That doesn't sound promising. Did you find him or not?"

"We're almost sure, and we didn't just find him. We found him with a GBU-12 Paveway II laser-guided bomb, from one of our Reapers. If you'd care to take a seat, Sir, I'll run the video."

He sat and watched the film. It was surprisingly sharp, and in color. Not at all like those grainy images that used to come out of his gun camera when he was attending post mission debriefs on his carrier off the coast of South Vietnam. He saw the man with the eye patch, and saw the smoke and debris. He watched for several minutes as it slowly cleared. The Reaper was circling, keeping the camera focused on the target. Then it cleared, and there was a heap of bodies and scraps of equipment.

"Is he dead? Really dead?"

"We think so, Sir."

He fixed his Chief of Staff with a hard gaze. "I'm not so sure. Number one priority, General. Find out the truth. Is the reward still in place?"

"Yessir, ten million dollars. American."

"Ok. Make it public that the reward stands, dead or alive. I want to see a body. Is that clear?"

"Yes, Sir, I'll get straight on to it."

"Good. But well done, everyone, and you can send my congratulations to that drone pilot."

He strode out. Please God, let it be true. If he could wind down the war in Afghanistan, and start bringing the troops back, his second term would be a kick-in.

* * *

The debrief was like a thick fog, and I fought my way through it, trying to keep my mind focused, but it was hard, very hard. Art Schramm was dead. Two hours before, a bomber had left his vehicle outside the hotel where he was entertaining his girlfriend. The explosion destroyed most of the building, killing Art, his girl and three other mercenaries from his unit, as well as scores of other civilians in the vicinity. After all the actions he'd fought through, the enemies he'd defeated and killed, to be murdered in his bed left me with a sense of disbelief and outrage. I knew who was responsible. There was no question. Ashford. He'd put the word out as soon as we took off from Peshawar. I knew it was a warning to my crew and me. I shouldn't have used Art Schramm's name as a threat to him. I realized my mistake and felt responsible. Yet deep down I knew that there was only one person responsible for the bomb, Joe Ashford. One day, I'd find a way to get even. The only way to achieve that end was to kill him. From that moment on, Ashford and I would be mortal enemies, and we both knew it. Each of us could harm the other immensely, that was obvious. I would have to be patient. 'Revenge was a dish best served cold', I believe that was the old saying. The Pashtuns had a better proverb. 'A man taking revenge one hundred years after a slight to his ancestor, would fret that he had acted in haste.' I didn't plan to wait that long, but killing Ashford would from here on in would be part of the fabric of my life. One day, I'd find a way to rid South East Asia of his pestilential schemes without any comebacks on me, my friends and my partner, Rachel.

"To sum up, the operation was a mixed success," General Westwood said. I looked up. I hadn't even realized the debriefing was almost over.

"There were some good points and some bad points.

I've recommended Lieutenant Rains for a medal, and I expect it to be approved by the time his body is shipped home. More good news, and this time it's about Mullah Omar. One of our drones got a hit on a party that was climbing the mountain right above where you lost contact with his people. They managed to drop a laser-guided bomb on the party, and as far as they know, all of them were killed. We're working now to get independent confirmation that Mullah Omar was in that party, but it'll take time. However, there's a good chance that he was there. So well done, all of you. Colonel Brooks, would you like to play the video and show these folks what went down."?

"Yes, Sir."

The blinds were already closed. Someone switched off the light and a video projector came to life. I saw the wide angle shot taken from high altitude, and then the rocky landscape came closer as the drone swooped down low. We could see them clearly now, a group of heavily armed insurgents. They looked up in alarm and launched a couple of RPG shoulder launched missiles. One of the men did appear to have a patch over one eye, but that was not conclusive. In a land of little or no medical care like Afghanistan, many men wore eye patches. Several of them fired their assault rifles, and then the bomb launched to arc down, exploding on the exposed mountainside. When the smoke cleared, there was just bodies. Then the lights came on.

"We're certain that we got him. The guy with the eye patch looked pretty conclusive. Our surmise is that you forced him out into the open when you attacked that village. Well done all of you. As soon as we know for sure, we'll let you know."

But I knew then. I had an icy feeling in my guts that it wasn't him. I could still remember that man in the village of Yaluk staring at me. That stare carried a power that was almost as powerful as the laser that had guided the bomb down to the party of insurgents. The man I'd seen looked similar, except for that one difference. He looked too ordinary. I hoped I was wrong. Mullah Omar's death could be the catalyst that begun the process of healing to end the war in Afghanistan. But I didn't think I was wrong. Like everything else in this country, time would give the answers, one way or the other.

"Lastly, we're sorry to hear about the death of Art Schramm and his men. I'd ask you to stand and salute the man who fought so long and so hard for what was right."

We stood, the men in uniform saluted, and us civilians put our hands over our hearts. Then it was over. There was only one place in Kabul for us to head for, Abe Woltz's bar. General Westwood laid on a Humvee to take us there but asked me into his office for a quiet word before I left. Rachel didn't like being excluded, but she gave in.

"Sit down, Hoffman. This won't take long, but we may

as well be comfortable."

I hesitated, but only for a second or two. When Generals give orders, even invitations, they have a way of making the subject go along with them. I sat down.

"What is it, General? I've a lot to do and people waiting for me. Can you make it quick?"

"Sure, but this business in Yaluk, hunting down Mullah Omar. You did well, damn well."

"If he's dead," I replied.

He looked and stared at me. "I gather you're not sure."

"No, I'm not. Frankly, I doubt it."

He nodded. "I see. In that case, it makes what I have to say more important. You know that US policy is to employ more security contractors and run down our troop strength?"

"Of course I do, that's common knowledge. It cuts down the number of soldiers being shipped home in body bags."

"That's not the sole reason," he objected. But then he smiled. "But I guess it figures pretty high in the politicians' thinking. Did you know I offered Art Schramm a long term contract?"

I wasn't surprised. "He was a good soldier. He would have been an asset."

"Yeah. The thing is, I also need someone who is more mobile, who can fly shipments and personnel around for me. Would you be interested? The money is good. I understand you've overcome your immediate problems, but this would guarantee a good future for your airline, even expansion."

"Who told you about our problems?"

He waved the question away. "I heard it somewhere. But what do you think, an exclusive contract to fly for the military in Afghanistan?"

"I'm not comfortable with it, General. I have a policy of not flying weapons and soldiers."

"Not what I heard," he grinned. "But I guess you were forced into it by the CIA."

So he knew about Ashford. "That's right."

"It's like this, Hoffman. The Afghan government is starting to get serious about cowboy airlines flying all over their country."

"My outfit is legit, General, always has been."

"Sure, sure. But they're trying to encourage their own people to get involved more. I gather they'll be looking hard at license renewals for foreigners, and I believe yours is up in a few months time?"

It all clicked into place then, the quid pro quo. Fly for us, and we'll keep your licenses valid. Refuse, and you'll find yourself grounded. Permanently. I felt bitter, and it was a stab in the back. But I guessed it was the way things played out in this country.

"I'll think about it, General."

"Of course you will. Good man. The kind of thing I

envisage is worthwhile, believe me. Extracting casualties from outlying areas, troops who fall sick. Maybe even picking up troops held prisoner by the insurgents, if it's ever needed."

My mind was diverted, thinking about how to transport sick people in the Twin Otter, when my brain picked up the word prisoners.

"I'm sorry, you said prisoners. That suggests to me that they'd be in enemy hands."

"That's right, yes."

"General, what you're describing is more than flying sick troops. You're talking armed operations into enemy held territory."

"Am I? Well, I guess it could come to that. That's why I'd be able to offer to employ Art's contractors as part of the deal. It would mean you'd have an armed escort, permanently attached to your staff."

I was stupid. He'd led up to this, and I hadn't seen it coming. So what he wanted was a convenient way to extract soldiers trapped or held captive in enemy territory. If he got his men back, it would be a feather in his cap for everyone who came home. If we got shot at and suffered casualties along the way, we'd just be another figure on a Washington balance sheet.

"No way, General. I'm not here to commit suicide."

He smiled. "Think about it, that's all I'm asking. You haven't asked about the money."

"No, I have not."

"I'd quadruple your normal charter rates, double pay for every person who you recruit, and full insurance and equipment back up. Isn't your Twin Otter due for a full engine overhaul soon? That'll be expensive. Anything you want, it's yours. Call in and see me tomorrow."

I left him in a daze and called a cab to take Rachel and me into the city. On the way I told her what he'd said.

"Jesus Christ, Max, that's amazing. We'd get the airline off the ground for sure, new aircraft. Think of it, we could even go international if we made enough money."

"If we're still alive," I grumbled.

There were twelve of Art Schramm's men drinking in Abe Woltz's bar. Luk was there with Najela, and Abe was busy running around with the drinks. He greeted me with a huge smile.

"Glad to see you're back, Max. Let me get you a drink. Are you joining the boys?"

"Yes, for a while."

They nodded when I asked if we could join them at their table. Art's second in command, Trip Wennerstrom, looked at me when I said how sorry I was.

"He was a great man, Art. The best. We'll miss him," was his eulogy.

"What are you going to do now?" I asked him.

"I've no idea. We need to find a new contract. The money from that last one will keep us going for a short while, but we all have bills to pay. Wives, children. They all need money."

"You mean you have families?" I was astonished.

"Of course we have. After Iraq, we left the army and found that there's precious little work in the US, because of the downturn. Most of us have kids in school, big mortgages, credit cards, you know how it is."

I nodded. "Yeah, something like that."

We spent a half hour with them and then left them to drown their sorrows while we moved to another table and ordered some food. Abe brought it out, and I asked him to join us while we talked about Westwood's offer. His eyes narrowed.

"The conniving bastard. They never change. They did something of the same to your grandfather in 'Nam."

"I didn't know that. All I was told was to avoid the CIA like the plague."

"Yep, that's sound advice. So what are you going to do?"

"Rachel, you're in favor, I gather?"

Her eyes were dilated, bright with excitement. "You can count me in, any day."

"Luk?"

"I've had enough of tending bar," he muttered. "Sorry, Dad."

"That's ok," Abe reassured him. "A man has to make his own way."

"Is it ok with you?" he asked Najela.

She nodded shyly. He told us what she had signed. 'What's the difference? The war is everywhere. Last time we were here the war was outside, when those bombs went off.'

She sure had a point. I went over to the mercs. They were now Trip Wennerstrom's men, although it caused an ache in the heart to call them that. I explained the offer. Their answering roar was enough. I went back to our table.

"It seems we have a contract," I informed them.

Abe Woltz could not hide the excitement in his face. "You know what his means? The Devil's Guard is back."

"Hey, hold up," I grinned at him. "We'll be flying sick soldiers and casualties out of the remote areas."

"Yeah, right. I'll call your men over, and we'd better celebrate with another drink."

I had the feeling that things wouldn't ever be the same again for us, for Rachel and me, for Luk and Najela. For Afghanistan.

Lightning Source UK Ltd.
Milton Keynes UK
UKHW010704040121
376386UK00003B/633